~ 1 ~

The Mystic Stone

Graham Adams

1: <u>The Gift</u>

The seascape along the coast of Southbourne as far as Hengistbury Head is absolutely breath-taking, in any season. Late autumn and winter though, is the best time for people who like to be alone and allow the biting winds to enter their very soul.

Gary and Eloise staggered to the brow of the cliff top that overlooked an October sea, grey and wild. The wind was whipping up fine sand in their faces which was hard to keep out of their stinging eyes. They had at least the sense to dress for such unpredictable British autumn weather, well equipped for their early morning walk.

They were honeymooners and had decided to spend their first time as man and wife together in Southbourne, which lies between Christchurch and Bournemouth. At this time of year, the coastal area is quite empty, except for the occasional dog walkers who would brave the cold winds that roar across the sandy escarpment.

'It's deserted' she shouted, almost falling over in the wind, saved only by the coarse grass on the ledge tangling around her jeans' bottoms. When she scanned the scene to the left and as far as the eye could see, the arc line of sand culminated in a large rocky outcrop called Hengistbury Head. The young woman could barely see the end of the bay as it was shrouded by the misty clouds of spray caused by the loudly crashing white surf. The huge waves thundered as they smashed on to the shingle and she felt exhilarated.

'You ready?' he shouted, as he caught his breath, gritted his teeth and gripped her hand. They struggled with the loose sand that was deposited onto the winding path that led steeply down to the wet shingle waiting below.

The sea's roar rose to an even more deafening crescendo as it pounded on to the beach, the surf caused clouds of white suds to blow towards the cliffs, swirling as if they had escaped from a giant washing machine. About half way down the path they stopped to take a breather.

'Look' she pointed, 'we aren't alone at all.'

Some five hundred metres from where they were standing Ellie could make out a solitary figure facing the roaring tide in a long black trench coat, an old western style one with long tails flapping in the wind, 'Funny' she thought to herself, 'I could have sworn the beach was deserted from the cliff top'.

'I don't like this Ellie, it doesn't seem quite right to me' Gary shouted at the top of his voice, 'perhaps we ought to turn around now before we get to the bottom.'

'How can you say that now, when I distinctly remember at breakfast how you mentioned how much those people at the office bored you and couldn't wait to get away from their pettiness. Well here we are quite away from them – so let's go for it,' she said.

'Yeah but look at the state of the sea, it seems to be getting worse' Gary shouted.

'We'll be fine, whatever happened to your sense of adventure?' With that she gripped his hand and ran down the rest of the pathway, stumbling and nearly falling, but soon reached their destination – the beach.

'What about him?' He tried to shout above the roar, but his voice went unheard as she ran to the water's edge, spinning and jumping like a child. He followed her to the edge, laughing as he caught her in his arms and enjoyed the beautiful moment.

They screamed and shouted as they avoided the waves that threatened to engulf their shoes. He picked up as many wet stones as he could, spinning them over the waves, all to fail miserably as the rough sea gobbled up each effort without a trace.

Suddenly a high-pitched screech caught their ears. At first it stopped them in their tracks, until they noticed a flock of black and white terns flying above them. The seabirds hovered on the wind, using its force to fly stationary, as if by magic. One hovered in front of them over the churning water and then it suddenly dived into the sea like an arrow and in a blink of an eye it reappeared, fish in beak.

In a second the birds were gone, but the onlookers stood quite still for a moment stunned. The whole episode had happened so quickly and for a moment they were unable to speak to each-other, instead just stood there holding hands amazed. As she looked up at him after the flock had gone, they were left alone again and kissed each other warmly.

Suddenly, the sea didn't seem so loud, the wind was not so fierce in their faces and a sort of calm had descended, he glanced at his watch, relieved that it was still only 9am. The heavy grey overcast envelope that had been the sky ten minutes ago, somehow looked thinner and they could see a thin line of gold on the horizon and over to the right, a real break in the cloud.

Soon a larger patch of azure blue was reflecting on the sea and their weather blown faces lit up as the rays of the low sun flashed in their eyes. It was still not warm, but they felt the sky's promise of change to come. As they looked eastwards along the bay, the previously ghostly looking headland was now showing off its coloured rock face, of a mixture of sandstone and granite. The wild surf had subsided and the waves broke more gently onto the sandy beach.

Gary caught his breath for a moment as they stared at this beautiful English seascape, he pulled his wife near and felt her warmth, she responded, looking up into his eyes smiling, nothing could take that moment away, he thought happily.

About an hour had passed since they first stood on the cliff top and twenty-four hours before that, each of them had been embroiled in mundane jobs in the now far off city.

'We could easily be in another world right now,' she mused contently.

'Shall we walk towards the headland, darling?" he asked.

His question was immediately answered by a tug on his sleeve. Suddenly they were sprinting towards the first of the groynes, which separated the beach into sections. The local council had, at great pains, built these structures to encourage the sand to build-up on the beach – promising idea at the time, but had not been that successful.

They had reached the first structure which was constructed of huge blocks of sandstone, which began in a line from the base of the cliff and ended jutting out into the sea. On their way to the structure, she picked up all sorts of flotsam and jetsam that had been thrown up onto the beach by the fierce action of the sea. There were clumps of brown and green seaweed, cold and wet, that she tried to hit him with. Together they gathered up a few interesting shells and some selected smooth pebbles, with amazingly coloured formations.

Ellie and Gary struggled to reach the top boulder of the groyne and he helped her jump over the other side onto the damp soft sand whilst the warm sun shone on their bare heads. He turned to her smiling, but quickly noticed that she wasn't looking back at him, but over his shoulder.

Strangely, without any reason, the whole atmosphere had changed again. The sun seemed to have disappeared behind a cloud for a moment and the grey October cool wind blew in their faces again. They looked at each other and did not speak, but quietly knew each-others' thoughts.

As quickly as it came, the dark moment was gone. The sun re-appeared from the cloud so they continued to walk along the beach, towards the solitary figure who seemed to be motionless at the water's edge. On the way, they continued to pick up the odd pebble, or sometimes they would peer at a shell or two, but slowly and surely the solitary figure was getting nearer as if he was a fisherman reeling them in.

Soon he was only ten metres away, he was probably less than six-foot-tall, but the long black leather overcoat and black wide-brimmed hat gave him height. Ellie had a sense of foreboding and as she nervously gripped Gary's hand tight, they tried to nonchalantly walk by him.

"Good morning". A cultured voice without a discernible accent startled them and they stopped and stared at him. It was the first voice other than their own that they had heard since leaving their hotel over two hours ago!

"S...sorry! Good morning, you must think us extremely rude but..." Gary spluttered, almost tripping on his words, his companion's long blonde hair caught the breeze covering her face and she struggled to remove it.

"I know." The man said smiling. "You don't usually get to speak to anyone down here – it's a very private place, if you know what I mean."

Suddenly, the tension between them had disappeared when they considered his face. It was well worn and weathered, yet he seemed to have a kind and distinguished demeanour.

"I'm Gary and this is my wife Eloise, we are, sort of, er, on holiday, aren't we dear?"

"He means that we are on honeymoon and this is our first day of surfacing, if you know what I mean," She said, blushing.

"Perfect for you or what?" he said, "My name is Edmund."

"Do you live here?" Gary asked.

"Not too far away, but this is my favourite place, winter or summer. Early in the mornings, I very often have the place to myself; it helps one to think you know." Edmund answered wistfully.

Just for a moment, Ellie looked closely at the man, he looked around sixty years old, yet healthy with a warm smile. She had never met him before, yet somehow, deep down, there was a sort of friendliness that she felt towards him, as if she had, in some other life.

Edmund could see that they wanted to move on, so with a wave of his hand and a quick goodbye, they parted company. They proceeded towards the headland and the stranger had turned to head back towards the cliff path.

"Oh, hold on just a minute." A voice shouted, stopping them in their tracks. They turned around to face the stranger and as he held out his hand, they peered into it.

In the centre of his hand was something that looked like a piece of quartz, the colour of a small smoky brown egg, translucent in appearance, very smooth and oval.

'I think it is a moonstone, quite rare. How it got onto the beach, is anyone's guess, but I'd like you to have it. Let's say that it's a good luck charm for your new start in life together, please take it." The stranger smiled, eagerly offering the gift.

Gary stood stock still, not sure what to do, but suddenly Ellie rushed over to the old man took the stone out of his hand and then totally out of character, gave him a hug and then quickly ran back to her husband.

Gary stared at the beautiful stone nestling in her hand, looked at Ellie's face and then turned back to the giver to thank him, but the unusual meeting was over and the stranger was already some distance away from them.

Ellie put the stone in her jeans pocket and as they continued their walk, her hand was holding it, smooth and cool. Why would that stranger give her that gift and did he really find it on that beach?

She quietly struggled in her mind to find an answer, to which there was none.

2: Looking back

Hideaway

Edmund sighed as he clambered up the sandy path of the cliff. At the top of the path he turned to look back towards the distant arc of the beach. The two small ant-like figures were just discernible at the edge of the sea and he smiled to himself. There was a small bench at the top of the cliff, so he decided to rest there for a while, to take in the beautiful views and the bracing sea air.

'Job done, the old prophesy has been fulfilled," he said to himself.

Looking back, as he often did those days, he thought of how different life would have been, but for the chance meeting forty years ago...

He took his mind back to his roots; a town in Derbyshire surrounded by coalmines, which by that time had mostly been played out. Those that still wanted to work in that black subterranean world had to travel northeast to north Nottinghamshire coalfields to unearth the 'black gold' called coal.

Traditions however, do not die so easily. The harsh intolerant nature of the local inhabitants still existed in the early sixties, when prowess of consumption of the local ale was deemed more important than any other 'gifts' that any young man might possess. He had dabbled into that way of life for several of his early years, but always suffered with the after effects the next morning.

At this point Edmund had reached a bench, some way from the cliff edge, he sat on it to regain his breath and began to try and picture in his mind again, his young life and what his first job was like.

Stanton, originally a village settlement, just south of his hometown, was at the time totally encircled by a vast sprawling belching giant steelworks, which never slept.

Over fourteen thousand people, all from the surrounding district toiled there. Whilst some workers were sleeping, having done their shift of heavy toil, others at the same time, were just raising their heads from their slumber, ready to begin their next shift.

Although his successful graduation from the local grammar school had made his mother proud, he was still destined to be drawn to the steel giant, to cut his teeth within its working environment, alongside his own father and elder brother and all those strong men of industry.

The structure of the ironworks was basically two steel productions areas; each one had two blast furnaces strategically built so that all the other functions could feed them with coke and iron ore. This constant huge material consumption finally resulted in great ingots of finished iron. The waste material, or locally called 'slag' was shipped out of the furnace in fiery hoppers and the resulting heat from them took many days to cool in their specially constructed sidings.

It was an awe-inspiring first visit to the steel works by Edmund and like all the other prospective office workers, they would be filled with fear and awe. Forty-foot-high towers of continuous deafening sound and blistering heat, was impossible to get near.

During the tour, to make things more graphic, the guide would intersperse his descriptive speech of the basic workings of the furnaces with stories of men falling into newly filled hoppers of molten steel and their bodies would be never found. The guide would laugh as he watched the blood drain from his young listeners' faces as they all imagined the workers' horrible fate.

After the tour was completed, each prospective new starter was told to which department they were going to be allocated. Edmund was informed that he would be working at the Coke Ovens plant offices which happened to be set apart from the centre of the other manufacturing activities. Naively the newly appointed junior office boy was initially relieved to be some distance from the awe-inspiring furnaces, that is, until he was shown the route to find the destination of his new job.

Starting from the head offices in the centre of the works, he walked two miles over railway lines and through narrow tunnels and after having asked several times weakly, 'am I on the right road to the Coke Ovens?'

He was given the same response each time that he asked; 'what the hell are you going there for?' and was gruffly shown the next part of his route.

The clean white shirt that his mother had proudly supplied soon became grubby, exposed to the grey dust that covered everything from huge Lorries that rushed by him, throwing up a choking cloud in their wake.

After an hour of struggling, finally he saw the first sign, battered and filthy which read 'To Coke Ovens Plant' and pointed into another tunnel, about the width of a lorry, with a narrow footpath just discernible on one side. As he peered into the black abyss, the light at the other end seemed so small it seemed as if it was miles away.

'Surely that isn't the way, is it?' He said to himself as he looked around, but there seemed no other road or pathway to take.

Just before starting off, he peered into the black hole again. The light at the other end had gone out; and he just pulled back in time as an open top truck loaded to the gunnels with something that was steaming, suddenly rushed out of his end with a roar and a mighty clatter. Two more vehicles quickly followed the first and then all went silent again.

He noticed the light at the top of the tunnel's archway had changed from red to green, so he listened. Nothing coming towards him but before he had a chance to proceed, the light changed from green to red again and further huge trucks came rushing towards him again.

Realising now that the light controlled the traffic, he now knew that he must run down the side pathway towards the pinhole of light, as soon as the light changed to green again.

He finally emerged out of the long dark tunnel and prayed that the light hadn't changed to green for the oncoming traffic whilst he was in the tunnel. Edmund tried to focus in the bright sunlight as he emerged and he filled his lungs with the acrid air gasping for breath. He saw that he was at the bottom of a street of tenement houses and searched the area for signs of the works. There it was to the left, a huge metal gateway with a sign 'Coke Ovens Works' and alongside it another and much larger sign in red capitals,

'SMOKING AND NAKED LIGHTS PROHIBITED'.

Both signs were so badly damaged and the worse for wear, the wordings were barely discernible. Beyond the entrance he could see several plumes of smoke and steam which emanated from various chimneys and grim black buildings. His first impression was that of the painting he had once seen in a local exhibition called 'Dante's Inferno'.

In the foreground, he noticed a single storey; brick built building with a complete row of metal-framed windows from end to end and a pair of double doors in the centre. Through the windows he could just make out that lights were on inside, but years of grime had covered the panes, enough to filter most of the feeble light out.

As he approached the building he discerned that there was a sort of movement, which he guessed were from people working inside. He went through the double doors and into an ante room where there appeared two more doors. The left one was marked 'Laboratory Authorised entry only" and the right one was marked 'General Office'. He timidly knocked on the Office door and having heard nothing, he knocked louder and could just make out a muffled shout through the heavy door and went in.

He saw three men sitting at desks, but only one of them looked up to greet him. The others had not shown any sign of acknowledgement, which did not encourage him. As he looked towards the opposite wall there were two other doors made in beautiful red wood with gold plaques marked; 'Works Manager' and 'Director' and those were firmly shut!

His first job after leaving school then, was to be in this Dickensian workplace as an Office Junior and General 'dogsbody' for the next three years! It was not at all what he imagined or hoped for, having left the school with such good qualifications.

Edmund got up from the bench on the cliff-top and slowly walked back to his beloved two seater Morgan sports car parked nearby in a small car park. The two honeymooners that he had met earlier were well out of sight by then, so he smiled to himself as he fired the powerful engine into life and pointed the classic sports car towards his home.

Several villages sped by as he drove deeper into the New Forest National Park. He drove through the final village before home and just before the deep woods gave way to open country; the little Morgan turned sharp right down a hidden lane.

The entrance to his lane was somewhat overgrown and being situated on a sharp bend and unsurprisingly, other road users would quite easily miss his turn. At the entrance, there was an ivy-covered sign which read; 'To the Red Cottage'. Edmund never made any effort to clear the sign as he liked to maintain his anonymity.

The little Morgan bounced on the rutted lane and lurched around a few bends, until at last a small thatched roof came into view, which was built above squat red brick walls of his traditional cottage. A single light emanated from the small window, an oil table lamp with a Tiffany style shade which made a soft welcome for him as he approached it.

He slowly edged the car around the back of the cottage and it came to rest under a small lean-to for protection from the elements. A short sharp bark from inside the back door relaxed him and as he opened the door, a silver-grey border collie already holding its lead jumped up at him, pleadingly with her pale blue eyes.

'OK Zowie, let's go.' Edmund grabbed on old walking stick fashioned from an unusual twisted sapling, a result of some creative carving. He re-locked the back door and headed into the undergrowth to which there was no discernible path, but the collie raced ahead knowing exactly where they were going.

On the way, the dog periodically darted this way and that, following the scent of some animal that had recently crossed their path, but a short whistle brought her back to his side and she assumed the role of obedient companion. After about an hour she raced off into the distance, but this time he was not alarmed, as they were approaching their intended destination.

The thickly grown leafless winter trees gave way to an open area, where the receding sun was reflecting on the dark water of a small pond, almost circular with a diameter of about thirty feet. The atmosphere created by this area was of a peaceful silence and as he looked to the right near the edge of the pond, a sturdy rustic bench awaited him and at the closest end of it, sat the collie patiently awaiting her master.

As he rested on the bench, after he had cleared the leaves and debris blown on it during the day he allowed his soul to absorb the quietness and time stood still. This little beauty spot had been his joy over the years and the pleasure of having it all for himself, was like a gift from God.

Yet not very far from this very spot, campers and hikers would be struggling to find somewhere that came near to its beauty and solitude, but overcrowding had already become the main problem for this new National Park.

After what seemed a few minutes to them, (in fact probably more than an hour had passed), Edmund's sharp hearing picked up the stronger rustling of the surrounding trees, sure in the knowledge that as the weak sun dipped below the tree line, dusk was approaching and it was best to make a move. The dog had already sensed Edmund's mental decision to begin the return journey; she jumped up and ran in the direction from whence they had arrived.

The water in the pond had become even blacker as the light had faded and the soft silence was now punctuated by the rustling of the branches above his head. The decision to move was reinforced by the thought of the open log fire lighting up the main room of his cosy abode and the food he needed to cook.

Edmund took a different route back to the cottage which to him kept the exclusivity of the pond. The dog raced ahead at times, almost guiding the man and giving him assurance in the fading light. About halfway into the journey though, he caught up with the collie which was standing stock still, looking ahead and making a little whining sound.

As Edmund followed her gaze, towards a small copse of silver birch, he shivered as he noticed some sort of movement between the tree trunks. He blinked, stared again and held his breath, preparing for the worst and then as quickly as it appeared, it was gone. The silence was deafening, so much that he could hear his own heartbeat. Did he see something or was it just a trick of the light? Certainly, his dog had sensed something.

'Come Zowie' he pushed hard on the walking stick and quickly made for home, the dog firmly at his heel.

He felt a little breathless as he reached the back garden of the cottage and instinctively scanned around for any sign of an intruder, but there was nothing. The Morgan continued to rest under the awning at the rear of the cottage and a little beyond the sports car he checked that his Toyota Hi Ace pickup, with a somewhat beat up bodywork was also still there, perfect for use during the wild winter months.

He made a mental note to fire up the Toyota's engine the next day, although he didn't worry, as in his view, the old pickup was still undoubtedly, the most reliable four-wheeled vehicle in the world. That was the reason to own two different vehicles; Morgan sports cars are not that keen on the heavy-going Forest roads in the winter months.

'First job is to get the fire going and fire-up the stove' he said to his four-legged companion, he opened the cottage door and Zowie darted in.

The stove was an old wood-burner, with neither gas nor electricity available, he had to be self-sufficient and with a large helping of imagination; a comfortable life was easily achieved. However, living the life of a recluse in the twenty first century can sometimes be more difficult, especially when he was past retirement age.

The local village post office staff were most helpful. Any mail addressed to him was held for collection with an instruction to them, that if a month had passed without contact, the manager would call by and check that he was ok. His financial affairs were sourced through a normal bank account, which was of course well managed for him and had never required any correspondence from his bank.

'Funny!' he suddenly thought, 'I have been here now for nearly ten years and it's the first time that I actually feel lonely, or is it the fact that I'm actually now getting old?' He reflected.

It was not long before the logs were burning in the grate and the added warmth of the stove was working its magic on their simple food. Within the hour Edmund was sitting outstretched on his comfortable leather chair, with Zowie lying across his feet and it was at such a time that he found the time to think back over the day's events.

The stone had been passed on to its new owner as foretold to him many years ago, when he himself became the guardian of it. He was still amazed at its mighty power, not the power over him, but the power to show him opportunities on his journey. It was not therefore, with any sadness that he had finally passed it on, but instead with grateful joy that in the past forty years it had been his companion.

He thought about his action more deeply and maybe he should have said a little more about the stone to the young blonde woman, but he knew that perhaps if he had done so, she might have been somewhat frightened. Still it wouldn't be long until events of her ownership of the stone, would become evident for her.

It was already quite dark outside and the memory of the strange shadow in that copse of birch trees made him shudder again, so he stared into the wood embers, which took him back to many years ago of that first job and the fires that raged in the Coke Ovens plant at 'Dante's Inferno'.

3: <u>Baptism of Fire</u>

Coke Ovens plant

The young Accounts Clerk soon settled into his new job at the works offices; even the Dickensian environment soon became normal. His three co-habitants in the office soon tolerated him if he fell into the expected 'pecking order'.

His immediate senior, John, was a quiet and meek individual. He seemed to perfectly fit into the character of Bob Cratchet, in Dickens's 'Christmas Carol'. John was permanently nervous, as if he was being watched constantly and of course he was – from Harold who sat at the desk in the opposite corner, a small crippled man of harsh disposition who didn't seem to outwardly like anyone. Maybe he had been that way due to his physical disability, but one could assume that was the reason, as no discussion of any personal nature ever came from his thin lips.

Another Dickensian character came to Edmund's aid again when he looked at Harold; he became Uriah Heep in 'David Copperfield'. John instructed Edmund to call him Mr. Thompson for now, not wanting to invoke one of those withering stares that were commonplace from old 'Heep'.

The third member of the office 'team' was a large ginger headed man, somewhat younger than the other two. He rose from his desk and came over to where Edmund was and although his demeanour seemed somewhat of a superior nature, he did have a warm smile. He had introduced himself as Mr Campion and he was the assistant of George Ward and as he was speaking, he looked over to the closed door on the left facing him marked 'Works Manager' who in turn was subordinate to the man behind the door to the right, marked 'M. Newman, Director'.

He knew that his mother's advice to him before setting foot in the new job would be priceless, so armed with that he wouldn't be like a 'lamb to the slaughter'. His mother made it clear that Office Juniors tasks were always menial ones, but to start from the bottom of the ladder in an office, was a thousand times better than the toil of the factory floor, as endured by the rest of his family.

Over a period, he was given his own tasks, one of which was to liaise with the Laboratory staff next-door, collecting and collating data sheets for Mr Campion. The Laboratory's main function was quality control for the plant's output and most of the work the technicians did was to test samples of the chemicals and by-products produced by the coke making plant.

Edmund found that it was much easier to communicate with the laboratory technicians than with his clerical colleagues; most would happily pass the time of day with him, although if one of the technicians were to try to get into a deeper conversation, it was frowned upon by the strict management regime.

One morning Mr Campion asked Edmund to speak to the supervisor of the Laboratory and ask him to designate one of his staff to show him around the plant and at the same time take with him some blank circular graphs. To Edmund's surprise the supervisor asked the friendliest of the technicians to help him. As he and the supervisor approached the seated man, he rose from his chair. A huge man was towering down on the diminutive junior, six feet at least and built like a grizzly bear.

'This is Dmitri' the supervisor said and instructed him to show Edmund around and at the same time explain about the use of the graphs that the young man was holding. Dmitri leaned forward, pushed a great hairy arm out to shake his hand with a wide beaming smile on his face. Soon they set off through the works yard and headed towards the noise of the smoke-filled towers and black sombre buildings.

Edmund could feel the warmth of Dmitri's voice and immediately knew that they were going to be friends. He knew the names of all the machines and explained each of their function. Many of the operatives, who were all dressed in heavy protective clothing, knew Dmitri. Some stopped to speak to him, laughing as they looked at the diminutive young man accompanying him, but Edmund didn't feel embarrassed in fact he felt quite comfortable and safe with this big man.

Soon they were climbing some mezzanine steps and traversed a raised steel walkway. The sights and sounds of the huge Battery that constituted the beginning of the coke-making process were awesome. It was a box-like structure about thirty feet high and consisted of about twenty narrow doors two feet wide and as high as the structure itself.

As they proceeded along the raised pathway Dmitri described, as clearly as he could, the workings of the terrifying machinery, he was to witness an event that would stick in his mind for as long as he lived.

Halfway along the Battery, an operator appeared with a long metal pole. With the pole, he opened a latch on one of the narrow black doorways, which immediately flew open revealing a crimson band of fire. Edmund had to shield his eyes as the immense heat flushed his unsuspecting face.

The crimson mass began to edge out of the doorway towards the heavy chain secured across its path. As the hot burning lava-like material moved out quicker, the heavy chain began to make the fiery column break and fall into a huge hopper wagon waiting below. The screaming broken fiery mass continued to crash into the waiting wagon until the end of the 'pusher' could be seen in the doorway, indicating the end of that process.

The worker firmly closed the narrow door with a loud bang and deftly locked the latch shut. The whole operation took less than thirty seconds and they continued to stand and watch as small locomotive pulled the smouldering wagon's contents away to the right towards a cavernous brick tower, only stopping when the wagon was fully inside. Edmund glanced to the top of the Battery where he could see shadowy figures moving.

'How the hell can anyone be working on top of that?' He shouted at Dmitri over the melee of noise and fire.

Dmitri smiled down at the young man. 'They're used to it, just doing their job and some have been doing the same thing for twenty years!' He laughed loudly. 'Mostly they are Iti's, prisoners of war, who didn't return to Italy and they have made a home here and married some of your English girls.' He answered in his heavy accent.

His voice was drowned out by a claxon horn from the tower and they witnessed massive amounts of water that began falling from it on to the fiery wagon below, causing a huge amount of smoke and steam to be drafted up the tower and into the sky.

'That's two thousand degrees to one hundred and fifty degrees in thirty seconds and that is how we make the coke!' Dmitri said.

Edmund noticed that all that smoke and steam emanating from the top of the tower was being blown directly onto the row of houses next to the plant. Yet in their little gardens, the housewives were unaffected as they displayed the results of their morning's toil on their washing lines.

'How often does this happen?' He asked Dmitri

Dmitri rubbed his bristly chin. 'About every half hour' he said.

Dmitri proceeded to show Edmund where to place all the circular graphs in the appropriate places and at the same time replaced the ones that had finished recording from the previous day. They were situated all over the works, some in the Battery itself and others in the wide-ranging by-product area, each in their own glass cabinets.

He explained in detail to the young accounts junior the amazing workings of the 'Woodall Duckham' designed coke oven plant, which had been installed at the works not long before World War 1, when the initial production was intended for bomb making. At that time, not many people who lived in the area were aware of the incredible uses that were made from the by-products of the amazing black gold – coal!

The coke itself, having gone through the quenching process was then shipped by the internal rail system to the four blast furnaces as fuel. The smelting of the iron ore was shipped in from the ore fields both in the UK and abroad. Both the coke making and the smelting processes worked 24 hours a day and 365 days a year, hence the need for substantial numbers of operatives working on a continuous shift programme.

The whole instruction from Dmitri took most of the day and when they returned to base it was obvious to Edmund's colleagues that he had learned so much. Mr Campion was pleased that there was no need to question or doubt the value of the time spent with Dmitri. In fact, Edmund had learnt so well that the day following his instruction, he was able to replace and retrieve all the graphs from all over the plant on his own, without any further help. Each day he would be found witnessing the fiery spectacle of the coke-making and often stopped to chat with some of the very brave operatives.

Edmund and Dmitri became firm friends after that first meeting and soon Edmund was invited to the local pub, the Iron Man, at lunchtime by a group of the Lab technicians including Dmitri. To get to the pub, all they had to do was leave the factory gates and walk up Old Compton Street, which was flanked by two rows of terraced houses. These were the same houses that got continuously enveloped by the huge cloud of smoke and steam which emanated every thirty minutes from the quencher tower.

At the top of that hill there was a small corner shop, the Iron Man Pub and a brick built church with a squat tower. The whole walk, from the plant to the pub would take him about five minutes and it was most comforting to open the public bar door of the public house and be welcomed by smiling faces and there was always a drink on the table waiting for him.

Someone had selected a record on the little jukebox, Edmund recognised it as Frank Ifield's 'I remember you'. Many years later, should he hear this particular song, it would remind him of the amazing time spent there.

'Where do you come from Dmitri?' he asked. 'Are you Russian?'

'No Edmund, I'm Polish, but before I came here I was in Russia in a place called Siberia and I was a political prisoner.' He showed the young man the tattoo on his forearm, a long string of numbers was still visible. 'Every prisoner had one of these tattooed on their arms and no amount of washing will get it off.'

'Why did they send you to Siberia?' Edmund asked him.

'My brother and I didn't like the Russian occupation of Poland and I guess that someone informed about our dissent and we were sent to a logging camp in Siberia without any trial. The conditions were so bad that my brother cut off his hand and put it in a pile of logs that were going to Finland His intention was to put a note with it so the world would know how the bastard Ruskies treated us!'

'What happened to your brother?' Edmund was shocked.

'They discovered the hand and note in the woodpile before it left the camp and they shot my brother where he stood!'

Edmund looked at the big face and could see the pain in it and he was so greatly moved by the story, he just couldn't speak with the emotion that it had invoked in him.

Fortunately, he had cleverly let his office colleague John know where he was going for lunch, so when he returned, there were no recriminations, but they did notice how upset he looked and asked him what was wrong, but he said nothing to them.

At every opportunity, Edmund quizzed Dmitri about his time before coming to England and the stories that he prized out of the Pole were both shocking and nauseating and could not fail to impress the young man. In return Dmitri was so pleased that someone was showing an interest in the huge difficulties he'd undergone at the hands of his cruel captors it had only increased their friendship.

For three years he toiled in the dingy office and the paltry sum that he worked for had hardly increased at all. It seemed that working as an office junior on the bottom rung was all well and good, but a young man needs to be able to have something to show for his labours. With that in mind, he took the offer of further education at the local college for one day per week, with the aim to ultimately achieve the accountancy qualifications they offered.

One time of year, in October his local town held the Annual Fair which filled the whole of the Market Place with the usual fairground entertainments. The whole event was held over a three-night period from Thursday to Saturday. It was a brave person who would walk around the area after ten p.m. however. Edmund did just that on the Saturday night and witnessed an event that shook him greatly.

He was standing at a stall that sold candyfloss and the local delicacy, brandy snap. Across from where he was standing, he was deafened by the screams of the occupants of the 'Waltzer' that was spinning at breakneck speed to the sound of 'Pretty Woman' by the great Roy Orbison, being played at full bore.

Suddenly from out of the Market Inn door, flew a half empty pint glass and hit the head of the person serving on the stall. She was knocked out cold in front of him! He helped other witnesses to carry her away to a waiting St John's Ambulance vehicle. 'Pretty Woman' seemed rather ironic, he thought to himself, as blood was pouring from her wound.

To his disgust, no policeman was willing to enter the pub and track down the felon. Another witness to the event told Edmund that this was commonplace, confirming that the town was more like a lawless western town on a Saturday night. Civilised it was not!

The final straw for Edmund at his employment came during the winter of 1963. A continuous downpour over a period of two weeks resulted in a river of water pouring down Old

Crompton Street on one Sunday. This had caused a major flood at the plant where he worked.

Totally unaware at the time, Edmund alighted from the bus on the Monday morning and proceeded down the street to the plant. He hadn't noticed that the air seemed much cleaner that morning, or that the great Battery was silent. As he turned to walk through the huge gates, he stopped in surprise; a huge black lake had surrounded the squat offices. The water was not only dark but very oily.

Parked on the edge of the black lake was the red Rover 110 belonging to Mr Newman the Director. The window rolled down and a suited arm beckoned Edmund closer. Edmund tentatively approached the window and the old walrus leaned out.

'Edmund, go fetch me my Gold Block.' Mr Newman ordered, waving a crisp pound note.

Edmund as usual obeyed and ran back up the street automatically, but as he ran, he imagined what the flooded office would look like and if there was anyone in there.

'Maybe old Uriah Heep is crouched on his desk right now, unable to swim out'. He thought, almost laughing to himself.

In fifteen minutes, he had returned from the corner shop, with Mr Newman's tobacco and Edmund dropped it into the waiting hand.

'It will take a week for us to get back to normal at the plant so there'll be nothing for you to do until next Monday' the director said sharply.

'Yes, but what about...' Edmund stuttered in disbelief.

'Don't worry son, you will be paid, after all, it's not your fault' he replied, laughing cynically. 'I will inform Harold personally'

Edmund turned on his heels and ran up the street to the bus stop. He didn't thank him, why should he? On the miniscule wages he was receiving, they could take as long as they liked to get back to normal. A whole week off, he thought, with pay, that will do.' He thought and smiled to himself as he imagined old 'Uriah Heep' up to his neck in the filthy water.

The return home was by trolley bus powered by overhead cable. This bus was the type that ran on pneumatic tyres, there being no metal tracks on the road, locally called a 'trackless'. Home was in an eighteen-house cul-de-sac in the centre of a small council estate situated in the North area of the town.

Most weekends would be spent walking in the surrounding fields, woods and the remains of two closed coalmines. Old winding machines and huge spoil tips were common place in his area. There was a chain of spoil tips that looked like a small range of mountains and in the winter the snow stayed on the caps of them giving the landscape an alpine look. At the base of the first of these, where rainwater had collected over the years, a small reservoir had formed. Locally known as Nutbrook, it attracted wildlife and was a regular haunt of the local fishermen.

Roach, perch, barbell and tench were the main quarry along with a fabled giant pike that many of the fishermen had seen, but never caught. There was a small bridge, which bisected the lake and as one approached it over the brow of a hill, it was quite a peaceful sight to the eyes, even though it was formed originally from the waste of the coal mining industry, nature had a way of transforming it.

Nutbrook was very often the limit of the walk for Edmund, as it was about three miles from home and for variation he took a different route back to his house. On one walk, he had chosen a route from the lake that took him through a recently ploughed field. Many of the old locals in the area told him that an enemy aircraft had been shot down during the dogfights in the battle of Britain and had crash-landed there.

Constant ploughing over the following years had brought up relics of the wreckage, these were only small items such as nuts and bolts and sometimes tiny pieces of twisted metal, but each finder prized them greatly. Nothing that anyone had found could be identified as from a Stuker, Heinkel or Messerschmitt, but with a little imagination, was prized none the less.

This field was a big one and he struggled with his footing at times, as the soil was heavy due to recent farming activity. About halfway across Edmund heard his name being called, faintly but clearly. As he looked to the far edge there was a tiny figure waving. Unbeknown to him at the time, that moment was to be a pivotal one in his life. He picked up speed and as he approached the waiting figure, it wasn't too long before Edmund had recognised him.

'Paul, what are you doing here? I thought you were in 'Brum?' Edmund asked.

Paul was born only four doors away from Edmund and only four days apart. Their paths however were separated at the age of eleven. Paul was not the most gifted individual intellectually and was destined to spend his senior schooldays at the local Secondary Modern. Although leaving school at fifteen without much of an education, he was however a gifted footballer, both for school and as a junior member of the town team. At sixteen he was quickly spotted to join the ranks of the prestigious Aston Villa football club after successfully passing their trials.

'They didn't give me a chance in the first team, not a chance.' The look on Paul's face said it all.

'Still, mate, they did give you a good run, two years isn't bad' Edmund replied sympathetically.

Paul's pride had been badly shaken and what had made it worse, his father was so disappointed that his youngest son, who had shown such promise as a youngster, was not going to give him such bragging rights at the pub.

4: <u>**The Great Find for Ellie**</u>

The chain

Two weeks had passed since their honeymoon; Gary and Ellie were back at home in Oxford in their respective jobs. Both were relaxing in the warm living room of their modest semi, where a comfortable atmosphere pervaded.

Ellie peered over the top of her book and looked at Gary's face which reflected in the light of his laptop, his face was somewhat puzzled as he gazed into the computer.

'Hmm interesting' he mused.

'What's that?' Ellie looked up.

'That stone, the one that spooky guy gave you on the beach, I'm trying to identify it on a geological website and there is nothing like it here.' Gary peered into the screen.

Ellie put her book down, moved over to the couch and picked up the stone. She immediately felt a slight energy in her hand. Bringing it closer to the light and moving it in her hand there seemed to be an uncanny depth inside it, somehow. The stone vaguely resembled the shape of a teardrop and on closer inspection, she noticed a tiny hole pierced in the pointed end.

'Did you notice the hole in the stone darling?' she asked.

Gary looked up from the laptop. 'Hole, what hole? I didn't notice any hole. Let me see.' He shook his head 'Looks like I'm wasting my time with this, I think that we should ask your friend Ro to look at it. Maybe she might find us some answers.'

Ellie's best friend Rowena was once a jeweller in London, but had decided to get out of the rat race and was lucky enough to find a gift shop for sale in the medieval city of Salisbury, where she could use all her training, but in a more satisfying way.

She gradually changed the gift shop into a more up-market venture – changing the existing range of gifts to higher jewellery content so that she could utilise her long training in London.

Ellie rang Rowena straight away and she was most intrigued with what she had heard about the mystery stone, so she asked them to bring it to her on the coming Saturday.

However, when the Saturday arrived, Gary could not make it, since he was tied up with a business report for work and he had to present it to his boss on the following Monday.

Ellie finally arrived at the little shop in Salisbury, complete with the stone clutched in her hand. They were so happy to see each other again, but skipped all the pleasantries as Rowena held out her hand to Ellie.

  'Well, where is this mystery stone then?' Ellie promptly passed it over and Rowena held it into the light, turning it this way and that. 'What's the story Ellie, where did you get it from?'

'We were walking along the beach called Fisherman's Walk near to Bournemouth and caught up with this strange man, who asked if I would like the stone, he said he found it on the beach that day.' Ellie explained.After a brief silence, Rowena's eyes became dark and she furrowed her brow.

'I don't think this was lying on the beach Ellie, things like this don't wash up like a common pebble, love. What did the man look like, was he old, young, tall, short? Sorry about all the questions, but it might help me to identify it.' Rowena quizzed.

Ellie described the man and what he was wearing and that he didn't seem the ordinary type of person that one might meet on the sea front.

'Was there anything else you can remember?' Rowena asked.

'Well, the last thing I remember was that just after he gave it to me; he seemed to give me a smile, as if somehow he knew me, does that seem strange to you?' Ellie asked.

Rowena didn't directly answer the question, as she was deep in thought at the time, peering closely at the stone with her magnifying glass.

'Look, nothing rings a bell for me and if you want an answer, I would like to keep it for a few days. Of course, I will take care of it for you.' Rowena said.

Somehow, Ellie felt somewhat anxious with the thought of the stone being out of her possession, even for such a brief time, but she nodded her agreement to Rowena. Some customers arrived in the shop so she took the opportunity to leave, but not before she made Rowena promise to take care of her stone and to ring her in the week with the results.

As she drove back home, Ellie was trying to justify the mystifying feeling of anxiety that she had at being without her stone. She had only had it for a couple of weeks and yet already it seemed to be wielding its power on her.

'It's only a stone, no need to get too upset about it, don't you think?' Gary said dismissively as he noticed how his wife displayed such a concerned demeanour.

'I guess it's the not knowing that upsets me the most. Honestly I can't explain why I feel so bad about not holding it though.' She said.

Ellie tried hard to put the anxiousness behind her for the following days after her visit to Salisbury, tried to throw herself into her job and not to think about whether Rowena had found anything out or not. Sure enough, by the following Thursday, Ellie's mobile burst into life.

'Hi Ellie, its Rowena here, can we meet up for lunch next Saturday? I think I may have found something, not sure, but it's a start'

'What have you got Ro?' Ellie asked.

'Rather tell you face to face if that's alright' pleaded Rowena.

'Fine, that's OK. Why don't you come on over here instead? Come for dinner, Ro. Give me a chance to show off my cooking skills.'

'Sorry, would love to but I'm out on Saturday night in Bath and can't move it. Anyway, I feel that if you were to come over here in the shop, it might help you understand what I have found out for you. Please understand.' Rowena pleaded.

Ellie gave in easily to her friend, as she knew that she wasn't the best of cooks anyway.

'OK Ro I'll see you around mid-day at the shop then'

'You won't be disappointed Ellie.' And then she rang off.

It had been a long hard week for Ellie. In her waking hours, all she could think about were the unanswered questions and try as she might to answer them, all that came to her mind were more questions. At night it was no better, as soon as she nodded off, her mind kept going over to the man on the beach. Sometimes he looked angry, as if she shouldn't have let Rowena keep the stone and he was remonstrating with her. Even Gary remarked how 'peaky' she looked. She hoped that when Saturday had arrived she would feel much better with the stone back in her palm.

Gary arrived home late that night and didn't seem himself to Ellie. 'Are you drunk Gary?' She asked him.

'No, but I did have a couple of glasses of Barolo with the pasta' he said. 'But the meeting went very well. Do you have any news about the stone from Rowena?' He asked as he quickly changed the subject.

She had made the room cosy and welcoming for him, she peeled off his heavy overcoat and scarf and despatched them to the hallway.

'It seems she has got some news about the stone but she wouldn't tell me over the phone. I've agreed to go there again this Saturday' Ellie explained.

'Why doesn't she come here for a change?' Gary asked.

'I did invite her for dinner, but she couldn't make it'

'Well, Ellie, come to think of it, since my meeting tonight, I can't get there either.' He looked at her rather sheepishly. 'The work I have to do over the coming weekend could have a profound influence on both our futures, darling.'

Ellie looked at him with disappointment on her face. However, inside she was not too hurt, as she felt that maybe with the two girls together they would have a little more fun.

The next morning was the day of her visit and true to form, Ellie's mobile chirped a text, from Rowena; 'c u at 12, 1 or 2 for lunch?'

She looked up and Gary was already at his laptop and he sensed her stare. 'I've been at it since six this morning, but I hope to complete before you get back, darling' Gary looked at her apologetically.

Ellie texted her reply, 'Just me and you, see you soon'

To her relief the early start had meant that she missed the pre-Christmas shopping traffic on the way to Salisbury and was pleased there was no panic for parking, as her friend had saved her a space at the back of the shop. The spaces were quite small but it was no bother for Ellie, as her VW Polo was small enough.

Rowena too had made quite an effort for Ellie's visit. She had closed the shop for an extended lunch, even though it was usually her busiest period. Many of the visitors loved to wander along the riverside and watch the swans being fed by children and conveniently, her little shop was adjacent to the pathway.

After greeting Ellie, she shooed out the remaining stragglers and shut the shop, ushering her into the tiny backroom. Ellie gasped with surprise as she surveyed the wonderful banquet that Rowena had laid out for her. A large cafetiere of Columbian coffee was steaming in the middle of the table.

'Is that decaff?' Ellie asked, Rowena nodded and smiled knowingly. They settled down and attacked the smoked salmon.

Eagerly Ellie asked 'well, what have you found out Ro? I really can't hang on any longer.'

'It's a very interesting stone Ellie, so interesting that I really wished that I had more time with it.' Rowena looked at her friend, hoping that she might suggest her keeping it longer, but Ellie was in no mind to let her keep it one moment more. 'We haven't been able to tie down its origin, or its geological makeup. Usually these days with the tools available, just about all specimens on this earth have been classified and someone, somewhere has written a paper on it.'

'What have you done, Ro, have you chipped it or something?' Ellie blurted out feeling somewhat agitated.

'No definitely not. I think I can describe it to you, but can't tell you its origin. I have spoken to several eminent people in their field, one has even been down from London to see it, in fact, he wanted to take it back for further examination, but I knew you wouldn't approve.'

'Where is it now, Rowena, has someone still got it?' Ellie looked rather seriously at her friend and by then was beginning to panic.

Rowena walked over to a low cabinet with narrow drawers and ornate brass handles. She pulled out the top drawer, took out a purple ring box and gave it Ellie.

Ellie opened the box and nestling safe and sound on a purple cushion was her stone. It seemed darker than when she had handed it over last weekend and yet when Rowena dropped it into the palm of her hand, Ellie seemed to feel a warm glow and as she stared at the centre of it, she saw a reflexion of something, but not of anything in the room. As she was looking at the stone, she could perceive this distinct warmth moving up her arm, giving her quite a pleasant lift of some kind.

Rowena watched intently as this was happening, not alarmed, more interested, without showing any outward emotion to her friend. She had noticed the change in the stone when her friend held it, but even more, the changes in Ellie.

Ellie brought the stone up closer. 'Ro, what do you think the hole in the top of it was for? It seems such a small hole, not big enough for an ordinary chain.'

Rowena looked closely at the stone and not wanting to take it out of Ellie's hand, shook her head and did not reply. Nor did she tell her that, for all the time she and others had looked at the stone for the past week, there was no hole in it, as if it had only appeared when in Ellie's hand. It now seemed to her, that the stone somehow was reluctant to give up any of its secrets.

'No, that's not possible' she thought. She also sensed that Ellie was still looking for an answer to her question.

'I think that you have the most amazing stone that I have ever encountered, just for the reason, it is an enigma to me. Although I realise that you need some clear answers, I can only suggest now, that the only person that would know anything about it, is the man that gave it to you.' Rowena hoped that her answer would be of some help.

Ellie looked into her friend's eyes as she spoke, almost in a pleading way yet with a hint of fear in it. On reflexion, she decided not to ask any further questions, only to keep the words in her heart for the time being. She didn't want to return home just yet, so with Rowena's agreement she left her car at the shop and decided to explore the medieval city on foot.

Although there was the usual smattering of chain stores and supermarkets in the centre, the old city retained its quaintness of timber framed buildings and narrow alleyways to hold her interest and so with no restriction on her parking, she enjoyed the luxury of taking her time and drinking in the wonderful atmosphere.

She started down the first narrow alley, just off the Market Square, its Tudor buildings were almost touching on the first floor, hiding any light and here she opened a black windowless door to a small shop boasting 'Fifth Generation Jewellers'.

The shop area was very small and in a few steps from the door, she was leaning against a low glass cabinet acting as the shop counter. She could hear no sound as she peered around the shop, however as she turned around, she jumped as the old shopkeeper; a short, bespectacled man in his sixties was looking up at her smiling.

'H...Hello' stammered Ellie, 'er... I'm on the lookout for a very fine chain to fit this.' She pulled out the stone and showed the tiny gap in it. The jeweller took out his glass from his waistcoat pocket.

'Mmm, a very small gap for a chain, isn't it dear? Will you wait here while I look for you' and he disappeared into the backroom not waiting for her answer.

Ellie scanned the tiny shop for anything of interest and while she waited, she noticed in the corner, there was a table so dark, that it was hardly perceivable! As she approached it she could see that it was poorly made and only a couple of feet square, covered in small dog-eared brown cardboard boxes. They reminded her of the same type that Gary kept his spare screws in and she always found it very funny that he could never find the one that he was looking for.

As she got to the table, the old man appeared from the backroom and from the look on his face, she could tell that he couldn't find anything to fit her stone.

'What do you keep in the boxes over here?' she asked.

'Well, those are collections of leftover jewellery that customers have in the past, asked me to value or sell for them. They are usually the leftovers from a house clearance after their relative's deceased effects have been looked over, if you know what I mean. I am certain that there is nothing of any value there, but lately haven't had much time to look at them. You're welcome to have a look in the boxes and if you see anything of interest, give me a shout and I'm sure we can come to an understanding.' With that he shuffled back into the workshop.

'How trusting' thought Ellie, she looked at her watch, 'plenty of time', she thought again and started to rummage.

The first three boxes produced only gaudy costume jewellery and then just before she thought about giving up, she decided to try a slightly larger box at the far side of the table. When she had emptied the contents out of the box on a space she had made, it revealed more paste jewellery and a very thin necklace. She picked up the necklace for a closer look and repulsed at the state it was in!

The old clasp was broken as if someone had forced it and in the centre, was the remains of a mounting for a coin or a medal, but all that was left was a twisted half of a semi-circular mounting. Although seriously damaged, Ellie could see that the diameter of the chain would certainly fit into her stone.

'Excuse me!' shouted Ellie. The old man quickly appeared and smiled as her noticed Ellie hanging the chain through her fingers. 'Could I purchase this from you please?' She asked. 'What would you take for it?'

'Looks like a silver chain with some damage' and without taking it out of Ellie's hand, 'How about fifty pounds?' He offered, hoping for a quick sale.

'No, sorry', she said, 'I don't think it is worth that, considering the damage and all.'

The old shopkeeper looked at her quizzically and after a moment, took a closer look at the necklace.

'Can you see this, my dear? It is a very fine snake chain, beautifully made and probably Victorian and I cannot accept less than forty pounds.'

They finally agreed on thirty-five after Ellie stuck out for the damage element and with the Jeweller's receipt in her hand and the necklace in a smart little bag, she felt quite triumphant.

As she walked back to Rowena's shop, she passed a lovely teashop and decided to call in for a treat. A pot of tea and a warm fresh scone seemed the right way to celebrate her success, so she made room on her table for the contents of the small bag and took the stone out of her jeans pocket. The workmanship of the chain was very fine and with a closer inspection of the stone, there was no doubt it would thread through that hole! She had never seen a snake chain before and was amazed how the interlocking sections were like a snake and marvelled at such intricate workmanship. As she pulled the chain through her fingers it felt perfectly smooth as if it was made of one flexible piece.

After paying the waitress, she rushed back to Rowena's shop, excitedly looking forward to hearing what she would think of her purchase. There were two customers in the shop and fortunately they were just about to leave. Rowena was still writing on the counter as Ellie approached her.

'You look pleased with yourself, Ellie. What have you got there?' Rowena asked.

Ellie laid down the bracelet on the counter in front of Rowena, 'Can you look at this Ro? Ignore the damage and just look at the chain.'

Before Rowena answered, she pulled out a small box from underneath the counter, which she opened, revealing her treasured set of jeweller's tools. Some of them were so small that Ellie could hardly make out what they were for.

She quickly set to work releasing the central mounting, which was soon despatched to the bin and then set to work on the clasp. Clasp removed, Rowena took a small damp cloth and carefully pulled the chain along it, taking as much dirt off it as she could. The whole operation took no more than ten minutes and Ellie looked on admiringly.

Finally, Rowena placed the empty chain, which by now was sparkling, onto a square of purple cloth. Ellie gasped at the sheer beauty of the result of Rowena's work, a radiant circle of about sixteen inches circumference.

'Is it silver Ro? The old jeweller said it was, although he didn't look too closely.' Ellie asked.

'OK Ellie now please tell me where you got it and what did you pay for it?' Rowena asked patiently.

Ellie told her in full detail how she found the shop and how she came to buy it, handing over to her the shop receipt with a smile. Rowena looked at the receipt and laughed.

'Ellie, you have got one of the finest platinum snake chains that I have seen in all my time in this business and just as a blank chain, I would value it at least four hundred pounds and it is a hundred and fifteen years old according to the assayer's stamp.' She showed her friend the tiny marks on the pointed end of the chain.

'Do you think you could find a suitable clasp for it? I have no idea of what style; I'll leave that to you.' Ellie asked her friend, after she had got over the shock.

'Find one? I'm not going to find one. I'm going to make one for it, a very special one. This is a big challenge for me and I already have the design in my head. Look, Ellie, why not come here next Saturday, come to my house and I'll close the shop. We'll have a girly day out and do some shopping in Bath, what do you say? I shall have done the clasp by then too.'

That was just what Ellie wanted to do, take all the silly cobwebs out of her mind and have a good laugh with her best friend.

'It's a date!' she said, beaming with her good news, waved goodbye and began her journey home, with lots to tell Gary.

As she opened the front door, she expected Gary to be leant over the laptop as usual, but she was taken aback by the wonderful warm aroma of cooking that greeted her. She could smell onions particularly, but couldn't quite put a name to the dish that was cooking. The house was quiet and as she pushed open the kitchen door, the full rich aroma greeted her and most surprising of all, the kitchen was emanating an air of peace and order!

Gary gave a gasp of mock surprise as he entered the kitchen from the door leading from the downstairs cloakroom.

'This is a first darling,' he said, giving her a big hug. 'I finished the report for work and emailed it off not long after lunch, so I thought about making my favourite dish for you as a surprise'.

'Shepherd's Pie.' she laughed, 'that's just what I fancied.' What Ellie was more pleased about, was that he had given her some thought instead of as his all-consuming career.

'Well, that's one thing I can't get wrong,' he said. 'How was your day, exciting?'

'Darling, yes it was exciting but, let me shower and in a couple of ticks I'll be down to eat your creation and then I can tell you the news.' She laughed, running up the stairs.

In ten minutes Ellie was making the gravy that was not his forte. But she knew that even with the gravy, he would be still pouring on his HP as was his wont. It was past eight before they had cleared up and settled down on the couch, the second helping of the Shepherd's Pie had filled them up completely, no room at all for afters.

'That's what you call comfort food. I'm stuffed' Gary wheezed. 'Just stretch out darling and tell me about your day.'

Ellie did her best to tell him what had happened since she had left home that morning. Gary wasn't surprised that Rowena hadn't been able to identify the stone as he had looked at every Internet site that was connected in any way to crystals and stone sites. He was, though, very impressed with her success in getting the chain so cheaply.

'Maybe I should go back to the shop when Ro has completed the clasp and give the old jeweller a bit more money, considering its real worth.'

'I'm sure that the thirty-five pounds you gave him, had already exceeded what he had expected, considering the state of it when you found it.' He gazed into her green eyes. 'Anyway, I don't suppose he would recognise it after all that you and Rowena have done to bring it up to scratch.'

'Have you thought about the whole chain of events that had happened to me today?' Ellie mused.

'Do you mean that you think they are connected in some way?' Gary asked.

'Not really darling, sorry, it was just a thought that passed into my mind, as if something is controlling events today, just silly thoughts that's all!' She was just about to suggest an early night when he interrupted.

'Well darling, I told you that I had sent the report off about one today and I was just about to power the computer down, when I got a reply in the inbox'

'So, who was it from?' She sat up straight, now fully awake.

'It was from old Freddy Aldwinkle'

'Isn't that the....'

'Oh yes, he's the head honcho and he wants to see me urgently on Monday' he said.

'What can that mean, Gary, are you losing your job? Ellie looked worried.'

'I don't think so, love, quite the opposite, anyway if that was the case I would get a letter and even if anything like that would be happening, the old honcho wouldn't be contacting me personally.'

'So, what you're saying, is it promotion?' Ellie excitedly asked.

A couple of weeks had elapsed since the first contact from his boss, the old 'Honcho'. Since then it had transpired that the size of the promotion for Gary was staggering! His current job was based at the Oxford site and he rarely needed to be away from home. His new post in the company was, from his job as divisional works manager, to the post of full Commercial Operations Director reporting directly to the CEO Mr Aldwinkle.

The offer of salary was breath-taking and so were the benefits, but Ellie thought, 'at what price?' She was at pains to point out the possible downside of the offer to her husband; he was going to be based in Belfast, where the Head Office was situated. Not only that, but the promotion would mean that he would be doing a lot of travelling within the Group and perhaps elsewhere. They had given him two weeks to mull it over and the final day for decision had come.

Of course, Gary was ecstatic about the offer and in response to Ellie's words of caution, his final words were always 'well, who wouldn't be over the moon?' Over the past two weeks neither of them could change each other's mind on the matter.

To Ellie it was very frustrating, it seemed as if he was blind and deaf to any of her arguments and understandably he was obviously on 'cloud nine' about the whole thing. She knew that Gary was just waiting for her to give him the nod and time was running out.

'Look Gary, we've talked and talked about it and I know that you can't see any of my arguments, but I need to stay here in Oxford a while to get my life sorted, can't you see that?'

'You mean about that bloody Stone?' he blurted out, clearly losing his composure.

She ran to the door, picked up her overcoat, slipped her boots on and ran outside slamming the door behind her and ran down the street into the night.

'Ellie! Ellie!' He shouted, but there was no reply from her.

The frosty night had cleared her head, especially from the pressure of constantly trying to get her point of view into Gary's head. It felt as if he had a head made of stone!

That thought immediately prompted her memory that she had to ring Rowena. Such a lot had happened since they last met, with so much going on, she had considered to say that she couldn't make the planned trip to Bath.

'Hi Ro.' Ellie's mobile had rung for quite a while before Rowena answered.

'Ellie, do you know what time it is? What's up?'

Ellie looked at her wristwatch 12.20am. 'I'm really sorry Ro; I just wanted to hear your voice. Gary is being so exasperating right now, so I'm outside cooling off.'

'Look Ellie, it's late; too late to get here, can you go home tonight and come over tomorrow?' Rowena asked.

'Thanks Ro, I really need someone to talk to, I just need to get away from here for a bit.' Ellie seemed calmer, 'I'll ring in to work and get a day's holiday and it should be OK, thanks.'

'Listen, go on home and get some sleep, if you can and we'll have a heart to heart when you get here, I'll clear the day and we'll sort something out. And, hey, there's something waiting here for you.' Rowena reminded her.

Suddenly all the tension had left Ellie and she looked towards home. Although she had been out for an hour, she hadn't walked that far and had quickly reached their front door. Gary had left the porch light on; she was just about to look for the key as Gary opened the door for her. He smiled warmly and stood aside as she passed by him into the warm room and took her coat.

'I had to ring them to confirm his offer Ellie, time had run out.'

'I suppose you didn't mention to the 'head honcho' that I wasn't happy?' Ellie asked

'I think they guessed that it was a difficult decision, so it was easy to wring out a concession from him. We will not have to move there for six months to give us time to get used to the changes.' He explained.

She looked up at him, but tiredness took over and she went up to bed without any response. All she could feel was defeated and deflated. He'd won this battle, but what about the war? That would perhaps be a different kettle of fish she thought.

After a restless night for both, the morning light had greeted them tense and not really sparking. Ellie finally decided to make the effort and fortunately there were enough ingredients to make him a real cooked breakfast with his favourite HP sauce.

She was right, the tension had finally broken and they got to talk about all the timings that the change entailed, starting from that morning.

'Gary, I'm not angry with you, really I'm not and I do want you to understand that I am prepared to make sacrifices so that you can get the job offer of your dreams. I really don't want to stand in your way, but I do want you to realise that there are things in this job that you cannot possibly foresee. I'm just praying that you take this job with your eyes fully open. It does sound like they are aware of the cataclysmic changes that it will make for us. Please promise me that you will keep your feet on the ground and don't say yes to anything without thinking about it. Darling, all I really want is the best for you and us.' She looked deep into his eyes; he was full up with emotion.

'I promise' he said to her.

'I've arranged to see Ro today, I've fixed a day's holiday with work, she's finished the clasp on the chain and I'm

looking forward to seeing that. Will you be home tonight?'
she asked.

'No, I'm booked on a flight to Belfast at lunchtime, but
should be back for the weekend.' She looked a bit downcast
and so as an afterthought he said, 'but I'll ring you at nine
tonight, OK?'

She wasn't surprised and showed little emotion outwardly,
but inwardly she knew this day was the beginning of a huge
change in their relationship. To him, career will be the big
part, to her, well who knows? She looked back at him,
smiled, picked up her coat and opened the door.

'Till tonight then.' She whispered.

Rowena's advice about going home that night was a very
good one. Who knows what could have happened if she had
left Gary to brood overnight on his own. Quite possibly he
would have made decisions without any consideration for
her feelings and things may have gone beyond any chance
of a repair in their relationship.

She slid into the driving seat of the Polo, turned the ignition
and didn't look back. He, on the other hand watched
through the front window as she disappeared around the
corner.

5: <u>French Adventures</u>

<u>**Cannes**</u>

Edmund had just returned from the local post office in the village, to pick up his post and smiled, noticing that there was an airmail letter with a New York franking mark on it. Smiling to himself, he knew that was from Paul. His old friend had moved to the USA in the late eighties. The dream of an acting career had never taken off in the UK, but with an offer of work in Los Angeles, he just couldn't turn it down. Several moves within the States later he finally settled in the Big Apple. He had found a place to live strangely in the Dakota building, on the same floor level where John Lennon had lived, before his sad assassination.

Many of Paul's letters described the small park where he often visited, situated within the nearby Central Park, dedicated to John's memory called 'Strawberry Fields', a song that will be forever embedded in both of their memories.

Edmund opened his old friend's letter and as usual Paul began with all the famous and not so famous, names of people he had met in New York, dined with or simply screwed. 'Oh yeah!' he smiled to himself being the sceptical one.

Paul was closer to him than his own brother and he knew that Paul could not resist the temptation to bend the truth a little, just for effect. The letter ended as usual with a fervent invitation to go over there and visit him and finally with the usual words:

'You just don't know what you're missing in the Big Apple, Eddie'

Edmund never usually replied to any of the letters that he had received from Paul. Basically, he felt true contentment in his life and trying to describe that to Paul would be a waste of paper. He also knew that Paul would not have been too upset with the lack of response from his friend either, as even at 66, he was just too busy with his New Yorker life to worry about it.

A recent investment in a wind-up radio gave him all the companionship he needed in his cottage. One afternoon having turned his radio on, he found himself in the middle of Dave Cash's programme, which was playing a selection of hits from the past. That night it featured 1964 and the Kinks were blaring out 'You really got me!' As he dozed off in the chair, his mind travelled back to that momentous time in his life, a time when the entire world was changing, *especially his*.

The winter of 1963/4 was a very hard one; the very cold spell had taken until May to finally break. The construction industry was hit the hardest in Edmund's area. The snow had remained over the ground up to the end of April and even when it had melted, it was so cold that the ground had quickly frozen over again. This situation created a thick layer of perma-frost well over ten feet deep under the ground. Building contracts that were due to be started, were held up because even the most powerful diggers could not penetrate to dig out the foundations.

His father was laid off work because of this arctic blast and he remembered what was said at the time in his household.

'If the wind comes by the North Sea in winter, then it originates from Siberia and nothing good ever came from there!' His dad would often remark.

By the following summer, Edmund had already left his first job at the Coke Ovens. Pay and working conditions were the main reasons for leaving and after three years, there seemed no opportunity of any career improvement at the grim offices where he worked. The Head Office was over a mile away and the only prospect of promotion was to get in those central offices and away from the grim outpost he was languishing in.

His pay had moved from £3.10s per week in 1960 to the measly sum of £4.2s.6d in 3 years. He had to get out of there and although he had made some good friends in the laboratory, he decided to move out of office work into factory work. A new factory had been built to house a new operation assembling wooden TV cabinets for the latest Decca model. At that time, it was the state of the art and after his training he was paid the princely sum of £15 per week. An amazing improvement, he just couldn't believe it! The only thing he regretted was that he didn't finish his studies and get his accounting qualification, but he knew there would always be time later to complete them.

By June 1964, Edmund and Paul had become firm friends since their chance meeting. Paul had also found work in the same factory and for a year they both enjoyed the trappings of a good income at the very time when young people were finding new freedoms. By this time, they had planned at length the ways of making their escape from their uninspiring environment. The sixties had exploded around them, so for young twenty-year olds the time had come to decide. They knew that old rulebook of their life ahead was to be thrown away and replaced with only one rule, that their new future was based on no rules at all.

One of the greatest influences was from the then banned film, The Wild One starring, in their opinion, the greatest actor of them all, Marlon Brando. From that film, there was a quote that stuck with them for a long time. It was in the scene where the young girl at the bar asks Johnny the question, 'what are you rebelling against?' Back came the reply from leather jacketed Johnny; 'Whaddya gat?' The whole idea of rebelling about everything and everyone appealed greatly to them.

Another character that struck a chord was Albert Finney's portrayal of Arthur in the film 'Saturday Night and Sunday Morning'. This was filmed much closer to home; in and around Nottingham. Allan Sillito's screenplay of the Nottingham factory worker was unnervingly correct in the narrow-minded and short-sighted attitudes that abounded in the locality, those types that Paul and Edmund dearly wanted to escape from.

Clutching their new passports and battered suitcases they walked down the hill to the bus stop to take them to the station in Nottingham. Within no time at all they were boarding the boat train at London Victoria. The young men were embarking on their most exciting escapade, they were on their way to Paris and they were breaking free!

Paris Gare du Nord was as far away from them, a week ago, as the surface of the planet Mars and an hour after they had alighted from the train, they were walking along the Champs Elysee in the most fantastic city in the world. Edmund was floating on air as he drank in the atmosphere.

No one gave them any advice on how to survive in this engagingly beautiful city; they just had to fly by the seat of their pants. Half of their savings were gone in just a few days. The only foreign language that they had between them was Edmund's schoolboy French, which in this great city was less than useless. However, as luck would have it, they fell into a friendship with a group of German teenagers who were on holiday travelling around France.

The great benefit of teaming up with this group was patently obvious, that their command of French was very useful and what's more, their command of English was even better! In some way, it made Edmund feel a bit inferior, but he soon got used to that.

In their favour, being English in the sixties was a great advantage. No other country in Europe had the great asset of being the hotbed of the revolution in pop music. The girls in the German group were just mad for that music and Paul was determined to take as much advantage of that fact as possible! They quickly found out that the Germans were leaving Paris for the Cote d'Azure the next day, so they quickly decided to join them.

The train journey was long and tedious, taking over twenty-four hours, not so bad for Paul, having wiled his way into the arms of the best-looking girl as usual. They decided to get off the train at St Raphael, a lesser-known resort, quite small and with lots of leaf covered beaches to wander on. Two of the German group's girls decided to explore the town with the two 'Englisher' men and waved off the rest of the group, promising to meet up again in Nice. Money was getting tight, but with the help of the two girls, they could rent a room over a Bouillabaisse café, situated in a backstreet. To Paul's dismay they didn't want to stay and try out the bed and instead they wanted to re-join their group in Nice.

As soon as the locals found out that they were English, it seemed to lower the temperature everywhere they went, Edmund just couldn't understand it at all. This weighed heavily on them both, enough to make them quite unhappy and it regularly crept into their conversation. It was at that point that the idea they might have to return home and their money was running out too.

Heavy hearted, they called in at the nearest beach café for perhaps their last drink before packing. On the next table a group of four guys in sailor uniforms were talking in loud American English.

'Hey buddy, you speaky da English?' A young American sailor was looking at Edmund, probably thinking he was French.

'I am English' he said with his best English accent.

'What are you Limeys doing here?' He shouted. The other three sailors looked over. One of them, as big and wide as the door butted in, 'can you find us some cold cans of coke Mr Limey?'

As quick as a flash, Paul got up from his seat. 'Yes, we know where to get your drinks pal'

'OK Pal' he answered a bit threateningly. 'Go and fetch us a six pack,' passing a twenty-dollar bill over to Paul.

Paul was a bit stunned; he suddenly felt exposed. Edmund acted quickly and snatched the money off his friend and ran down the street, not knowing at that time where the hell he was going. He asked a dozen people in his broken French, but most of the passers-by just shook their heads.

'What are you looking for sir?' Once again it was a German, who was speaking perfect English that rescued him.

'Thanks, yes I'm looking for somewhere I can buy some Coca Cola for some friends and where they might change this for me' Edmund asked, realising that US Dollars were not the local currency. The German took Edmund to a small bar only two streets away from the café where the Yanks were. The very kind German translated to the owner and even made sure that the French shopkeeper didn't short change Edmund. Before he went back to the café with his booty, Edmund made sure that he got the German's name and where he lived, so that they both could thank him properly later.

He had in fact bought twelve small bottles of Pepsi from the bar for the princely sum of five dollars and he had fifteen in change, ten for the Yanks and five for going, stuffed in his back pocket. When he got back to the café the yanks roared in approval and were also amazed to get ten bucks back. The sailor closest to Edmund shot out a huge hand to shake and when Edmund offered his hand, the American just about shook his arm off.

Edmund signalled to Paul that they were leaving, but not without a huge amount of good-natured back slapping from the four sailors. They also told Edmund that they were passing on to their fellow shipmates about them and hoped to see them again. As they walked back to their room, Edmund stopped and looked at Paul's puzzled face.

'Listen Paul, we have found an opening at last'

'Opening, what do you mean?' Paul looked puzzled.

'This is the payment for our trouble and they were happy to get their cokes and ten dollars change, weren't they?' Edmund laughed as he pulled the five-dollar bill out of his back pocket.

A smile filled Pauls face and he now could see a chance to make some money at last. Edmund also explained that without the help of another German, none of this could have happened.

'Who won the war again?' Edmund asked with a smile, they both laughed, more in relief than anything else.

For once Paul could see the benefit of Edmund's education. Before that day, he thought that the only way to get ahead was by using his charm and looks. But in a hostile environment such as this one, Edmund had seized the opportunity offered to him with both hands and here was the result; five dollars. Edmund however, had made it very clear to Paul that although the situation with the American sailors could be a money-spinning one; he saw it only as a short-term solution.

'Why do think that Eddie?' he asked.

With his newly acquired confidence, he explained that the American fleet would only be visiting the area for a brief time. He had overheard one of the sailors say about two weeks. He also said that the locals wouldn't let them take any money-making opportunity from them for long and that he wouldn't be surprised if they had already spotted what was going on.

'Yeah, but things are in our favour just now. They're French and we're English and it doesn't look like the Yankee sailors speak French either'. Paul said.

'Good point there, so we've got to make hay while the sun shines and whilst luck is on our side, but we must keep our eyes peeled and not be greedy.' Edmund said.

'What about the night time?' Paul asked.

'I have thought about that Paul, think on. Yes, there could be more Yanks about, but they will all be boozing and when booze is about there is always trouble, what do you think about that?' Edmund asked.

'We don't want any trouble mate, do we?' Paul admitted.

'No, so let's make some money and keep our noses clean at night, agreed?'

'Yup, let's go for it buddy.' said Paul in his best Midwest accent.

For nearly two weeks they both kept to their rules and for quite a small effort, the two lads had amassed a tidy sum of $350, but there were two things that made Edmund concerned. By now there were fewer sailors going into their café and Edmund had noticed that on the last two evenings they were being followed by two of the locals on the way back to their lodgings.

The other worry for Edmund, was that Paul was also playing with fire. In the last few days he had struck up a relationship with a French girl. Nothing wrong with that, but he felt that Paul's new relationship had coincided with them being tailed.

'Mate, we have got to stop now and get out of here.' Edmund looked worried as they sat on the bed counting their loot.

'You're joking, aren't you? Paul asked.

'Trust me mate, there are some fireworks brewing and very soon. We have to get out of here, at the latest tomorrow, or we risk losing everything.' Deep down Edmund feared that Paul would blow up a storm, especially when he was getting tied up with Marie-Pierre.

Paul looked worried, 'Where are we going Eddie, home?' He looked so downcast.

'Not that I don't trust you Paul, but I'll tell you where we are going, when you get back from seeing Marie tonight. My advice is to tell her nothing about this, but if she presses you, tell her that we are planning to return to England next week and whatever you do, don't say anything about tomorrow savvy?' Edmund's face looked tense, 'I really mean this Paul, there is going to be trouble and soon, I can feel it. I don't know whether the bird has something to do with it or not, but we've got to move out of here.'

Paul looked at his friend with new eyes, 'where had that spotty-faced office boy gone' he thought to himself.

'Without much help from me, here we are with a good pile of dollars stashed away.' Paul looked straight at his friend. 'Shit to the French bird, there's plenty more where that came from. Let's move out matey.' Paul smiled as he realised the situation that they were in.

'I wasn't thinking of going to England mate. Oh no, twenty miles up the coast is a town called Cannes and we can catch a bus to there from just down the road.' The relief on Edmund's face was plain to see.

'What are we waiting for? Let's go tonight!' Paul shouted.

Leaving the room that night was no problem, the café owner had received his rent for the week and as they expected he said, 'don't expect a refund monsieur.'

In a very brief time, they were sitting on the bus bound for Cannes. The route through St Raphael passed the café and Paul stuck two fingers up at it as they went by. Living on their wits and against the odds, they had grown street-wise in this foreign country and they were now escaping the trouble that they would have most certainly encountered and were escaping totally unscathed.

In less than an hour the bus had deposited them outside the Imperial Hotel on the Cannes seafront boulevard. For a while they stood still taking in the sights. Across the boulevard was the beach, which edged up to the azure sea and in the distance, white sails of numerous yachts were bobbing gently on the swell. Along the boulevard huge palms were swaying in the light warm breeze and the high-class promenade disappeared into the distance.

Behind them were the white edifices of the huge hotels and rising behind them in the lush green hills were dotted the villas of the super-rich.

'Look. They're getting ready for the Film Festival.' Paul pointed to the banners, flapping in the wind.

His eyes were popping out of his head; even Edmund had to admit it was the most incredible sight that either of them had ever seen in all their lives.

'Look Paul, the sun will be down very soon and we need somewhere to bed for the night. And don't think we're staying in one of them.' Edmund pointed at the hotel that they were still standing in front of.

He finally got Paul down to earth and they went down the nearest back street and luckily found a small lodging house, they secured a reasonable room and after Edmund's good haggling, at a reasonable price.

Being the height of the season and nearing the Festival time, the owner had no problem accepting dollars. After all the work in St Raphael, Edmund made sure that they weren't duped in the exchange, by not too much anyway. Paul was like a dog on heat, so after a quick splash and unpack, he was ready to take the beach.

In less than an hour after arriving in Cannes, they were back on the seafront. The sun was leaving the sky on the horizon, with a range of bright yellow colours, fading into a scarlet hue on the horizon. The cloudless sky was streaked by the white vapour trails of jet aircraft. It was truly a magical place.

'Look Eddie, over there!' Paul shouted.

The beachfront gave way to a sumptuous yacht marina, where hundreds of Sunseeker yachts and huge touring launches were bobbing together.

'Let's go and have a look at them.' Edmund replied.

As they came closer, the huge 'gin palaces' came into view. As the two young men walked by, the crowds of beautiful girls and poser guys looked haughtily at them.

'All waiting for the film producer to walk by, I expect.' Paul said through his teeth.

Edmund knew that looking at this vista alone was enough to make a life-changing impression on Paul and it would drive him into the show business world for the rest of his life. The money flowing into this place was immense, way beyond their dreams and Edmund knew that there were 'no easy pickings' here.

As they headed back to the digs, there was a local bar on the same back street, one the locals had frequented, so they picked up a bottle of wine and then two baguettes and some local cheese from the next-door boulangerie.

In their sparse surroundings, they ate and drank their purchases and made their plans for the next day in that beautiful French town of opportunity.

They agreed not to take all their cash out with them. Each would take $50 and leave the balance in the concierge's safe in the vestibule of the hotel, in all about $250. Paul couldn't wait to get out there in the sunshine and try to make his impression on some of the starlets. They agreed to split up, as Paul knew that Edmund wasn't that impressed with the showbiz types and decided to leave all that to Paul.

Everything was so fresh and bright on the seafront boulevard and the sunshine almost blinded them as they emerged from the darkened backstreet. In a flash, Paul headed into the crowd, which soon swallowed him up and he didn't look back.

Edmund headed back to the marina, where he remembered that he had noticed there was one boat moored there which was not lit up like a Christmas tree and didn't have all those flashy types parading on deck. He easily found the gangway he was looking for. The prow was topped with a steel handrail jutting out and was overhanging the walkway that he stood on.

He had soon strolled by the beautiful yacht and soon arrived at the end of the boardwalk, so he turned on his heels and continued back the way he had come. As he passed the boat for the second time, he was unaware that he was being watched.

'Hey buddy, you looking for someone?' Edmund turned and as he looked upwards, there was a friendly face peering over the huge prow and a hand beckoning him over. 'Do you speak English?'

'I am English, I'm just out for a stroll' said Edmund innocently smiling back.

'Well then, why not come aboard and join us for some coffee, that is, if you have the time.'

Edmund nervously climbed aboard and held tightly on to the shiny rails as he went down into a sumptuous saloon.

'I've never been on one of these before.' Suddenly he felt very nervous.

The man pointed to a soft leather seat and soon they were chatting. Edmund stood up as in walked a small but well-proportioned woman in her thirties with a tray of coffee.

'Let me introduce myself. I'm Ben and this is my wife Vera.' They shook hands and Edmund introduced himself and started to relax a little.

'Hope you don't mind me asking Ben, but what do you do for a living?' He asked as he surveyed the sumptuous interior of the yacht.

'Well Edmund, I'm a stockbroker on Wall Street and Vera er...' Vera smiled at him, 'I paint a little' she said, looking at Ben. 'She paints a little - only has an exhibition in 46th Street!' Ben laughed awkwardly.

Edmund decided to tell them truthfully what he had been up to since arriving in the South of France. He felt somewhat embarrassed that he had taken advantage of some of their countrymen.

'Yeah, I guess they deserved it too eh Vera?' They both laughed loudly.

Edmund noticed from the beginning, even though they had this luxury, they seemed genuine people; Ben particularly was not at all what he had expected. Instead of spouting off about his achievements, he was more interested in Edmund's meagre ones. Time had passed so quickly, Edmund got up to leave, but Vera would have none of it.

'Will you please stay for lunch Edmund? It won't be much, but you're surely welcome'

'Listen Vera, I can tell you that you don't eat much when you're living on your wits in a foreign country every day.'

Edmund told Ben that he was down in Cannes with his best pal, who was more interested in the trappings of show business, so they had agreed to split up during that day. He explained that because of his humble beginnings at the steel plant, he stressed that there were other things in life that interested him, more than trying to get into the false world of glitz and glamour.

As they ate, Ben told Edmund that he was still very close to his mother who was a widow living in an apartment in Manhattan. His father had died when he was quite young, so she had brought him up on her own.

'New York is a tough place when you don't have money Edmund.' His mother had got him through college and now he was a rising star, making deals 'that would curl your hair buddy.'

He told Edmund that his mother was not happy in New York anymore, especially as she was worried about the rising gun crime. What she wanted more than anything would be to live in the UK. She had a pen friend in Bournemouth and had recently been to visit her and was very impressed with it.

Later in the afternoon Edmund decided it was time to leave his hosts, but not before offering to contribute to the wonderful meal he had shared with them.

'It's good money Ben, as you now know, it's care of the US Navy.' They both laughed so much that Ben's eyes were streaming.

'We'd love you to come and visit us tomorrow, would you join us Edmund? I particularly would like to hear more of your life in the UK'. Vera asked him. Ben was still recovering from Edmund's last remark.

'Look buddy, we both would love to see you again, with comedy like that, I could get you on the Ed Sullivan Show.' Ben gave Edmund his business card and shook his hand mightily. 'Come if you can Edmund, it's been great to have your company. Bring your friend with you next time.'

As he walked down the floating gangway, he looked back. They were on deck, waving. He waved back, clutching Ben's card. On his way back to the room, there was a real warm feeling inside him, not from the food, but the genuine hospitality, from two people, very rich people who, if they had been British, they would have treated him so differently!

Stretched out on the bed he quietly thought about the day he had had and dozed off with Ben's card still in his hand. He woke up with a jerk, the small amount of light had disappeared from the window and he looked at his watch. Eight o'clock.

'Where the hell are you Paul?' He asked out loud.

Edmund was just thinking that Paul had finally scored with one of the myriad of starlets who were also looking for fame, when he heard the downstairs door slam. He swung his feet off the bed, out of the bedroom door and onto the landing. He spied Paul struggling to get up the stairs swaying from side to side as he just managed to put one step in front of the other.

'What the hell, what's going on mate?' Edmund asked concernedly.

Paul looked up at his friend, grimacing with pain. There was blood on his face and his right coat sleeve was torn at the shoulder. His clothes were dirty and the knees of his jeans were scuffed and black.

'I've just been run over by a horse and cart.' Paul struggled to say.

Trying to laugh, Edmund knew what he meant. Paul was referring to Albert Finney's character Arthur in 'Saturday Night and Sunday Morning' when he had explained the severe beating up that he sustained at the fairground.

As Edmund helped him into the room, Paul explained that two men had jumped him from behind about an hour before. He had taken punches in the face and had several kicks to his side.

'Get on the bed Paul and I'll go and get us something to eat and drink.' The sense of wellbeing he felt had quickly vanished.

As he walked to the shop, he weighed up in his mind what the reason could have been for Paul's beating. Either it was a simple robbery or perhaps some sort of reprisal for the time they had in St Raphael. He soon returned to the hotel room laden with the regulation baguettes and cheese along with a big bottle of local wine.

Paul had showered and got into bed and as Edmund entered the room, he stifled a smile and he certainly had the stuffing knocked out of him. The bruises on his face were forming and no doubt several on his body were forming too!

They talked into the night. Before Paul had suffered the beating, he had had a delightful day and met some interesting people and even 'nearly scored' with a gorgeous blonde, the thought of which helped him slightly with the pain.

Of course, Edmund was more concerned with the reason for the beating, but they agreed to see how he felt the next morning before deciding on what action they might take. When it finally came to Edmund's turn in describing his day, he glossed over it somewhat and made light of it, considering what Paul had been through.

The next morning Paul was in no fit state to go chasing the starlets so Edmund suggested that they make their way to the Marina, not just because Ben and Vera had invited him, but maybe they could help to get Paul checked out in case he had broken anything. Quite frankly, there was nowhere else for them to turn, so Paul agreed.

As they approached the floating gangway, Paul stood there for a while, catching his breath and Edmund hurried on towards the yacht. He called Ben from the side of the boat and fortunately he appeared quickly.

'Ben, I need a favour from you, my friend has been badly beaten up and is in some pain, do you think you could help? I've brought him here and he's just along the gangway. It would be an immense help if you could look at him for me.' Edmund asked.

Ben ran along the gangway with Edmund towards his injured friend and Vera was not too far behind. With some difficulty, Paul was pulled on board and down into the saloon where he was stretched out on the long leather couches.

'What happened buddy?' Ben asked Paul, his face grim with the pain. Paul had undone his shirt revealing two heavy bruises.

'Vera has had first aid training, Paul and she is going to check if anything's broken under there, whilst I get us some coffee.' It didn't take her long to ascertain that there were no bones broken, to everyone's relief.

'I guess you ain't going nowhere today old buddy, why not stay on board and we'll take care of you,' Ben said to Paul and then to Edmund. 'I guess that you don't want the cops to be involved, is that right?'

Edmund nodded. 'Thanks Ben, I'm really sorry to drag you into this, but quite honestly we hadn't got anyone else to turn to.'

Vera passed Paul some aspirin for the pain, covered him with a blanket and in a few minutes, he closed his eyes as the pain diminished. 'We've paid for another night at the hotel and we'll go back there a bit later, then tomorrow I have decided that we will be making our way back to Blighty'

'Blighty? Where's that, Edmund.' Ben said looking puzzled.

'Sorry Ben, I mean England; it's an old nickname for home.' Ben stifled a laugh looking at Paul's prostrate body. 'This really changed my plans Ben, as I was looking forward to hearing about yourselves and your life in the States. One thing is for sure though, I have your card and when I can, I will contact you and one day I will be in New York to thank you personally for your kindness and hospitality. Paul wants to be an actor, I know that, but since I have met you, I think I know what I want to be now.'

'What's that old buddy?' Ben asked.

'Just bloody rich Ben, bloody rich!' They both laughed and as Edmund looked at Vera, she was laughing too.

Later that afternoon, after a sumptuous lunch with the Americans, Edmund decided that it was time to take their leave and another surprise occurred. Ben had radioed for a taxi to take them to their hotel. Edmund protested weakly, but Ben would hear nothing of it. The taxi driver helped Paul along the gangway to the waiting Peugeot, followed by Ben, Vera and Edmund.

'Shalom dear friends, I will see you again God willing.' Edmund shouted.

'Until then, Edmund, God be with you.' Ben shouted back.

'And may God also be with you Vera and with you Ben.' Edmund hugged both and slid into the Peugeot.

'Till then' Ben shouted, but the two young men were already on their way back to their digs in town in the prepaid taxi.

6: <u>More Questions than Answers</u>

Pulteney Bridge Bath

As Ellie pointed her car on the route to Salisbury, she knew that Gary would soon forget the friction that there had been between them. He would soon be on the plane to Belfast, the excitement of his new job would fill his thinking. Sometimes careers absorb everything in ambitious people, even love.

'Who knows?' she thought to herself.

She soon arrived at Rowena's new little semi and parked across her driveway. Just as she opened the Polo's door, Rowena was standing at the front door, tall and beautiful.

'Not dressed to stay at home' she thought.

'Where are we going Ro?' Ellie asked.

'I think we deserve to go on that shopping trip to Bath. If you recall, we were going a couple of weeks ago but....'

'Yes, I know something had got in the way! Whose car are we taking?' Ellie interrupted.

'We'll take mine.' Rowena smiled wistfully, as if she had a secret. 'But first come in I want to show you something.'

Ellie ran into the house. 'It's not much Ellie, but I made it myself.' She handed over the chain, which she had displayed in a flat presentation box.

Ellie extracted the chain carefully from the box. It was fastened together and she looked carefully at the clasp. It was made quite small, to match the size of the chain. The clasp was fashioned in the shape of a dragon's head, just as if it had grown out of the end of the chain. The flat part of the head was lit on each side by the smallest of red rubies representing the fiery eyes; the whole thing was totally enchanting.

Rowena showed Ellie how to unfasten the clasp with a perfectly soft click, revealing the head on one side and a pointed tail-like sculpture on the other end. Rowena showed her friend the Celtic engraving she had done on the tail, Ellie gasped with delight, utterly speechless. Rowena then gave her lessons on how to fasten and unfasten the chain so that she didn't either damage the mechanism or scratch herself in the process.

Ellie got her breath back as she undid the chain and laid it in the box.

'Ro darling this is so beautiful, you are so talented.'

Rowena smiled, 'you know Ellie, I really enjoyed making the clasp and it took me back to my training in London.'

'The stone, we've forgotten the stone.' Ellie pulled it out of her trouser pocket and straight away began to thread the engraved tail of the chain through the tiny hole in the stone.

She pulled the chain gently along, then suddenly it stopped, as if it was jammed. Instead of yanking the stone any further along the chain, she carefully handed the whole thing over to Rowena. Rowena carefully laid the assembled necklace onto the soft cloth and fastened the clasp.

'Look Ellie, look where the stone has stopped, precisely in the middle of the chain.' Rowena exclaimed.

Uncannily the stone had stuck exactly where it should have done; opposite to the clasp so that it was indeed perfect to wear.

'You certainly won't have to worry now, it will always be in the right place for you.' She handed the necklace to Ellie, who excitedly put it on for the first time.

Ellie looked at the wall mirror. 'It's perfect Ro. Look how perfectly the clasp matches the chain and the stone matches it too.'

'Let's get going to Bath, Ellie, or we won't have time to look around, I love exploring that place, don't you?' Rowena quickly changed the subject as she didn't want Ellie to talk about payment. They quickly swapped the car positions in Rowena's drive and were soon on their way in Rowena's little car.

An hour or so later they were edging their way towards their destination and Ellie pointed out a car park notice as they approached the Georgian city, but Rowena carried on, she knew where there was a better one and it was right in the centre of the Georgian city.

The Abbey loomed closer and Ellie was getting a bit nervous, thinking that there couldn't be much space around that congested area, when Rowena turned sharp left on a narrow alley between two sandstone buildings.

'No turning back now' Ellie said.

Suddenly at the end of the block, the road opened out briefly, they drove under an arch and there it was: a tiny parking space for about twenty cars. As Rowena followed the arrows painted on the floor, she looked intently for a space; Ellie spotted the white lights of a reversing car, in the far corner.

'Bingo!' She shouted and pointed to the exiting car.

As Rowena drove carefully towards it, Ellie noticed that it was a big executive car, a very big one and the driver was struggling to miss a car parked opposite. Ellie quickly jumped out of the Golf and ran toward the car. It was a silver blue Bentley Continental, she caught the driver's attention and guided him out of the space beautifully. The driver stopped the Bentley and got out.

'That was most kind of you my dear.' A tall, impeccably dressed man in his late forties walked up to Ellie, smiling at her with grey-blue eyes. 'This must be your lucky day.'

Ellie blushed deeply, 'my lucky day, why is that?'

He handed her a parking ticket. Printed on it there was an expiry time with five hours remaining on it, she gasped when she looked at the price of the ticket; £15.

'I've had to cut short my visit, urgent call from the hospital.' He then looked beyond Ellie to the approaching

Golf and waved to Rowena and he then gently took Ellie's hand and kissed it. She felt a tender lip on the back of her hand and she quivered inside. Before she could say anything, he slid back into the plush white leather, gunned the engine and was gone.

Rowena was in the space like a flash, opened the door and watched the Bentley disappear around the corner. She managed to get the number plate 'ZB 1'.

 'I think I know who that is', she thought to herself and decided she wouldn't tell Ellie at the time, but keep it for later.

Ellie handed Rowena the unexpired ticket and her eyes widened at the time on it.

 'What a stroke of luck Ro' Ellie giggled like a school girl. 'Five hours for nothing!'

In only a few steps they were in the throngs of shoppers and tourists. To the right towered the Abbey, but they went straight on for a while and then into the maze of tiny narrow alleyways that Bath was famous for.

For ten minutes, they were dashing down one alley then the next, passing by most of the little shop fronts that were tempting them to go in. Finally, they both stood outside a little shop which seemed devoid of colour, quite dark really and above the narrow door there was a squeaking black metal sign, with gold lettering on it.

 'It's not in a language I know, Ellie' said Rowena.

'I think that language is Cyrillic. Bulgarian or Russian, sort of Eastern European' Ellie boldly opened the door and walked in.

Rowena was surprised at Ellie's prompt response, but followed her in the little shop. The well-lit alley seemed quite a contrast to the room they had just entered; they had to adjust their eyes for a moment.

The only light that they could perceive came from the opposite doorway and even that seemed very low as a curtain of beads shielded it. A short-crouched figure came into the shop and peered at the two young women with a strange smile and beckoned them closer.

'Have you come in for a reading?' The old woman inquired.

Rowena stifled a laugh nervously. 'No, we haven't, we just came in through curiosity, as we couldn't understand the writing on your sign.'

'You, the blonde one, come and sit here.' Ellie was startled for a moment. 'What is your name?' The woman asked.

'I'm Ellie, why do you want to know?' Ellie gulped.

'Come sit on this chair, I wish to talk with you.' The old woman ignored her question.

Somehow Ellie found it hard to resist the old woman and impulsively sat on the wicker chair, which wobbled when she sat on it. She looked back at Rowena who stood quietly watching, just as puzzled as her friend.

'What is Ellie? Is that your real name?' The woman asked

'Eloise, it is Eloise'

'I see the sun in your name and you will be famous in battle and you will live by the sea.' The woman stood closer to Ellie and as she walked a little around her, she bent closer to her, as if she was looking at something.

Ellie turned and looked up at the woman's face and saw that she was staring at her neck. She also noticed that the woman's face had changed from a light smiling one to a somewhat darker feature. Her very dark eyes also seemed to get colder.

Ellie recoiled, 'what is it? What are you looking at?'

Although the woman had stood back somewhat, she continued to look intensely at Ellie 'Where did you get the serpent from my dear?'

Ellie pulled the chain out revealing the stone. 'Do you mean this?' She lifted the chain from her neck, revealing the stone to the woman. The old woman stood transfixed on the spot, she seemed to be in some sort of shock. Rowena walked towards the woman who waved her away, having quickly recovered.

'My blonde lady, thank you, but I cannot see any more for you. Now I will speak with your dark friend'.

Ellie looked at the old woman and rose from the chair a little disappointedly. She had expected something a little more interesting. The old woman didn't look at Ellie again; in fact, it seemed that she had lost interest in her and was beckoning Rowena to the chair for her to have a go. As Rowena approached Ellie, she touched her hand.

'I'll only be a few minutes Ellie, see you outside.'

'I'll have a little scout around, I think I saw a gift shop a couple of doors down, I'll see you in there Ro' Ellie said as she walked out of the shop door.

As Rowena sat on the chair, she looked up at the old woman, whose face was fixed on the door, as if she could still see Ellie, who was already out of sight.

'Well do you want to speak to me or not? It's no bother to me; I'll just as soon as leave now.' Rowena said indignantly.

'My apologies dark lady, now tell me what is your name?'

'Rowena' she answered.

'Ah, Rowena, you are the Saxon princess. Your name gives you fame and boundless joy in your life.' The woman was still looking at the door as if Ellie was coming back. 'You are the most gifted one, do you work with your hands perhaps?'

'Yes, I do, in fact I am.....'

The old lady cut her short. 'Your friend the blonde one, Eloise, is she close to you?'

'She is my very best friend' Rowena answered.

'I want to tell you something about your friend that is very important, but you do not tell her. You must swear that you will never reveal to her what I tell you.' The old woman insisted.

'I swear'

'Swear on your life!' The old woman's eyes darkened again.

'I swear on my life.' Rowena became scared, but the old woman's eyes strangely filled with power.

'I'm very sorry that I couldn't read into your friend's future.' The old woman said.

'What are you talking about?' Rowena snapped at her.

'Her protector was stopping me my dear.' The woman looked at the doorway again.

'Protector, what protector do you mean?' Rowena was getting a little angry with this woman.

'She wears her protector. Around her neck the stone and the snake, they are very powerful, very strong, even stronger than....' The old woman stopped herself from saying anymore and her eyes looked far away.

She then regained some composure. 'Something good will happen to your blonde friend today, something very good. It will take her on a new pathway, but she must decide for herself. No-one, not even the protector can tell her what to decide.'

Rowena thought that she would try and get some information from this woman, so she asked, 'my friend and I want to know something about the stone, what do you know about it?'

'I can tell you nothing, I am but a vessel in all this, it is not of my choosing. Go now dark lady and seek out your friend, but say nothing of what I have said to you to anyone and that you be sure to remember your oath.'

'Yes, I remember, don't worry, I can keep secrets.'

Rowena got up and walked through the door and didn't look back. 'I wish that I'd never been in that place!' Rowena thought to herself.

'I haven't seen anything I like Ro.' Ellie caught her friends arm lovingly as they walked out of the gift shop and made their way towards the Abbey and the light of the wider streets of the ancient city. The whole episode in that little shop was one that they both needed to get out of their thoughts; Rowena knew that Ellie was frightened even if she didn't show it.

As they approached the impressive Abbey, they were busy looking up at it from the pavement, when an open top bus pulled up alongside them. The bus emptied its contents of happy, chatting tourists. The driver then unfolded an 'A' frame advertising the next Bath tour.

'C'mon let's go on it.' Ellie shouted to her friend. 'How long does the tour take?' She asked the driver.

'Around forty minutes Miss.' He answered; they looked at each other and laughed.

Ellie paid for the two nine pound tickets and they ran upstairs. They were the first ones to embark, the open top was still empty and so they chose the seats at the back. As they sat down, there were two pairs of headphones slotted in the seats in front.

Not long before, the guide would use a microphone to point out the sights and due to the traffic noise, had to shout, but this had caused trouble with the locals on the route. Some residents had even poured water from their upstairs windows on the visitors, so eventually the tour operators were forced to change the information method to headphones, which finally appeased them.

The bus started to fill up and Rowena looked around to see the beautiful Poultney Bridge and their new perspective on the Abbey from the top of the bus. She then glanced at Ellie, who was picking up a discarded newspaper which had been left on the seat on the other seat next to her. As she opened the paper, the Bath Chronicle, Ellie noticed that it was folded showing the classified section. Her eyes immediately moved towards an entry in one of the columns, which had been circled in thick black marker ink.

'Ro, look at this.' Ellie shouted and read out the notice that was circled. 'We are trying to trace the whereabouts of an E.M. McIntyre who originates from Bradford on Avon. Please ring the following number. Do you think that could be me Ro?'

Rowena swallowed hard, 'Is this what the old woman was on about?' she thought to herself.

'Ro, Ro! Can you hear me? Do you think that is this about me?' Ellie shouted above the chatter from the passengers, as she grabbed her friend's hand.

'Sorry Ellie, I was miles away for a minute.' She looked at the entry that Ellie gave her. 'Let's find out, you know what they say: nothing ventured.'

'Nothing gained,' laughed Ellie and pulled out her mobile phone.

After a couple of rings, a voice answered 'Vizards, can I help you?'

'Would you mind telling me who Vizards are please?' Ellie asked assertively.

'We are the leading firm of solicitors in Glasgow, madam' said the voice haughtily.

'My name is Eloise Monks, er I mean McIntyre, which is, or was my maiden name and someone is looking for me according to the Bath Chronicle advert'.

'Hold on please, I will put you through to someone.'

'What shall I say?' Ellie asked urgently.

'Just tell them who you are, be natural.' Rowena answered.

'Hello?' A deep voice with a strong Scottish accent came on. Ellie put the mobile on loudspeaker for Rowena's benefit. 'Mrs Monks, would you mind if I ask you a couple of questions please?'

'Go ahead.' Ellie said.

'Three simple questions if you wouldn't mind answering them: your date of birth, your mother's maiden name and finally your father's mothers first name, can you do that for me.'

Ellie reeled off the answers without hesitation, which immediately put the man at ease.

'Eloise, it is of foremost importance that we meet as soon as possible. Can you get up here to my office in Glasgow? Oh, how very rude of me, my name is Alex Macduff; I'm the senior partner of this firm.'

'Just a moment please Mr Macduff.' Ellie put the speaker on mute as she looked at Rowena.

'Tell him to come to you, if it's that important.' Rowena advised in a whisper.

Restoring the loudspeaker on the phone, Ellie spoke to him and at the same time she was absent-mindedly clutching the stone from around her neck.

'Sorry I cannot get to Scotland now, I would prefer it if you came to see me nearer my home.'

'We have offices in London, if that would be of any help,' he said. 'I will text you back as soon as possible with the time and date; it certainly will be within the next seven days. Is that acceptable to you?' The lawyer asked.

'Yes, it is, but before you ring off, can you give some information about what this meeting is about Mr Macduff?' Ellie felt her confidence surge as she gripped the stone again.

'I cannot of course reveal too much detail, but I can reveal that you are the beneficiary of a will and the inheritance is quite substantial. Will that do for now?' he answered.

'Thank you, yes' Ellie looked wide-eyed at Rowena.

'I will contact you as soon I have dates and times. Until then, Mrs Monks, goodbye.'

'Goodbye Mr Macduff.' Ellie breathed in deeply as she closed the connection.

Ellie looked at Rowena. 'After all that, I don't feel like I want a bus tour, I really want to go somewhere quiet and talk this over, OK with you Ro?'

The bus engine started, so they quickly chased downstairs before it moved off. The driver was a bit grumpy about refunding, but with a little persuading sold the tickets to disappointed tourists standing at the bus stop. They then rushed down the road in search of a quiet teashop. A small one near a beautiful sandstone crescent was ideal. It was off the beaten track and almost empty.

'Look Ro, everything has happened so quickly today, I can't seem to catch my breath. This latest thing, the inheritance, it's so uncanny that someone had that advert circled, as if they knew I was going to be on that bus at that time. It's crazy, but not just that Ro all the other things too, they all seemed to be leading somewhere, none of them appear like accidents. Please tell me you think the same.' Ellie looked pleadingly at her friend.

Of course, Rowena had also been tracking those amazing events and that meeting with the old lady today confirmed to her that those were no coincidences. 'But,' she thought, 'what could I say to Ellie?' Rowena knew that she had to say something.

'It does look a bit strange Ellie and if you stretch your imagination, anything could be connected in some way, but I don't really think that myself.' Rowena then gave her a big hug, hoping that Ellie couldn't read anything in her face, as she hated lying to her.

Ellie drank up her tea, leaving the cake, 'I'm ready to go back home now Ro and I feel all washed up.'

They chatted in the car once they were out of town. Ellie said to Rowena, 'I really don't want to go to London to see Macduff or anyone else for that matter'

'Maybe Gary would go with you.' Rowena bit her lip, 'Sorry, I forgot about him being in Belfast. Well, I could go with you but I'll need a bit of notice, the shop you know, no cover.'

Ellie unconsciously held the stone for a moment as she was thinking of how to get out of the visit to London, when her mobile rang, interrupting her thought.

'Mrs Monks?' The voice asked.

'Hello, is that Mr Macduff?' Ellie inquired.

'Good news Mrs Monks, I felt that calling you to London would be a little unfair, so I have made arrangements for one of my colleagues in the London office to meet you in Salisbury at a day convenient to you. My colleague's name is Clive Jameson, please feel free to ring the number which I will text to you directly and arrange it with him. I have instructed him personally, to comply fully with your requirements.'

'Goodbye Mrs Monks.'

'Goodbye.' Ellie closed the line.

'Wow Ellie! That was amazing. No sooner had you said that you didn't want to go to London and the solution happens.' Ellie's mobile bleeped again with the promised number and she saved it with 'Jameson London' as the name.

Rowena also noticed that Ellie was holding the stone just before the phone call, but again refrained from saying anything to her. As they reached Salisbury, Ellie turned down Rowena's offer to stay the night, as she remembered that Gary was ringing her at nine.

Ellie parked her little Polo on the drive and saw that the house was in darkness. On the way home, she recalled all the amazing events of the day and only when she had arrived, did her heart sink as she realised that there was no one at home to greet her.

As she opened the front door she remembered that the heating timer hadn't been changed and the atmosphere was cold, as well as empty. She put the coffee filter on the hob and waited for the heating to kick in. The two hours before Gary's call would be enough for a good long soak and maybe something out of the freezer to put in the microwave for dinner. 'Not too bad' she thought to herself.

Taking her clothes off to prepare for a bath, she glimpsed herself in the full-length mirror. In the reflexion, she saw the stone and necklace that she was wearing for the first time. The stone was gently glowing in the dim light and suddenly felt her spirit lift with a sense of anticipation. Maybe this was the moment that would change her life. She must be prepared.

'Life can be a wonderful thing, if you seize the opportunity.' She mused. 'The first thing though, is to recognise the opportunity.' She surprised herself with the wisdom she felt within.

As she soaked in the hot tub, she planned not to mention anything about the conversation with the lawyer yet there weren't any details to tell Gary, only the word 'inheritance' and that could be anything. 'Anyway, there'll be plenty to talk about besides that,' she thought.

She glanced at the clock, eight thirty and time to move. Dry and warm, she lounged on the couch, phone by her side and awaited his call and he did ring, spot on time.

'I'm on the eleventh floor of the Europa Hotel, darling.' Gary started the conversation a little hesitantly, as he was aware of the icy atmosphere between them when she drove off to see Rowena the night before.

'I expect you've had lots of meetings with your boss and things are going well,' she said a little cynically, 'how long are you going to be there Gary? I've got so much to tell you and it's not so easy on the phone.'

The phone went quiet for a few moments. 'I won't be able to get back until a week on Monday darling. There's so much to do and you know that everything hinges on this working out for us. I'm really sorry though, do you understand?' He asked, a little pleadingly.

'I'm fine about it. I guess that deep down I expected it, considering what you've been offered. I don't want you to spend a week over there being anxious about me not understanding, because I do understand.' Ellie explained.

'Thanks Ellie thanks a lot.' He breathed a sigh of relief. 'Honestly I have made them all aware how big this is for you as well. The wonderful thing is, that they want to make it work too, so they will bend over backwards, I promise you that!'

Ellie sensed the conversation had become more relaxed now that was out of the way, so she decided to break the news that she had previously promised not to tell.

'Gary, I have had a phone call from some big shot lawyers in Scotland. They wouldn't go into detail but there is something about an inheritance coming my way.'

'What? I didn't get that; did you say something about an inheritance Ellie?'

'Yes, I did.' She replied. 'They wanted me to go up to Scotland next week, but I refused to go.'

'Why?' He asked

'I told them that if they wanted to see me they had better make better arrangements. So, they called back and agreed to meet me in Salisbury to give me the details! What do you think of that?'

'What news Ellie? I think it's just great, looks like it's not just me, eh?'

'And I'm so happy for you Gary, I really am darling'

'I love you Ellie and I'll ring you same time tomorrow. Any 'probs call me on the mobile.'

'Love you too, bye.'

'Bye Ellie.' Then the phone went dead.

Ellie was shattered. She remembered the jar of Belgian drinking chocolate in the kitchen cabinet and decided that was what she would take to bed with her. Winding down, after the phone call, she put the empty mug on the bedside cabinet and felt satisfied with her day. Gary was happy and so was she.

'It's time to settle down and get some sleep.' She said to herself.

After less than an hour of fitful sleep she awoke with thoughts going around in her head. She couldn't shift them, so she puffed up her pillows and gave in to them. The meeting on the forthcoming Wednesday in Salisbury had suddenly become the focus.

'I am going to receive a substantial inheritance, or so the man said' she said out loud. 'Yes, but who do I know, that knows me enough to leave me anything? I really don't know anyone.'

'The lawyer comes from Scotland, so the person must have lived in Scotland and I went to Herriot Watt in Edinburgh. Did I meet any rich person when I was there? No.'

Her mind started to wander from Scotland and then to her parents. She was brought up in the beautiful town of Bradford on Avon. The house she lived in all her young life was a local stone-built, quite substantial three-bedroom property. Her mother had never worked and dad only worked part time, as he was in poor health. She had never questioned their life before, but well, how did they afford that way of life? Many of her friends, whom she went to school with, were from wealthy parents and they certainly didn't work part time!

She qualified to go to Herriot Watt University to read Mathematics and Computer sciences. There was no question of applying for any help and whilst there she could rent a nice little flat in the suburbs of Edinburgh for the duration of her time there. Many of her fellow students were often short of funds and had to increase the student loans. But she didn't even have one!

'Come to think of it, who did I meet in Edinburgh whilst I was at University?' She asked herself. She had led quite a monastic life in Scotland. During the day, when not in class, she would be at the nearby park reading, or in the flat doing the same. There was this woman, who seemed somewhat shabbily dressed and often sat on the same bench feeding the ducks and often got to talk, but it was just small talk. In fact, Ellie had felt sorry for her and sometimes shared her sandwiches, ones that she had prepared at the flat.

As Ellie thought more deeply, she remembered that whilst she was looking at the ducks she noticed that a stranger was looking at them closely from the next bench. The poor woman next to her seemed so alone Ellie remembered what her name was, 'Mary, that's it Mary.' That's the same one as my own middle name.' She thought but dismissed it as a coincidence.

She remembered the massive upheaval when, after she had qualified, her parents decided to sell their house and immigrate to South Africa. Dad was nearing retirement and his health was deteriorating. His doctor recommended a warmer climate. They did ask if she would like to join them, but she declined. Gary was on the horizon and she wasn't prepared for the obvious changes that South Africa would impose on them. Looking back though, they didn't try too hard to get her to go with them. What was the real reason they were leaving? How could they afford to move there in the first place? Was she that selfish that she had never thought of this before?

She had been very busy with her job, then the marriage. She realised there had been little contact with her parents. Of course, she had invited them to her wedding, but due to dad's health problems they couldn't make the long journey from South Africa.

Finally, exhausted she dropped off to sleep, but still she had not been able to answer any of her own questions.

7: <u>Zowie's Friends</u>

Zowie's bark had awakened Edmund out of a dream. It was a recurring one, chasing a dark figure down a wide street, which was flanked by very tall buildings, like skyscrapers. He seemed to be catching up to the cloaked figure when suddenly it stopped on the corner of the street and looked around at him. The figure was wearing a hood and as he got closer still, he could detect a smile under it. An arm reached out of the cloak and pointed upwards. Edmund followed the direction of the long finger up the side of a huge wall of windows, so tall that it disappeared into the sky. The mouth underneath the hood began to speak, but he couldn't make out what was being said. The face came up to him and as it did, it contorted into a dragon's head. Closer and closer, the huge mouth had a forked tongue, which looked like a whip!

As he woke up and cleared his head, he looked around the small bedroom, the only upstairs room in the cottage. The sloping sides of the ceiling made the headroom quite low, but as usual in a cottage of this type, it was quite warm even in the coldest winters, helped by the deep thatch on the roof. There was only one small window in the roof area which gave dim light.

Zowie barked again. 'All right girl, I'm on my way.' He stumbled into the downstairs room.

This room also was very dark and low ceilinged. He rubbed his hands together to generate some warmth. She stood at the front door, which they didn't use that often and was bolted as well as locked. Edmund struggled with drawing the bolt back as he heard an engine start. He opened the old door, just in time to see a little Suzuki Jeep disappearing down the lane, too far away to get the driver to stop by then.

He racked his brain to try to remember if he knew anyone owning that sort of car, but without success. The engine noise faded into the distance as he turned to look at the little porch way, scanned for a letter or something the caller might have left behind.

'Yes, there it is' he thought. In the old broken latticework, which Edmund had guessed had once been used to support climbing roses or honeysuckle; someone had lodged a small calling card.

Not in any hurry to read the card, he placed it on the small oak table and prepared some breakfast for the pair of them. Purposely taking his time to clear up, he let Zowie out for her run and then picked up the card again.

On one side, there was just one word printed in heavy block capitals '**VIZARDS**'. The reverse side was blank, with no message. Edmund turned the card over again and stared at the name. He knew what it meant however, the name alone was enough to tell him that stage one had been performed as he had instructed them.

Suddenly he wanted to go out and impulsively, down at the beach was where he wanted to be. It had been several weeks since his last visit there. Christmas had come and gone, along with a spate of heavy weather, unusually quite nasty for that part of the world. Outside of the cottage it was full of puddles and the ground was wet and soft, no good for his Morgan, so the Toyota pickup became the order of the day.

It was Zowie's favourite vehicle and when they travelled anywhere in it, she would be on the flat tailback and loved to bark at any dogs as she passed them. She would growl and bark, especially if they were big dogs. Edmund would smile to himself as he knew it was all bravado, they couldn't catch her at the back of his car and she knew it too.

It felt good to be out again. Edmund rarely felt lonely, but the severe weather had forced them to be housebound for longer than usual, so it felt great to be back on their usual route and to get some fresh sea air again. As the Toyota headed through Christchurch, Zowie began barking again, she knew some of her pals would be there; Freddie and Indie the Bichon Frise twins, Murphy the black Labrador and finally, her best pal Mollie, another Border collie.

Mollie was unusual for the breed; she loved to swim in the sea. Edmund could smell the sea as they approached the Overcliff Drive at Southbourne, where he parked the pickup next to the small café called 'Delice' situated near the zigzag path and the cliff lift.

They walked past the café, which had beautiful views all around the bay as far as the Isle of Wight to the east and Swanage to the west. They walked down the zigzag and Edmund let Zowie off the lead about halfway down. She stayed at heel until they reached the bottom and then looked at her master and with a single wave from him she was off to the water's edge.

The space of about three wooden sea groynes ahead of them, Edmund could make out a single figure with two tiny white specks moving around it. They were heading towards them, so in no time at all, the 'boys' as Ursula called them, were running rings around Zowie jumping, barking and madly excited to see her.

'A Happy New Year to you!' Edmund shouted.

'And I wish the same to you too. We haven't seen you for a while Edmund, I do hope that you are well.' Ursula answered.

Ursula was in her seventies by then, but still was very fit thanks to her walking regime. Her accent was Austro Swiss, even though she had lived in the UK for over forty years, it was still strong. When they first met he mistakenly thought she was South African but she soon forgave him.

After a friendly hug, they continued their way. It took a little persuading from Ursula to get Indy and Freddy away from Zowie, but after few minutes they became tiny specs again.

About a mile along the beach, Edmund looked towards the cliff. Perched on the top, a little way from the edge, was a large brick and sandstone structure he knew as the Breakwaters, a large apartment block. He remembered that he had watched it being built in the late '90s. It was perhaps on the best site for views across the bay. It was once his biggest project and a very important one too.

Looking back at the sea, the waves were quite small, as the prevailing winds were from the north and were blowing towards the sea. People reminded him of the sea, expect calm and you get rough and vice-versa, he never got what he expected. This reminded him of the two people he had met in Cannes on their yacht, Ben and Vera. Rich people in a yacht in Cannes, who would have expected them to be as kind and generous as they were to him and Paul at that time?

He scanned the sweeping coastline for any sign of Tim and Murphy the black Lab, or John and Mollie the swimming collie, but it was completely empty, but none the less it remained so very inspiring to him.

Although it was wintertime and the northerly wind bit through his overcoat, there was a sense of pride that came over him. He had the whole beach, about three miles of it, to himself. As he looked towards the horizon, he perceived a large band of very black cloud, laden with rain heading his way.

'Time to get back girl' and they headed back to the pickup truck, hopefully to miss the worst of the weather as it rushed towards them.

It started to rain just as he clambered into the Toyota's cabin and Zowie jumped inside this time. As they headed back through Christchurch, the radio was playing 'Inchworm' by Sinatra. He recalled how his old pal Paul imitated another famous song by Frank many years ago, which brought a smile to his face again.

8: Can this be Love?

Canterbury

After Paul had received such a horrible beating in Cannes, it had left him with a bit of a complex and so it wasn't difficult to persuade him that it was time to head north from the French south coast and home. Paul left it to Edmund to change their remaining dollars to the local currency at the local bank exchange counter and buy two train tickets for Paris.

On their way to the station, Paul continually looked over his shoulder, expecting the thugs to return, but his face soon relaxed when they were safely on the train, making their way out of the place. Edmund this time, had paid for better seats and SNCF didn't let them down.

The journey was a bit of a blur for Paul, A comfortable seat had relieved the tensions and Edmund didn't feel like talking much anyway. He was thinking about Ben, who was only a few years older than himself and Paul and yet the American had achieved so much. As Paul slept soundly he stared at Ben's business card and wondered what their next adventure was going to be.

The next morning, they were on the ferry to Folkestone and they disembarked from the boat and into customs. Paul passed right through and waited on the other side whilst the officer scanned Edmund's passport photo against the person who was standing in front of him.

'What the hell is up?' Edmund thought. 'After coming all this way, now they won't let me back in the country!'

'Could you please state your date of birth and where you were born?' The customs officer said as he looked at Edmund gravely.

Edmund reeled the answers off, which seemed to appease the officer and he reluctantly stamped the passport and let him through without apology. Edmund looked again at the picture in his passport and compared his reflexion in a parked car window. The passport displayed a white faced pasty boy and in such a brief time had changed into a healthy, bronzed and fuller faced young man!

Their great adventure in France was now officially over. They both breathed in the Folkestone air and crossed the road heading towards the High Street. The street itself did not reflect what its name depicted. It was in fact a very narrow cobbled street with tourist shops and the like flanking both sides. The road was quite steep and as they reached the top they stopped for breath. To the left, along the side of a wall there was a white frieze of some kind depicting ancient warriors and their horses prancing and above this was one word 'Acropolis'.

There was an aroma of freshly brewed coffee coming out of the open door, so they turned and automatically walked in.

It took a few moments to adjust their eyes to the very dark atmosphere inside the café. To the left was the bar that was lit by the huge 'Gaggia' coffee machine. Looking around the room, there were wooden carved tables spread out and above them there was a low ceiling covered in plastic vines and hanging bunches of plastic grapes suggesting the atmosphere of the Mediterranean. In the middle of the room a huge jukebox was emanating its garish red and green lights.

The music that was playing Edmund did not recognise at all. He later found out it was Howling Wolf's 'Little Red Rooster', one that the Rolling Stones were to copy soon after. Only one of the tables was occupied. In fact, two tables had been drawn together and about eight figures had turned around looking at the newcomers.

A smiling face below a shock of black curly hair shouted 'Hello!' to them, as they approached the bar.

'We would like two coffees but we only have this, Paul said, pointing to a handful of small denomination francs. 'We have just come off the ferry and it's all we have.' Paul looked at him and smiled one of his disarming smiles.

'I don't understand you sir, are you French?'

'No, we're not French. We have just come from there.' Edmund said, standing on tiptoe and still smiling at him.

'Well, we are Greek Cypriots here.' The man smiled back at him. 'Look, never mind about the money, we trust you and have two coffees on us.' The two visitors were amazed at such generosity, shook his hand and turned to find somewhere to sit.

The group of people at the tables near the doorway waved them over and even pulled two chairs from elsewhere so that the newcomers could join them.

Within a short space of time they had got an invitation to the latest party, an address of a lodging house, even a chance of a job at Strickland's, the local bakery. To top it all, Paul started a relationship with one of the girls called Rosalind. They certainly had arrived home in style much to Edmund's surprise, so different to where they had just left.

Paul handed over the handful of insignificant change in Francs to Rosalind and she persuaded the owner to exchange them for a couple of Greek style sandwiches. It was the best welcome to England they could have wished for. After securing their job at the bakery and with Ros's help, the landlady of their new digs was happy to let them pay their rent at the end of their first week at the bakery. They were overwhelmed by the trusting nature of the people of Folkestone.

The job at the bakery was no picnic. Edmund's job was in the bread production department which was permanently hot and reminded him of his days at the Coke Ovens plant, with only one benefit, you could eat what the bakery produced.

Paul, on the other hand worked upstairs in the confectionery department, predominantly staffed by women. To Edmund, his friend had once again 'fell on his feet', although in Paul's mind he had just arrived from Cannes and the film festival and filling doughnuts with jam just didn't light his fire.

As expected, Paul soon got the sack for larking about and, even worse, putting an extra squirt of raspberry jam in all the doughnuts, which was a cardinal offence. In all, they lasted three weeks.

'But hey, it's still summertime; let's get a job outside somewhere.' Paul said irrepressibly.

Edmund showed Paul a job advert in the Folkestone Messenger. 'Staff wanted urgently until the end of the season at Maddieson's Holiday Camp at St Margaret's Bay. Apply at the camp'.

'I reckon we might be able to stay there in one of their chalets if we're lucky.' Edmund said.

'Let's go for it, mate, it looks a breeze.' Paul enthused.

So, they did and got set on straight away. Paul wangled himself a job to clean the entertainment area after each nightly show and Edmund became a breakfast chef's assistant.

'Bet you don't get a job on the stage Paul. If you do, you could do your impression of Frank Sinatra, singing 'A new kind of love' like you did at Strickland's and get us the sack again' Edmund laughed.

Edmund did not like working in a kitchen environment, it was just about the lowest of the low for him, but Paul was better suited to the stage, even though he was only cleaning it.

'You never know mate, I might get a chance to shine.' Paul said.

'Yeh, like the shine you're giving to the stage floor.' Edmund answered and laughed loudly.

The season had two months to go, so Edmund packed in his unsuitable job in the kitchens, took the wages owed him and caught the bus to Deal, just down the coast from St Margaret's bay.

It was midweek and the local jobcentre was advertising for staff at the shoe factory just north of the town. He originally applied for a vacancy on the factory floor, but the woman who interviewed him was impressed with his level of education and where he had worked before. She offered him a job in the Purchasing Office, which he grabbed with both hands. Before he left the personnel office, he asked the woman if she knew of any digs nearby. What a stroke of luck; she had an aged aunt who lived in a cottage in a nearby village called Sholden and just happened to be looking for lodgers.

Edmund was settling down for a while; nice digs and a lenient landlady, a steady job where he quickly excelled and was even encouraged to improve the system where he saw fit, on top of that, there was Pauline.

Pauline was the most beautiful girl he had ever seen. Her father owned a chain of ice cream parlours of which two were on the Deal beachfront. The name of the chain was Divito's. Saturdays were spent drinking coffee in the café where she worked. Edmund would be found sitting at his usual table near the window, ever hoping for a chance to speak to her, but so far he had had no success.

Deal was famous for one thing; Julius Caesar was expanding his empire and it was soon time for him to conquer Britannia, but he hadn't bargained on Deal.

The invasion fleet was turned back by the blue painted Briton warriors waiting for them at the coast of Deal! Not only that, when he did succeed in getting a foothold on the island, he had to move further down the coast to do it so that he avoided further conflict by the ferocious Deal residents.

At one time, there must have been a very clever cartoonist who was a regular to Divito's. On each table, there was the result of his work, depicting Julius's failure. For example, the table where Edmund usually sat, underneath the glass top, he had drawn the great Roman eating one of Divito's Knickerbocker Glories and in the process of spitting it out. The caption then said:

'Let's go back to Italy where we can get real ice cream.' Surprisingly, Mr Divito must have had a sense of humour after all!

The Divito family were part Scottish and part Italian and Pauline was the beautiful result of this union. She had long black wavy hair, a dark smooth complexion and deep brown eyes that could flash at the least little thing. Not surprisingly Edmund was totally smitten with her.

At this time, there was one American female singer of the day whose songs were often copied by British singers like Sandy Shaw and Cilla Black, though to him they could not match her voice.

That artist was the legendary Dionne Warwick. Her version of Bacharach and David's 'Walk on by' was played endlessly in the café and the words were very poignant to Edmund, as they matched his feelings of his unrequited love for Pauline. Sadly, he was too shy to show it, or perhaps too scared of her reaction.

A few weeks had gone by and Edmund wondered if he would ever get the chance, but come it did. She was chatting to people on the next table and he overheard that she was going to Canterbury on the next Saturday, so when she returned to the counter, he took his chance. On the pretext of ordering a sandwich, he knew that he would have to wait whilst she cut the cheese from the huge block behind her.

'I'm going to Canterbury next Saturday; would you like some company on the bus?'

He leant backwards a little away from the counter in anticipation of a large slab of cheese being thrown at him.

'Yes, that would be nice Edmund, can you be at the bus station at about ten; it leaves at ten past'

'Did you say yes?' He wanted to hug her but was too scared.

Someone on a table behind him chirped up. 'Are you deaf mate?'

He walked away from the table with his sandwich, 'Edmund!' He turned around, wondering what she wanted, was it that she had already changed her mind?

'You haven't paid for the sandwich yet' Pauline retorted.

'Sorry, I was miles away' Edmund blushed.

'Yeah, in Canterbury.' piped the voice from the table, making all and sundry laugh at him but he didn't care, he had finally broken the ice.

Paul had finished the season at Maddieson's Holiday camp and to Edmund's surprise, he did get a chance to perform on that stage, in a supporting song and dance part. He had apparently impressed the entertainments manager at the camp. Edmund used his influence with Sheila, the Personnel Officer at the shoe factory to give him a job on the factory floor, sticking soles on shoes.

As usual, instead of working, he was entertaining the factory girls with the newly found song and dance act he'd learnt at the holiday camp. Working at Strickland's Bakery also taught him a lesson too; not be discovered larking about when authority was watching. However, he did escape with the skin of his teeth on a few occasions.

During most of the weekends and evenings, Paul spent at either Rosalind's house, or rehearsing a play with the Deal amateurs. He was introduced to the group by Rosalind's parents who were avid thespians themselves. Edmund often smiled to himself, realising that her parents had called her Rosalind after the character in the Shakespeare play 'As you like it'.

The East Kent Mercury ran an advert about a forthcoming play that Paul was in: Terrance Rattigan's 'Separate tables'. Paul made a point of showing Edmund his name advertised as one of the cast. This was his first real play and everyone was going to know about it.

The following week dragged interminably, Saturday took so long to come around and then finally Edmund and his 'dream girl' were sitting together on the bus on their way to Canterbury. Pauline smelled like wild flowers and she was smiling at him, although she was a little detached, when he tried to make conversation.

As they approached Canterbury bus station he realised that no matter how hard he had tried during the journey, he couldn't get her to start a conversation, even though he did his best to find out what she liked to talk about.

They separated in town, her on a pretext of meeting a relative and only at the persistence of Edmund did she agree to meet up outside the cathedral later in the afternoon and go for a coffee with him.

'She never actually said that she would walk around with me' he thought to himself, but walking on his own was not what he had planned. 'I know' looking in an antique jeweller's shop window, 'I'll buy her this diamond ring and when we meet, she'll be so overwhelmed that she'll marry me at the Cathedral! I'm a stupid idiot.' He said to himself. To think that he had been longing for this day to come all week long and yet it turned out a damp squib.

Around three o'clock, he was standing outside the black gates to the Cathedral looking across the Butter Market and up Burgate. It was very crowded with shoppers and tourists in the area, but from a long way off he caught a glimpse of her jet-black hair bouncing as she walked. As she got closer he could see she was not alone and she was holding someone's hand as they walked together laughing.

'I've got to get out of here before she sees me' he thought and quickly dashed into the thronging crowd.

He stayed within view of the cathedral gates and wondered if they would stop and wait for him, but they didn't. They walked straight on by, looking and laughing at each other, oblivious of his own pain and disappointment. Dejectedly he then headed back to the bus station, his heart was broken!

'She never promised anything Edmund' 'It's not her fault that I still love her with all my heart.' He said to himself as he trudged back to the bus station.

It was only four o'clock by the old clock on Deal Town hall as he alighted from the bus and the pubs were not open until six. 'Paul is getting ready for the last performance of Separate Tables tonight, so he won't want to be bothered by my problems', he thought to himself. Once again, his thoughts wandered to Canterbury, wondering what she would be doing now.

'No. It's over! I can't go on torturing myself like this' he said out loud. 'What would Paul do in this situation? For a start, he wouldn't be as timid as me. I suppose if I told him, he would just laugh, he wouldn't understand my plight, I bet.'

Edmund was walking on the shingle beach and the sea was grey and lifeless. There happened to be one of the fishing boats moored near the esplanade and he sat on the shingle close to it, trying to figure out what to do next.

'Sometimes we can't get everything we deserve in life, instead we have to recognise the opportunities as they come along. Maybe tomorrow is my day' he thought to himself.

9: <u>The Breakwaters</u>

The beach view

'Hello, can I speak with Mr Clive Jameson please!'

'Can I say who is calling?'

'Mrs Monks'

'Putting you through now'

'Mrs Monks?' A strong south-western accent came through to her.

'I am ringing to arrange a meeting with you in Salisbury. Has Alex Macduff contacted you about me?' Ellie tried to be as professional as she could.

'Indeed, he has Mrs Monks; I am at your service and can comply with all of your requests. Have you a day in mind for the meeting madam?'

'Would you be able to make this Wednesday Mr Jameson?'

'Certainly, Mrs Monks, may I suggest the Courtyard suite at the Red Lion Hotel on Milford Street, at eleven in the morning? Mr Macduff has instructed me to offer you lunch afterwards.'

'Yes, that would be fine.' Ellie was most impressed.

'Mrs Monks, may I respectfully request that you bring certain papers with you to the meeting?'

'What are they?' Ellie asked.

'Your birth certificate, your marriage certificate and some proof of address, like a bank statement or utility bill. I trust this will not cause you a problem Mrs Monks.'

'No problem, however I would like to bring along a close friend, as my husband is currently in Belfast and cannot accompany me.'

'Can I call you back on that Mrs Monks as I don't have authority to grant that request? I do apologise.' Ellie gave him her mobile number and he promised to ring back within the hour. While she waited for him to call back, she rang Rowena and got her agreement to go with her.

On the Wednesday morning, Ellie was turning into Rowena's shop car parking space. It had been only a few weeks since she had been to visit her friend, but in that brief time, so much had happened to her. What with the stone, the necklace and the beautiful clasp that she had made and now this!

When Jameson had rung back with his approval for Rowena to accompany her, Ellie had taken the opportunity to ask him a question.

'Couldn't you have sent all this in the post, surely it's not such a big deal that we have to meet, is it?'

'Mrs Monks, believe me, if I could deal with this by post, I most surely would, but this is no ordinary inheritance. In my view, Mrs Monks, this is a substantial one. I am looking forward to meeting you both on Wednesday and all will be revealed to you then.'

Ellie knew that Rowena was the best person she could have possibly wished for to accompany her on this. She was cool-headed and sensible and she would keep her feet on the ground. At that moment however, her mind was racing with so many questions. She unconsciously felt the stone around her neck as she walked to Rowena's shop and suddenly her self-confidence was boosted, she straightened her back and walked in.

They arrived at the Red Lion and walked through the archway into the courtyard. An American hotel group owned the hotel, but long ago it was a prominent coaching house dating back several hundred years.

When they walked into the cobbled courtyard, she looked back to the archway and Ellie could imagine a gold and black mail coach thundering under it, on their way to London. The archway itself was quite high and she imagined that she could hear the echo of the post horn blaring out as they entered Milford Street.

The courtyard was tastefully furnished with tables and comfortable chairs on top of old flagstones. They were almost an hour early so they sat at one of the tables and a waiter brought them coffee. Ellie fumbled with her purse, but the waiter waved his hand.

'You are Mrs Monks, aren't you?' Ellie nodded at him. 'A Mr Jameson has instructed me to offer you anything from the menu, madam. I believe you have an appointment at eleven, your meeting room is over there.' He pointed to a door to the left.

'Would you like something Ro?' Ellie asked.

'Coffee's fine.' She shook her head in reply.

Ellie had time to explain the last conversation with Mr Jamieson, particularly about the size of the inheritance. As usual Rowena did her best to keep her excitement to herself so as not to make Ellie lose her calmness. She knew that meetings with lawyers under any circumstances are a daunting prospect for anyone.

A youngish man, of about twenty-five, was standing at the doorway, the same one indicated by the waiter earlier. He was waving at them to try and get their attention. Rowena tapped Ellie's arm, very gently so as not to alarm her, as Ellie turned her head, she knew immediately who it was. They quickly left their coffees half drunk and walked over to him.

He looked at them as they approached him. One was a tall, dark olive-skinned woman in a full-length maroon coat and the other was two to three inches shorter, with shoulder length, wavy blonde hair, in a three-quarter length grey overcoat with black velvet collar. Both were stunning, he thought to himself.

'Mrs Monks?' Reaching out to shake Ellie's hand, 'and Ms Ffitch, I trust I have guessed correctly?'

As he ushered them into a formal but warm meeting room, he carefully pointed to the chairs for them to sit. On the table in front of them were pens and a note pad to take notes if they wished.

'May we dispense with the formal names Mrs Monks, if that is acceptable to you? I feel that it helps in these circumstances.' They both nodded their approval. 'My name is Clive.'

'This is my friend Rowena and I am Ellie'. She gave him a warm smile and the tension was gone.

'We have a good amount of space on the table, so I can lay out all the relevant papers for your perusal. Do you have the paperwork that we asked for, when we talked on Monday, Ellie?'

Ellie quickly zipped open the briefcase that she had taken from Gary's wardrobe and passed him the proof documents. Clive quickly scanned them and smiled.

'Thank you all is fine.' He said.

There was a small photocopier in the room, so he quickly copied everything, gave them back to her and placed the copies in his large case. He took out a large manila folder bound in red silk and started to read the contents to them.

'This is the last will and testament of Miss Eloise Mary McBride' He read out in the usual legal jargon that Ellie was the main beneficiary of the will, after detailing small bequests to some societies and charities that she favoured. Then he came to the crux of the will.

'And to Eloise Mary Monks, I bequeath the full deeds of The Breakwaters, Southbourne Overcliffe Drive, Bournemouth and the balance of any other properties and cash at the time this will and testament is activated'

'Ellie, are you alright love?' Rowena held her hand tightly as Ellie was just staring at the ceiling. She heard the words from the will, but they hadn't gone in.

'Clive, please explain to us the extent of the other properties apart from the house.' Rowena took charge whilst Ellie was staring into space.

'I think that we should take a break, if that's alright with you' Clive picked up the phone and the waiter quickly appeared with some coffee and biscuits.

Clive rose out of his chair and began to pour out the coffee for them both. He was very aware that this news had been more shocking to Ellie than he had imagined as he watched as Rowena put her arm around her friend, comforting her.

'Clive, did you say that the person who has left me this has the same name as mine?' Unconsciously she pulled out the stone and held it for a moment. Clive stood right next to her and observed the beautiful chain held together by the head of a snake with two bright red eyes.

'Ellie, that is the most stunning piece of jewellery that I have ever seen, it's a snake chain, isn't it?' Clive remarked, hoping to lighten the atmosphere that pervaded over the room.

'It's her Protector, Clive' Rowena said.

'What do you mean?' Ellie looked at her puzzled.

'Sorry Ellie, I don't know what I mean,' Ellie watched as Rowena sucked in her bottom lip and seemed a bit nervous about what she had said.

'Let's get on with it, I'm OK now, but please take it slowly.' Ellie suddenly gathered her confidence, smiled back at Clive and nodded at him.

Clive could not explain the question about the name on the will being the same as Ellie's, but he was successful in detailing what the rest of the will entailed. She was to receive just over one hundred thousand pounds in cash, as well as the property, which he explained to her was not a house, as she had originally thought.

They declined his offer of lunch and Ellie thanked him for his efforts. She gave him a hug, not the usual response to a lawyer, but Clive enjoyed it, he looked a little embarrassed and his face was a little flushed. He finally handed over another manila folder, identical to the one he read the will from, also bound in red silk.

'All you need to know is in here Ellie, all the details of the property that you have inherited. Off the record, this whole inheritance is subject to the usual taxes and my advice is to get a reputable financial advisor, but may I remind you that their advice is not free.' Clive explained.

'My husband has contacts in that area Clive, I'll speak to him about that. What about your firm's charges?' Ellie asked him.

'They have been taken care of Ellie, so you need not worry about that. Finally, I have been instructed to let you know that Mr Macduff in the Glasgow office wishes to meet you within the next three weeks when he hopes to be available for any questions you may have when you have viewed your new property. This offer is quite free of course.'

With the folder securely in the briefcase, Ellie and Rowena walked arm in arm out into the bright sunlight of Milford Street. Ellie looked up at the high arch as they passed under it and would have loved to have blown the hunting horn as loud as she could.

'Rowena, you are the best friend that I have ever had. I really don't know how I would have got through this morning without you.' Ellie said, hugging her arm.

They decided to walk back to Rowena's shop, which she had closed for the day, but on the way Rowena came up with an idea.

'Look Ellie, Bournemouth isn't too far away, why don't we go over there now, I know a little café on the cliff top called Café Viva, or something like that and we can sit down and have a little lunch before we explore the area and find that property of yours.'

'Great idea, that's just what I want to do too! My treat for lunch and I'll drive.' Ellie looked excited at last.

Southbourne was only forty minutes from Salisbury and half of that journey was a dual carriageway. It certainly was an excellent choice, free parking on the road adjacent to the café and only two of the tables occupied inside. The table that they chose overlooked the sea, as they looked to the right; they could see the cliffs of Old Harry Rocks and to the left, Hengistbury Head and the Isle of Wight.

They chose the daily specials on the board, Mushroom Soup followed by Macaroni Cheese. They two diners drank their cup of tea and Ellie excitedly pulled out the folder tied up with red ribbon that Clive had given her. The top section related to The Breakwaters and they were drawn to an Estate Agent's description of the property, including photos.

The Breakwaters, Southbourne Overcliffe Drive, was written under the company name proclaiming 'Southbourne's leading Estate Agents'. The blurb continued 'Situated on the eastern end of this sought-after road, a prestigious apartment block tastefully managed by ourselves and maintained to the very highest specification'

The pictures were amazing, three floors and each floor had a balcony circling the whole building, with its own car park in the front of it. Rowena knew that not every picture on an Estate Agent's brochure depicted the real thing but this one looked amazing to her.

'Let's go and find it.' Rowena said.

They drove eastwards towards Hengistbury, passing other apartment blocks and large houses; everyone looked large and expensive. They approached a small mini roundabout, the first exit seemed to direct them into the shopping area and the next one was signposted; 'To Hengistbury'.

That road followed the cliff edge, the only properties were to the left for a good quarter of a mile and Rowena told Ellie to slow down. Most of the properties along this road were large houses and all were on the left side of the road. In the distance however, they perceived a large square building, which happened to be the first one on their right on the cliff edge.

'Ro, this can't be it, can it?' Ellie asked her friend as they approached.

They slowed right down and then stopped alongside an impressive sandstone wall each side of the car park entrance, built into the wall there was bronze-coloured plaque which read: 'THE BREAKWATERS', in very large letters.

There was a fair amount of land surrounding the property which was grassed and looked like public access, so they left the car on the road and walked towards the cliff edge towards a fence, put up for safety.

They looked up at the block of flats in awe; it seemed quite a newly constructed building and each of the external verandas were large enough for tables and chairs and each flat had its own glass partition giving both privacy and protection from any winds.

Ellie looked at Rowena and then suddenly burst into tears. She sobbed loudly, loud enough to catch the notice of passers-by, although fortunately no one had looked out of their apartment windows. As Rowena held her close, she could feel Ellie shaking with emotion.

'Let's get back to the car Ellie.' Rowena said in a comforting tone.

As they got back into the little Polo and closed the doors, Ellie was still sobbing, Rowena found a box of Kleenex and passed some over without speaking. Then she whispered to Ellie, 'are you ready to go back home now?'

'I'll be OK in a minute Ro; it's just been all too much for me to take in. Nobody inherits a place like this do they Ro? I thought it might be an old run-down block of flats, needing lots of money needing to be spent on it' Ellie started to sob again like a little girl.

'Look, we're going home, come back again when you've taken it all in.' Rowena held her hand.

'No. I want to know if this is a dream and I'm going to wake up with it all gone.' Ellie opened the folder on her lap, found the phone number of the agent and quickly rang it on her mobile.

'Ruddock and Partners, can I help you?' A cultured voice answered.

'My name in Eloise Monks, I wish to speak to someone about the Breakwaters.'

'Mrs Monks, I have been told to expect your call, is there anything I can do for you, my name is Brian Mulholland?'

'Are you free to meet me now Brian?'

'Yes, I am, Mrs Monks. Would you like to come to my office?'

'I am parked on the road outside Breakwaters right now, can you come here?'

'I will be with you in fifteen minutes and please drive your car into the car park in front of the apartment block and I will join you there. If anyone asks what you are doing there, just tell them you are viewing and that I am on my way.'

'I am in a black Polo' Ellie said and terminated the call.

Rowena lovingly gazed into Ellie's eyes and marvelled at her courage, noticing that Ellie had been clutching her stone again as she spoke to the estate agent. Only a few minutes before, she had witnessed Ellie in a state of complete helplessness!

Less than ten minutes had elapsed when a red Mini Cooper slid alongside them. Ellie jumped out of the Polo and Rowena got out more slowly.

'Mrs Monks, what a great pleasure it is to meet you.' Brian held out his hand to her.

'This is my friend, Rowena. I'm very keen that she is party to all our conversations and that she accompanies us throughout.' Ellie shook his hand.

'Yes of course Mrs Monks, I am at your service. Would you please follow me?' As they both followed him, Rowena squeezed Ellie's hand as if to say how proud she was of her.

From a substantial ring of keys, he unlocked the front door which was a very wide solid one that opened noiselessly. The hallway was oak panelled from floor to ceiling and the floor covering was a heavy pile blue Wilton carpet. Brian pointed to a door at the far end of the room, mahogany coloured with a bronze coloured plaque on it marked 'PRIVATE'

'We use this room when we need to interview any prospective new tenants, before we show them around.'

As they were seated around a large heavy table, Ellie spoke to Brian in a hushed tone.

'Now Brian, please answer me this question before we go any further. Are you telling me that the whole of this building now belongs to me?'

'Yes, Mrs Monks, the whole of this apartment block is now in your ownership. Also, if I may, I would like to show you something else.' Brian said with a knowing smile.

They came out of the room and went through the next mahogany door marked 'West Wing Lift'. He closed the sliding doors inside the lift and they noticed that there were three buttons to press 'G, 1 and 2 and above that, a keyhole with a number three against it. He took a key from the ring and pushed it in. As soon as he turned the key, the lift began to rise.

'This is your private apartment, Mrs Monks, with your personal access only.' Brian said.

As they came out of the lift on to the thickly carpeted hallway, they could smell the newness and yet they already knew that it was over ten years old.

'It is my responsibility to ensure everything on this floor is kept pristine, although no one has ever lived here.' Brian stated proudly.

He opened the door into a three-bedroom apartment tastefully furnished. The views over the western part of the bay were breath-taking. The lounge had a large sliding glass door opening on to the balcony. There was the usual outside furniture but she noticed that there were also plants thriving there. In the fully equipped kitchen, the appliances shone in the light, just waiting to be used.

'It looks as though someone has stepped outside for a moment, to allow us to look around.' Rowena gasped.

'Is the apartment building fully occupied Brian?' Ellie asked, as she had neither seen anyone no heard anything.

'Yes, it is Mrs Monks, although some of your tenants may be abroad now, as they often winter in warmer climates. But even if it were fully occupied, it is so designed that the sound proofing is of the highest standard and would be just as quiet.' Brian answered.

'This is just perfect Ellie, don't you think?' Rowena looked at Ellie and smiled at her.

Bursting to scream with excitement, but keeping a lid on it, Ellie turned again to Brian. 'I have one more question for you Brian, for the moment. I see that you have come with keys to the property, I don't suppose you have a set for the new owner?'

Ever the professional, Brian smiled at her and out of his other coat pocket he pulled another set of keys for her. As he held them up for her to see, he explained what they were.

'This is the front door key, the elevator's third floor key and skeleton key for all the internal doors. As the agent, I retain the same set subject to your approval Mrs Monks' Brian led the way out of the apartment and closed the door. 'Would you like to lock the door of your new apartment for the first time, Mrs Monks?'

'Thank you, Brian, thank you very much!'

'When we get outside Mrs Monks, I have a file showing the tenant income details as well as the information concerning our management charges. Everything in this folder, is in order for you.'

Brian reached into the backseat of his Mini and passed her another manila folder, which she promptly slid into the briefcase.

'Thank you for your time Brian, you have been most courteous and very helpful, we will be in touch soon.' Ellie surprised herself with the coolness of her words.

Brian shook both of their hands and quickly got in his car and drove away. Ellie watched him disappear around the corner and then pulled Rowena close and gave her the biggest hug that her strength could summon.

Now that Ellie was clear in her mind exactly what she had inherited, she was back at home in Oxford, there was plenty of time on her hands to take stock of everything.

'You've got to get used to it Ellie' she said to herself. 'All these things are happening for a reason'. She was finally using what wisdom she had, to not to be overawed with it all and it wasn't long before she had formulated a plan.

First, she had to be sure whether Gary had changed his mind about when he was coming home from Belfast, so she rung his mobile straight away.

'Hi Gary, I'm just checking that you are ringing tonight.' Relieved that she could get through.

'Yes, I'll be ringing you about eight thirty when I get back to the Europa.' Gary answered.

'Talk to you then love.' Ellie smiled to herself.

'OK, bye' Gary closed the line.

Ellie had dropped Rowena off and was home by five in the evening. After a long hot bath and a quick snack, it was still only seven so she decided to take time out and get her head around the paperwork that she'd brought home.

She pulled the briefcase off the floor and opened it on the couch. On top, there was the file from Brian, neatly headed 'The Breakwaters'. Dividers neatly separated each section and she could clearly see that the top section covered the financial income, followed by the individual files on all the current tenants.

For the time being she just looked at the top section. She scanned the details; rent, ground rent, ancillary charges and management charges and finally at the bottom of the statement it showed the net rent payable to the owner.

The bottom line, the net rent payable to her was £1200 per apartment. She mentally calculated that the income she would receive per year was £115,200. She checked the maths on the calculator and after estimating the income tax payable on the sum, she was still going to receive an amount of about seventy thousand pounds.

'That is a lot of shoes!' She gulped.

With that figure buzzing around her head, she started to think of her life options. 'Do I need to carry on working? If I stop working, what do I do with myself?' She said out loud.

'No wait, I'm getting ahead of myself, slow down and just leave the figures alone for a bit.'

Ellie's subconscious was working at breakneck speed. She instinctively knew that it was better to keep her feet on the ground, but she always liked to go against the grain and swim against the tide. She decided to leave the financial questions alone for now and concentrate on the other questions she had yet to ask herself.

Firstly, the person who has left her this inheritance: Who was she? Why did she have the same name as her own? What role did her mum and dad play in all this? Did they know this woman? They certainly had the same surname name also. Then there was the man who gave her the stone, did he have a part in this? Then finally she remembered something.

Clive Jameson had clearly said that Alex Macduff offered to answer any questions that she might have. 'That's it!' she said out loud, 'I've got to go and see Macduff, he will have all the answers, of course he will. I'm going to Scotland as soon as I can, to get this well and truly sorted!'

She stood up from the couch and felt a great weight lift from her. She unconsciously held the stone in her hand and felt a surge of something inside her.

'Power - Knowledge is power!' She shouted out loud and just at that moment the phone rang.

'Hi sweetie, it's Gary here.'

'Great to hear your voice darling, how are you? Ellie asked. Gary started to describe his day and the plans for him for the rest of the week, when Ellie asked, 'what about the weekend, any chance of getting home? I've got so much to tell you.'

'Ellie, I realise this is difficult for you and I would feel the same in your place, but I've got to hold myself available to the rest of the board for this coming weekend, there is so much planning to do.' He answered.

'Don't they realise that you have a life too?' She pleaded.

'Please don't be upset darling, I realise that important things are happening to you as well, but please be patient. I must do this and you'll see it will all turn out for the best for both of us'

Ellie decided to play down the details of the inheritance at that time, as all of that, could only confuse and possibly increase the tension between them.

'OK Gary, that's fine, I do understand, just don't overdo it darling, I need you back in one piece.'

She distinctly heard Gary breathe a sigh of relief and the tension between them had swiftly disappeared.

'Tell you what, I will not stay over next weekend, I'll come home by next Friday instead, hell or high water. I promise you that.' Gary said determinedly.

'Gary, I'll let you get some rest in a minute, but I want to tell you quickly that the inheritance is quite complicated and I need to go to Glasgow to see that Macduff fellow who seems to have all the answers. Do you have any objections to me going?' Ellie asked him.

'Of course not darling, why should I object? I know that this is very important to you and you must do what you can. If you want to discuss anything whilst you're up there please ring me anytime.'

'OK darling I'll speak to you soon. Goodnight and take care of yourself. By the way how are you getting your laundry done?' Ellie asked.

'The company has taken care of everything. Goodnight my love.'

'Bye Gary'

'Bye Ellie'

After replacing the receiver, she felt a little guilty not spelling out the full details of the inheritance, but overcame that after she realised all the pressure Gary was under and a body can only take so much. She decided that she would ring Macduff first thing in the morning and take at least the rest of the week off from work.

'What can they do, sack me?' She smiled at her own sardonic comment. She looked at the time, nine fifteen and just one more thing to do.

'Hi Rowena.' Ellie said.

'Hi Ellie, what's up?' Rowena asked. Ellie told her what she had decided to do over the next few days including, she hoped, a nice break in Scotland. 'I think it's great, you seem to be more assertive, now you are a woman of substance.'

'You've got it in one Ro.' Ellie couldn't stop herself from a giggle.

'Keep in touch! Oh, by the way I want to tell you something' Rowena's voice seemed to go a little serious.

'What is it Ro, are you alright? It just seems to be all about me now, what am I missing, do tell!'

'Well Ellie, er...'

'Go on.' Ellie urged.

'Well do you remember that man in the car park in Bath, the one you helped direct his car for him?'

'Do I remember him? That kiss on my hand sent shivers up my spine!' Ellie admitted.

'Well. Er, well, we are seeing each other, I mean we're an item, I mean that I love him.' It all came out in rather a rush on the phone.

Ellie screamed down the phone, so loud it just about burst Rowena's eardrums! 'It's amazing, it's wonderful, I love you Ro. I'm so happy for you. He's gorgeous.'

Even Rowena didn't expect such a response from Ellie and she was delighted by it. 'Thanks Ellie, thanks a lot.'

As Ellie put the phone down, tears were streaming down her face with happiness for her best friend. It was the best news that she had heard all day. As she got ready for bed she was still smiling at Rowena's news.

'What a wonderful thing to end the day with.' Ellie thought to herself.

10: Spike

The Pelican Deal

Saturday at the Brickmakers was usually quite a lively affair, for Deal that is. The pub didn't have the usual jukebox, but instead, in the corner of the main bar room there was a record player and any customer could bring along their favourite records and play them for the appreciation, or otherwise, of the rest of the customers. The unwritten rule was that no one could bring more than three records per night and they had to be singles.

This Saturday, Edmund was not in the best of moods, although he realised that the company of a noisy pub would be a better choice than sitting in his room thinking about the afternoon of disappointment with Pauline, so he thought he would give it a try. It was very hard for him to forget that trip to Canterbury, but after a few pints he soon got into the swing of it and although not drunk, he had been successful in putting the whole incident to the back of his mind.

Closing time at the Brickmakers was ten o'clock. He decided not to drag out the final ten minutes drinking up time and to make his way back to Sholden, down the long London Road. The last song on the record player was Sandie Shaw's 'Girl Don't Come' and he was humming it as he walked down the road. He straightened up a little as he noticed someone standing on the pavement blocking his way. As he got closer, he could see that it was an old lady wearing an old-fashioned pinafore, just like his grandmother used to wear. She looked agitated and worried.

'Are you waiting for someone love?' Edmund asked her.

'Can you help me young man? I have got a leak in the kitchen and I have got water all over the floor.'

'I'm no plumber, but let me have a look for you.' Edmund replied.

The gate was just about hanging on its hinges and looking up at the house, it did look in quite a sorry state. The frontage of the cottage was made with bargeboards which at one time had been painted white, but the paint had long since peeled away leaving most of them back to the bare wood. One or two of them had also slipped as if the nails holding them had rusted away. Frankly it looked ready for demolition, but he ignored all that as he followed the old woman into the house.

The dark passageway had bare green painted walls and the flooring of the hallway was old fashioned brown linoleum. He could just perceive a dim light emanating from the open door at the far end. The other thing he noticed was how cold it seemed as he entered the run-down place. The kitchen, if you could call it that consisted of a square shaped sink propped up by a rusty metal frame. Under the frame there was a water pipe that seemed to be severed about two feet from the floor and water was just pouring out of it.

'Do you have a hammer dear?' Edmund asked her.

She came back with a large old-fashioned hammer, quite a heavy one. Edmund crouched under the sink and grabbed hold of the lead piping at the top and with some effort managed to bend it over.

Then, with the hammer, he gave the top of the bent pipe a couple of sharp blows, forcing it to kink in the middle. This stopped the flow immediately. Next to the sink was a metal bucket with an old mop sticking out of it and he did his best to get as much of the water from the floor as he could.

'Thank you my dear, you have done me a great service, I have no money to give you, but I can help you.' The old woman looked up at him and gave him a toothless grin.

'You, help me! I don't want any help thanks. Anyway, I just wanted to help you and I'm glad it's done.' Edmund looked towards the front door as if to leave.

'Yes, I know, but you must come in here, I won't be long, I will give you a reading for the good you have done.' She pushed him into a dimly lit sitting room that had bits of old furniture and a very tired looking settee. She pushed him towards the settee and beckoned to him to sit on it. Edmund gave in and sat on the old horsehair settee and as he did, noticed a mangy old dog asleep next to the couch. He could see that the dog's coat had virtually dropped off its back; he guessed it was a small mixed breed, perhaps a mongrel.

'Don't you worry about Rex dear, he won't bother you? I had him in the Blitz and his hair fell off with fright during the bombing.'

'Do you mean the air raids in the war?' Edmund asked.

'Yes, my dear, we lived in London then.' She answered.

'But that was over twenty years ago, surely not?' Edmund asked.

'Yes, that's right my dear, Rex is twenty-three years old.'

Edmund decided not to challenge the old woman any further, all he wanted to do right then was to get out of there and get to bed.

'Now my dear, what is your name?'

'It's Edmund.'

'Ah, Edmund, it suits you. Your name is from Saxon folklore and it means wealthy protector. You are a deep thinker and one day many people will rely on you. Now, give me that ring on your finger.' She demanded.

Edmund sighed and looked at her, but could see no way of getting out of this, so he reluctantly took off the ring from his little finger and she rubbed it in her hand.

Edmund rolled his eyes as if to say, 'why is this happening to me?' The old woman closed her eyes and hummed, he looked at her and rubbed his eyes in disbelief, she seemed to grow in stature right in front of him.

'You have a spiritual guide; he is called Abdul and he is watching over you. He tells me you will soon be travelling on water and there is a rope, but do not trust your life on this rope!' she uttered in a sort of disembodied voice.

Edmund blinked his eyes for a minute, the old woman returned the little signet ring and once again tried to get up off the settee, but she stopped him.

'You are a very special young man, Edmund and the reason I say this to you is that you helped me without asking why. For that kind gesture, I will give you this.'

She placed a small stone in the palm of his hand; it looked to him like a small crystal. 'Do not be afraid.' She added and as he looked at the strange object, the stone was small and smooth and it began to glow in his palm.

'What is it?' Edmund asked, a little afraid.

'This stone has great power for you and only you. It will not give you anything; instead it will open your eyes, before tonight your eyes were closed. It will not decide anything for you, but you will be helped when the time comes. The stone is your Great Protector and whilst you have it, it will only work for you, that is, until you decide the time that you pass it on to the next special person.'

'How will I know when to pass it on?' Edmund asked.

'Go, young man and remember all I have told you, now leave me.' She ignored his question and waved him out.

Edmund got up and walked to the open front door, through the rickety gate and ran down the road towards the shadowy tower of Sholden Church. Finally, he walked down the dark alley to the row of cottages and home. He felt the chill of the night, but he felt strange warmth in his pocket that he couldn't explain.

The next morning was Sunday and Edmund came into the little dining room. Paul was already eating his breakfast that Winnie had served up.

'What's this mate? You're usually up and gone before I get up! Where did you get to, yesterday? I thought you might have come to see the play.'

'I went to Canterbury.' Edmund told him the events of the afternoon with Pauline Divito.

'Well, things are looking up, you two an item then?' Paul asked.

'If only mate, if only.' Edmund's face dropped.

'Yes, but what made you so late? Did you go to a party or something?' Paul smiled as he asked him.

Edmund explained how he had helped this old lady with her plumbing and how she gave him a reading afterwards. He told him about the ancient dog, but carefully omitted some of the other things the old woman had said to him. Paul wouldn't have believed him anyway.

'Tell you what; we're going into town aren't we? Let's go the London Road way and you can show me the house.' Paul got out of his chair.

Winnie excelled herself that morning with a fried egg on toast! Whilst he was eating, Paul regaled him with his exploits on the stage and how they all liked his performance. Rosalind's father had told him that he knew someone in London that might be of use to Paul, he could see his name in lights already. Edmund, deep in thought, tried his best to look interested.

They both gave Winnie a little kiss and she giggled at them. They were her boys now! As they walked along the road Paul continued with his tales from the play and Edmund nodded absent-mindedly as he felt they were getting close to the old house from last night.

Edmund looked at each house in turn as they passed, especially about halfway, but as they carried on down the road, there was no sign of the old fence and gate. No sign of the dilapidated house, no sign at all! When they had finally reached the end of the road, Edmund stopped walking.

'Look, you carry on and I'll meet you in town. Are you going to the Pelican?' Edmund asked and Paul nodded. 'OK see you there.' Edmund said.

Edmund turned around and walked slowly back from where he came, stopping at every house this time. Every house was made of red brick. Most had either trimmed hedges in front or a low brick wall, certainly no rickety gate.

His heart sank as he reached half way. Everything seemed so real last night. 'Was it a dream?' He thought to himself. He was standing at the gate of a house which was about halfway along the road, when a man came out of his front door and was locking it when Edmund interrupted him.

'Excuse me, hello.' Edmund said loudly. The man turned around, didn't smile, just looked. 'I'm looking for a house down this road, mainly made of wood, like horizontal slats, painted white, do you know of one?'

'No there's none like that down here, I know of a row of houses like that in West Street, but not here! Sorry.' The man finally said.

The man didn't look like he wanted to be bothered anymore, so Edmund waved his thanks and moved on. An elderly couple were approaching with their dog; he stood in their path and smiled at them.

'Excuse me sorry to bother you, but I'm looking for an old wooden style house on this road, do you perhaps know of one?' Edmund asked with a smile.

The woman looked at her partner and looked back at Edmund. 'Around twenty years ago there was a little row of three wooden houses about halfway down this road but they got into a sorry state and got pulled down.'

'Twenty years ago? Did you say they were pulled down twenty years ago?' Edmund asked rather desperately.

'Yes, yes, that's about right dear, twenty years ago.' They looked at each other thinking that he probably looked a bit strange, so they quickly walked away from him. 'We must go now dear' the lady hurriedly said to her partner.

'Thanks' he said to himself. He was about to ask if they knew anyone who lived in the houses, but thought better of it as they seemed to be in a hurry.

There was no more to be done in his search, it seemed a futile quest. Who would believe him anyway? He thrust his hand in his pocket in frustration, only to find that stone, he pulled it out and it once again glowed a little in his hand.

'There's my proof. She gave me this and I'm not going to forget it, no matter what anyone says!' He said it out loud.

By the time he had reached the seafront in Deal, it was twelve o'clock and that time could only mean one thing, the Pelican was open. He turned eastwards on the coast road, past Divito's and purposely did not look in the window.

Lings, which was a very small cosy café run by a little Chinaman, was their favourite café for a cooked meal. He stopped for a moment to greet Mr Ling who was standing at the entrance beckoning him in, but Edmund smiled.

'Ah, you go to de Pelican no?' The Chinaman said in his broken English, 'your flend Paul, he just gone by.'

This part of town was quite often exposed to harsh weather from the sea and now it was blowing a gale offshore but he didn't mind that. It wasn't far to go before he entered the little roadside pub. It was no larger than a little terraced house with a bar in it.

Any stranger entering the bar would be quickly identified and, in most cases, the cold greeting would encourage them to drink up and leave after the first drink. Two or three acquaintances nodded at Edmund as he closed the door and Olive was already pulling his pint even before he had ordered. Paul sat at the first table on the right, his pint was nearly empty, Edmund gestured to him for a refill and of course, Paul needed no asking.

'Any luck with that house search Eddie?' Paul asked.

Edmund had no time to answer as his best friend in the pub had arrived. Spike, a bull terrier, the pub dog came up to him and placed his huge head on Edmund's knee as he sat down at the table. The powerful terrier was nearly all white except for the traditional black spot over his right eye, looking like a pirate, but a very threatening and dangerous pirate, especially if he had taken a dislike to you.

He was a guard dog that took no prisoners, but this time was different. In his mouth, he had a small stiff rubber ball and as much as Edmund tried not to notice him, he kept that heavy head on Edmund's knee and made the traditional bull terrier 'whine'. Edmund knew what he had to do; he placed two fingers each side of his jaws and gently pulled out the hard-wet ball.

The pub suddenly went quiet and the crowd of men dispersed a little. Edmund threw the ball across the pub floor and Spike whined again as he chased after it. Any empty tables or chairs in his way went spinning; he grabbed his quarry and sauntered back to the thrower.

 Once again Edmund tried to ignore him but it was futile. Spike gently laid his head on Edmund's knee again and offered him the wet ball. Edmund repeated the game two more times, but on the fourth time, Spike had laid his head on his knee and as Edmund reached inside for the ball.

Spike's enormous jaw muscles contracted like a vice! Edmund then grabbed hold of the ball, but Spike had held on to it, whining loudly. Edmund knew what he had to do. He picked up the ball with Spike still hanging on to it and wheeled him into the air around the bar area. It really was a fantastic sight and for some reason Spike had always chosen Edmund, from all the customers in the pub to do his trick. Edmund felt this was Spike's way of showing his power and authority and not one of the pub customers would argue with that!

The pub soon settled back to normal as Spike calmed down again. Edmund patted his powerful torso before the bull terrier sauntered back behind the bar, his party trick now over. Only then could they receive their Pelican Pie and Olive placed two plates of generous wedges of the famous pie on their table.

It was a richly made game pie with plenty of meat and very filling. Along with the pie were pickled onions and a good piece of cheddar. Olive of course knew that if anyone had consumed that meal, it was impossible to refuse another pint to wash it all down, all good for business of course.

'Not a sign of the house, as a matter of fact I spoke to an elderly couple who told me that one like I described to you had been demolished twenty years before.' Edmund finally answered Paul's question.

'You must have dreamt it mate. Perhaps you were pissed and the dream was a vivid one. Pity it wasn't about you know who.' Paul looked at Edmund and laughed.

Heading west back into town along the beach promenade they approached Divito's ice cream parlour and Paul wheeled inside so Edmund reluctantly followed him in.

They found a vacant table with a different cartoon under the glass; this one depicted the old Mr Divito, very skinny and bare-chested, being chased by a Roman soldier pointing his spear up his behind. Pauline came to the table and asked what they wanted, Edmund looked up, but she didn't respond.

'Is it guilt, or are you just plain stuck-up?' He asked himself.

Just as Pauline had gone back to the counter to make their coffees, the glass door opened and in came Joe.

'Hey, you two, I've been looking all over town for you.'

Joe was the son of a local butcher and was only a passing acquaintance; they had only met him a few times in the Brickmakers.

'Alice said you might be in here. Listen have you heard the Pirate Radio station called Invicta? It's really good, plays all the top twenty.' He was starting to shout with excitement by now, so Paul told him to calm down a bit. 'Well mates, have you heard about Tom Pepper?'

'Who's he when he's about?' Edmund asked.

Much quieter, Joe leaned closer to them. 'Well, dad told me that he's gone missing with two of the DJs'

'Gone missing? What's Tom Pepper got to do with Radio Invicta?' Edmund asked him.

'Tom owns the station and a load of fishing boats as well in Dover' Joe answered.

'How did he go missing Joe and what's it got to do with us?' Paul asked.

'Maybe he thinks we know where he is mate!' Edmund said and they both laughed.

'No, you got the wrong idea, looks like they got themselves drowned coming back from the station and I think my dad said their boat capsized in dangerous weather.' Joe raised his voice again.

Pauline was standing with the coffees and looking seriously interested. 'What do you want Paul and Edmund to do about it Joe?' She asked.

'Well, my dad told me they are looking for two unattached guys who might like to be DJ's on the station and I thought of you two!' Joe looked at the two friends.

'Look Joe, we don't know anything about being disc jockeys do we Paul?' Edmund looked at his friend.

'Don't worry guys; they'll train you at it, no problem. They want someone to cover for Christmas.' Joe looked convincingly at them.

'Hey, Paul, you're the show biz man, why don't you give it a shot?' One of the diners shouted at the next table.

'When do you need to know Joe?' asked Paul, though he was looking at Edmund for his reaction.

'I need to know right now, as I've got to tell dad whether his mate can come down to Deal from Ashford to arrange an interview for you.' Joe answered, breathlessly.

'I'm up for it mate, what about you?' Paul looked at his best friend, sort of knowing what his answer might be.

Edmund put his hand in his pocket and put the stone in his hand; he thought for a minute and looked up at Joe.

'Don't see why not Paul, let's go for it.'

'Are you sure?' Paul knew Edmund didn't make decisions lightly.

'Joe, go and tell your dad to arrange it with that bloke.'

Edmund looked up at Joe and then his eyes moved over to Pauline who was still standing looking at him, sucking in her lower lip, her dark eyes were looking worried.

'Stay here guys, I'll be back in a flash!' Joe ran out of the café and shot in the direction of the butcher shop, his family lived in the flat above.

'It sounds a bit dangerous to me guys, are you sure, especially with those poor men disappearing?' Pauline did not look directly at Edmund, but she did look sincere for once.

'Probably the good thing is that we don't have anyone who cares, or anywhere to go for Christmas. Don't you think so Paul?' Edmund responded in a flash.

'I guess so Eddie' Paul knew exactly what he was doing.

She turned away and rushed back to the counter, uncannily Edmund knew that although she was not really upset, but somehow, she may have regretted the treatment he received from her the day before in Canterbury. He never found out for sure, but it felt good inside anyway.

He was still thinking about Pauline when Joe burst back into the café. 'It's all arranged guys. He'll meet you outside the Brickmakers at eight tonight.' With that he was gone.

Paul finished up his coffee and stood up to leave. 'I'll see you at the Brickmakers at seven thirty.'

'Better not be late tonight, this could be your break into the big time, with Radio Invicta!' Edmund said to him sarcastically.

'For you as well don't forget.' Paul was laughing as he left Edmund on his own at the table.

There seemed to be a buzz around the tables, as if Edmund was the topic of their conversation, but apart from sideways looks, none of the other customers said anything to him.

'It does sound a bit scary though Edmund, you will be careful, won't you?' Pauline came over to his table, this time she looked at him directly.

'I don't suppose anyone would be crying in their beer if anything happened to me, Pauline. Look at this lot for instance.' He said it quite loud and as he looked around. The rest of the customers looked away, pretending to be deep in conversation with each other.

'Well, I care.' her voice was so soft when she spoke.

'Thanks anyway, Pauline.' He looked up at her for a reply, but she was already on her way back to the counter. 'Nice try love, but I don't think you really mean it.' He thought to himself as he finished his coffee and headed for the exit.

As he left the café, no one spoke to him, but he was sure that he wasn't going to lose any sleep about that either.

As they waited for the man from Ashford to arrive, Paul told Edmund that he had asked Rosalind's father to tell his agent friend in London where he was going over Christmas, but as soon as the job had finished with Invicta, he would contact him the possible agent.

A silver blue Humber Sceptre pulled up alongside them as they waited outside the pub and the driver indicated to them to get in the back seat. The brown leather seats smelled new and they were designed to wrap around them. The driver pulled away for a short distance and pulled up near the local park where it was quiet and dark.

'I'm David and I'm the Managing Director of the Ashford Engineering Company and because of the recent situation, we need some emergency cover for disc jockeys for the Christmas period.'

He continued with his spiel about the business, then turned around and offered them the job on the spot, without any interview.

Paul's eyes lit up, he couldn't believe it, but Edmund didn't. 'Hang on friend; we've got a few questions for you first.'

Up till then, only thing that the two friends could see of their interviewer was the back of his head and his eyes reflected in the rear-view mirror. David turned around and his heavily bearded face was not a pretty sight.

Edmund stood on Paul's foot as if to wake him up. 'Yes pal, what's the money you're offering?' Paul asked him, in a tone that came straight from a stage play.

David smiled at Paul unconvincingly and spelled out the terms. 'Three weeks working on the station and then one week off. You will be expected to work up to April, when by then we will know what we are doing with it. We will pay you £45 per week including the week off, that's £180 cash in hand, each month.

'How do we get there, that is, if we accept?' Edmund asked.

The beard looked at Edmund. 'The boat leaves on Monday morning from Whitstable Harbour'

'Like tomorrow morning?' Edmund asked.

'Yes, if you want the job, you will have to decide now, if it's yes from you, I will pick you up at Sholden Church at seven tomorrow. So, guys what do you say, Yes or no?' He looked at them unblinking.

Paul was thinking about the £180 in his hand and was itching to go for it, but Edmund trod on his foot again, harder than before which made him howl.

'Fifty a week and you're on!' Edmund said to the beard.

There was a stony silence as the man's eyes darkened for a moment and then he smiled and put out his hand.

'You've got a deal guys'. He shook Paul's hand and then shook Edmund's hand and before he let go of it he said, 'I think I've got to watch you, buddy, you've got a good friend there Paul.'

'Don't I know it Dave?' Paul laughed as they both disembarked out of the Humber. The car swished away into the distance. 'Back to his pad in Ashford I expect.' He mused.

'When we get back to our pad in Sholden, let's get an early night, we've got a lot to talk about.' Edmund said seriously.

They were walking down the London Road back to Sholden; it was the first time that Edmund had been down that road since the encounter with the old woman the night before. Edmund instinctively thrust his hands in his pocket and was tempted to tell Paul about the stone in his hand, but he decided against it.

'I know what you are going to say. It does, on the face of it, sound a bit dodgy, but you know us, we can turn this to our advantage and don't you think so?' Paul asked.

'OK I agree we've got to go for it. But I don't trust that Dave. There's more going on than we know, so we must be on our guard, considering what happened to the last two DJ's who are still missing don't forget.' Edmund shook his head ominously.

'Funny that Dave didn't speak about them, nor did he mention Tom Pepper by name, he seemed to be in too much of a hurry.' Paul remarked.

'Maybe we'll find out more tomorrow. I must tell Winnie to let Sheila know and hold my job at the shoe factory, if it all goes tits up at Invicta.' Edmund said, as they passed Sholden Church.

11: <u>Radio Waves</u>

The Mounsel Forts

One of the many very small oyster fishing boats was tied up at the side of the Whitstable harbour wall. There were some stone steps on the quayside to enable Edmund and Paul to get aboard and they tentatively held onto the rope and jumped into the hold. There was just enough room to sit and as soon as they were settled, the little boat's diesel engine jumped into life.

Whitstable harbour was calm and they had no trouble as they headed into the North Sea, but only a few hundred yards into open water, out of the shelter of the harbour, it began to swell. Small waves at first, but soon the little boat was tossing quite violently until it was like a little cork riding the waves.

The fisherman had told them that the forts were about nine miles out at sea in the Thames Estuary. Edmund had visions of an estuary like the mouth of a river, like in his geography lessons at school, but unfortunately it was nothing like that. Soon they were out of sight of land and they both stood up peering over their boat's superstructure scanning an empty grey sea of waves. Paul looked at his friend and didn't need to say anything, as his look of fear was enough.

Edmund shouted over the crashing noise of the waves at the standing fisherman. 'How long will it be till we get there, matey?

The fisherman grimly pointed forward. 'The Mounsel Forts are ahead!'

On the misty horizon, they could see a small shape appearing, but it seemed still far off. In about half an hour more of tossing about in the little boat, the shape had taken form. Having never seen any Defence Forts before, the shapes were totally alien to them. They formed a cluster of cylindrical structures each standing on four stilts that came out of the sea. Obviously, they were secured in the sand bars on the seabed, Edmund could make out five forts in a circle and then two others were further out in the estuary. A flimsy gangway was all that there was connecting each of them.

As the little boat pulled alongside the nearest fort, he could see how they were to get onto them. There was a platform built halfway up the stilts and from that platform a metal ladder ran from the side and down into the sea. With some difficulty, the fishing boat managed to get alongside this rusty fixed ladder, bobbing suddenly close, then away from it as the rough waves dictated.

The fisherman put his arm out to Edmund and helped him out of the hold. He couldn't speak due to the roaring noise produced by the waves crashing against the stilts, so he indicated to Edmund to stand with his back to the small span of rigging. He did that rather reluctantly and his knees were trembling in fear...

'When the boat rocks close to the ladder, let go of the rigging and then JUMP!' The fisherman then shouted in his ear.

The boat rocked close to the ladder, but Edmund held onto the rigging for dear life. He was really scared as he looked down at the churning sea below. The boat rocked a few times more, but Edmund couldn't release his hands from the rigging. He suddenly remembered the old lady's warning 'don't trust your life to a rope'.

Finally, the boat rocked close again and this time the fisherman pushed him violently in his back. Edmund let go and jumped for the rusty ladder, missing the first rung and just managed to grab the next one down. Holding on again for dear life, he looked down to see that the churning water was lapping on his shoe.

He scrambled up the ladder and was soon standing on the platform in a second. From his place of safety, he looked down at the raging sea and realised that if he had missed the second rung, it could have been curtains for him, swallowed up by the sea with no hope of rescue.

'No life jackets or anything else to save me!' He thought as he plunged his hand in his jeans pocket and gripped the stone and it felt comfortingly warm. Paul followed quickly, no looking down for him, swearing and cursing to hide his fear.

'Thank you!' Edmund thought to himself, as he clutched his stone.

The fisherman winched up their two little cases containing their clothes for them to unhook on the platform. The fisherman looked up at them just once, waved and turned the little boat around and set off back to the harbour. The sound of crashing by the grey menacing sea, sounded as if it was angry that it hadn't got them and in its violence soon drowned the little fishing boat's engine as it chugged away.

The only way now for them was to clamber up another rusty ladder leading to a trap door underneath the big metal structure. This time Paul went up first. He scrambled through and then held his arm out for his buddy. The trap door slammed shut and the silence was deafening.

'What the hell have we let ourselves in for Eddie?' Paul blurted out.

'Listen, did you hear that? Edmund pointed in the gloom.

They felt their way in semi darkness to the far end of the dank room to a door, up some more steps and then through another door.

'Sounds like music, over there.' Paul exclaimed.

They followed the ever-increasing sound upwards onto the next floor. This time the room was well lit and smaller. Paul rushed over and opened the door, still following the sound and suddenly discovered where it was coming from.

A man in a dark coat was crouched over two turntables. The table that the equipment was on was edged with large pieces of plywood and over the top of the make-piece structure was a large piece of material, like a blanket. This was attached to the top of some sheets of plywood. Amateur was not the word!

They recognised the song 'Satisfaction' by the Rolling Stones barely audible to them. The man turned to them with a sheepish smile and put a finger to his lips. They both had recognised the signal to be quiet as he was obviously on air.

He introduced himself to them. 'I'm Roy and am I glad to see you two? I've been on air for four hours and I need to go, if you know what I mean.'

He looked at Edmund who was unfortunately the one standing the closest to him. 'Look, put these headphones on, hold on to this mat, you see that the turntable beneath is still spinning. At the end of the Stones, flick this switch and introduce yourself to the audience, then introduce the record on the mat and let go of it. OK?'

The Stones last bars were fading, Edmund looked up at Roy who nodded at him. 'Hi, good morning I'm Bob and I'm here as your new DJ. I've just arrived on Radio Invicta and I need a shave' He let go of the mat and the Beatles 'I Feel Fine' began. The intro sounded a bit like an electric razor.

 'Bloody hell mate that was brilliant.' Paul shouted.

'About Fourteen million people could have heard you say that!' Roy clicked the microphone off quickly and looked sharply at Paul.

There was no time for recriminations, so Roy showed Edmund how to cue up the next record on the other turntable as the Beatles were playing and it then dawned on them both why they needed two turntables.

Paul looked at the second record. 'Hey pal, do you know this one; 'A walk in the Black Forest', by Horst Jankowski, bet you can't introduce this one.' he almost bust a gut trying to stop himself from laughing. The Beatles number was ending and Roy watched as Edmund switched the mike on.

'Hope you liked that. On my way, here today I noticed a row of trees and someone told me I was going for a walk in the Black Forest, see you there.' and let go of the mat.

Roy smiled and put his thumb up and indicated the 'mike off' switch and said that he was off to the toilet. Paul looked in the record pile that was ready to play. He picked up 'Shout' by Lulu, put it on the table, cued it up and lifted the mat for Edmund to hold. As Edmund got hold of the mat Paul pointed to Edmund's wrist, it was covered in blood! Edmund hadn't noticed that with all the excitement, he had caught his hand on one of the rusty rungs of the ladder when he had jumped off the boat.

Roy returned looking much better, just as Edmund introduced Lulu, not so slick this time, having noticed his wrist. Roy indicated for Edmund to get up out of the chair and for Paul to replace him, which they did. As Paul was rummaging for the next disc, Roy showed Edmund the rudimentary bathroom to clean up his wrist and told him to get back in the 'studio' as soon as he could.

Edmund was longer than he thought, as the facilities were as basic as they possible could be and it was ages before he could find even a plaster. When he finally returned to the studio, he needn't have worried as Paul was in his element, as usual. It was as if he had been born to it and there was no doubt on Roy's face either.

They both took turns, for three record plays, to get used to the system until Roy was happy that they were competent enough.

Between one of the sessions, he asked Paul if he could handle it on his own, for about half an hour, whilst he showed Edmund around the place. Paul stuck his thumb up at Roy, remembering that he was live on air.

'Ladies and Gents, your favourite DJ Gary Brando is now going to play you one of my all-time greats......'

'He's got it, that one.' Roy smiled at Edmund.

'I know Roy, he certainly has and he's a born performer, Mr. Brando.' Edmund laughed.

As they walked around the rooms, Roy explained that his real job on the station was Engineer, but we have had to turn our hands to everything at this tough time without any other staff.

He told Edmund that since the tragedy, he had been on his own, keeping the broadcast going for nearly a week and Edmund felt sorry for him.

'No wonder that Dave was in a bloody rush in that interview in the car.' He thought to himself.

Roy pointed to the wall that displayed a map of the layout of the forts, which were originally built as a line of defence for the shipping lanes into London during the war. The furthest fort from the main cluster, housed the generator. This had to be tended regularly with fuel and lubricants day and night. Roy promised to show them both what to do about the generator at the end of broadcasting.

'What do we do about food, Roy?' Edmund asked.

Roy showed Edmund the galley, for what it was! All the food came out of tins, but the most precious thing for them was water, which was stored in large plastic containers.

The only good thing that Edmund noticed, was the large cupboard by the table, which contained the booze and the fags, locked of course and Roy knowingly smiled and waved the key at him!

It wasn't long before the euphoria of being a DJ on a Pirate Radio station wore off for the young men, as the work was relentless! If they weren't spinning records, they had to take turns to fill up the Generator.

This entailed walking the tightrope over the swinging walkways, emptying two four-gallon containers of diesel into the generator's reservoir and checking the lubricant levels of the engine. Roy had made it very clear to them, that without the generator being attended, everything would stop and that wasn't just the turntables.

Also, their other tasks were to make some sort of meal from the meagre supplies, as well as find the time to prepare for the next show.

'Well Eddie, that's Show Business!' Paul's humour kept the other two going and they were very grateful for it.

The radio station was on air between 7am and 7pm. Paul and Edmund were expected to be on air at least five hours each day. Very often a show would last two hours, so planning for each production became a nightmare, as the record library was not the most extensive one. In the first week, the new DJs struggled greatly with the problem of keeping fresh for the listeners.

In the second week, however Paul (Gary Brando) hit on the idea of a tandem show with Edmund (Bob Gray). This added new life into the production; however, it was hard to tell whether it was a success, as they didn't receive any feedback from the listeners.

Roy was just so happy that the new DJs were using their initiative; it enabled him to get on with the upkeep of the equipment.

'Bob Gray' also came up with another idea for a show. He called it 'Pop Sticks' based on a request only programme. The problem that they immediately encountered was that there were no requests arriving at the fort. He got over this by sticking a pin in an old London phone directory and then making up a request, as if it had arrived in a letter from them. The two DJs used to take turns on this show and some of the requests they made up were so weird that it was very difficult to read them out without 'corpsing' on air!

Probably the worst thing about being on the forts however was the silence and it was the hardest to get used to. By the second week Roy had fixed up a short-wave radio and he was able to contact base. What a relief that was, as the first two weeks on the forts seemed to the new recruits as if there was no one else in the world.

In the third week, the water was running low, the beer was running low and, worst of all, the diesel for the generator was running out! Fortunately, Roy had finally reached someone in Whitstable on the short-wave radio and they were able to send out the lifeboat loaded with the new supplies.

That was the time that Roy informed them, that in four days' time their replacements would soon be arriving, which made Paul and Edmund suddenly long to get off the forts at last.

It was soon the third Sunday and at last there was one more night to endure their strange new life! Edmund was the last of the three to make that endless journey to the generator that time. It seemed to him such a pointless task, especially at night.

This night though, was the worst one that he had had to perform the job. It was early January and the wind was blowing up a gale. It was pitch black except for tiny bulbs that were attached to the side of the structures as he walked around them.

The walkways between the structures were about thirty feet long and were swaying violently in the wind. Roy told him that they were designed to sway, otherwise they would snap off with the wind and that didn't bear thinking about.

It had started to snow and as he looked down from the middle of one of the swaying gangways, he could see the white surf on the top of ferocious waves beneath him. He knew that because the North Sea is so shallow compared to other seas, this made it the roughest sea imaginable.

The tiny bulb on the last but one structure was flickering, which meant that the generator was running out of fuel. 'I must get there before it does!' he shouted.

He thrust his hand in his pocket took out the stone and shouted at it. 'Help me, get me there before it runs out, I need to get there.' He put the stone back in his pocket and trudged on and the weather was worsening. At last, he had made it to the final connecting gangway and it was swaying like hell, but he persevered, knowing that he was near to his goal.

'Hold on you bastard, Hold on!' He finally reached the generator and it was spluttering, on its last legs.

He started the lengthy process of pouring the diesel out of the heavy container into the engine's reservoir and to his relief it suddenly jumped into life again. His hands were frozen with the wind and wet snow, his clothes were sodden, but he had done it! He was part way back when Paul appeared around the corner.

'Shit mate, I thought you were a goner.'

'Tell you what Paul that was the worst thing I have ever endured in all my life and I don't mind admitting to you, that I have never been so scared.'

'When the lights started to dim, I thought you might have needed some help Eddie, poor old Roy is fast on, totally out of it. Anyway, mate you're a bloody hero in this lot, a bloody hero!' He shouted above the gale and slapped his friend's back.

The wind had worsened and the snowflakes were blinding. Through the cacophony of noise Edmund had never heard a word that Paul had said to him, but none the less, he was so glad to see him.

The next morning the sea was flat, the storm had blown itself out. Roy had slept right through it and they decided not to bother him with their troubles during the night. He wasn't getting off the forts as they were, not yet as he would have to show the newcomers the ropes as well. Paul the DJ hero was spinning the records, it was seven in the morning and they were having a Fray Bentos steak and kidney pie for breakfast.

'This is the last time I'm ever going to eat one of these.' Edmund said to himself.

Around ten, Roy came into the studio, stuck his thumb up at Edmund and that could only mean one thing, dry land next stop. It was a time to be inventive so Edmund switched on the mike and spoke to his 'adoring fans'.

'Dear friends, this is Bob here, I hope that you enjoyed listening to my choice of records over the last three weeks. I hope you don't mind listening to 'A Hard Day's Night' because that's just what we've had, here on Radio Invicta. Signing off and speak to you soon.'

Edmund switched off the mike. 'Roy, will you please see Paul and me off, I've loaded an LP on the turntable and that will keep them all happy until someone takes over the mike.'

Unusually for Roy, he smiled at Edmund and put his arm around his shoulders.

'I know what you did last night Edmund and I'm proud of you, proud of both of you.'

As the three of them arrived at the lower landing through the trapdoor from above, three men had already disembarked and stood on the platform, with two more on the way. Fortunately, Roy recognised two of them and they shook hands. Roy introduced Edmund and Paul to everyone.

'Which one of you is Gary Brando?' A tall blonde man asked.

'That's me' said Paul.

'Well you are really cool man, I like your style and my name is Dave Cash.'

'You related to Johnny Cash?' Paul asked, jokingly.

'You related to Marlon?' Dave quipped in return.

The whole crowd of men broke into laughter and the tension had gone! The replacements all shook hands with Paul and Edmund then they each climbed the ladder into the fort. Roy was last to go up after they both had given him a hug.

'Thanks, mate for all your help' Paul said.

'You both took to it like ducks to water, considering the circumstances' Roy's words were filled up with emotion.

'Yeh Roy, there's plenty of that around here' Edmund shouted as Roy disappeared through the trapdoor.

They boarded the homeward bound boat that was thankfully much bigger than the one they arrived on three weeks before. As they stood on the deck, they looked at each other and breathed a sigh of relief.

'You know what mate; I don't think those new guys will have it as tough as we did.' Edmund sighed in relief.

Paul nodded in agreement, but his eyes were forward, searching for land. Edmund tapped on Paul's shoulder, for him to look back. Already the forts were a very small pale blue dot on the horizon.

'Bloody good riddance to the place and yet I wouldn't have missed it for the world. When we get ashore and get paid that two hundred quid, I want to tell you something.' Paul said.

Edmund didn't reply, but instead just held the stone, still in his pocket. He realised that he was just glad to be alive and as he gazed toward the shore, he made out the low line of Whitstable harbour coming into view.

Edmund remembered that a few days after they arrived on the station, that he had found a letter from Decca records offering some commission to any of the DJ's on Invicta that would plug the new Twinkle's record called 'Terry', especially if it reached the top 5 in the charts.

'Talking of money, can you remember that letter I showed you about the Twinkle song from Decca?' Edmund asked.

'Do I remember? I think I must have worn the grooves out playing it.' Paul grinned as they were pulling up alongside the quay.

'Well, we need to check if it got into the top five whilst we were on the fort. If so we are owed some money there too!' Edmund shouted.

Paul ran up the harbour side steps and saw someone looking out of a little cabin. 'Where's Dave mate?'

'Are you two looking for your money? Got a message to tell you that you've to go to the office and collect it.' The man said.

'Where's the office?' Edmund asked.

'In Ashford,' he replied pointing over the road. 'The bus leaves in half an hour.'

Edmund walked up to the man in the shed. 'And how are we expected to get there without cash?' The man ducked back into his shed and came back flourishing a five-pound note.

'One of the others left it for you' he shouted, as they picked up their belongings and trudged across the road to the bus stop.

'Look for Ashford Engineering, ask for David Delaney and good luck.'

'That Dave is going to need all the luck if he doesn't have the money ready.' Paul growled to himself as he sat on the top of the East Kent double-decker bus.

'Edmund, I've been thinking about this DJ job.' Paul broke the silence.

'I know what you're going to say mate. I'm not going back on those filthy tin cans again either, for all the tea in China. Let's get what we are owed and we'll walk away without even telling them, what do you think?' Edmund said and Paul nodded in agreement.

'I'm not going back to Deal with you mate, Rosalind's dad has got me an interview with the director of that touring company I told you about. He thinks I've got a chance.'

'Do you mean that Shakespeare gig?' Edmund asked as Paul nodded. 'Wherefore art thou Romeo? Best of luck mate, you deserve it.' Edmund watched the Kent landscape flash by and then he looked again at Paul. 'I'm not staying in Deal either, at least not for very long. I know that. Well, er. Pauline wouldn't....'

Paul cut him off. 'Don't you worry mate, plenty more fish in the sea where that came from. You're far too good for her anyway. She might be good looking, but that's only skin deep.'

'Wow, Paul, first you're an actor, then a DJ hero and now a philosopher as well.' Edmund smiled at his buddy.

They both were laughing as the bus pulled into Ashford bus station. The engineering works were a good walk from the centre of that dreary town, but Paul kept rubbing his hands in anticipation.

Edmund however was less confident and hoped there wasn't going to be any trouble with that Dave. They were soon walking through some glass doors into a large modern reception area, with a girl sitting at a desk.

'David Delaney if you don't mind.' Paul smiled at the girl.

'He's out.' She looked back at him stony faced.

'Get him now and tell him that there are two people from Invicta waiting to see him. Do it now!' Paul's face went red and he came in close to her rather menacingly.

'Two men are here looking for David. Yes, I know. But I think you had better get him quick!' The poor girl looked scared to death and her hand was shaking as she lifted the receiver.

In two minutes a bearded man walked down the open staircase which was situated behind the reception desk. He wasn't smiling, but he did have something in his hand, two envelopes which he gingerly gave one to each of them. He then turned to go back up the stairs without speaking.

'Wait, you!' Paul shouted and the man stood stock-still. Paul indicated to Edmund that they should open the sealed envelopes and each counted £180. 'We agreed £200.'

'Yes but....' David stuttered.

'Go and get the other forty, now! We have kept your crummy radio station going over Christmas and by the way, what were you doing over Christmas friend?' Paul scowled at David.

'Wait, Mr Delaney!' He turned around to face Edmund this time. 'We also want the commission from Decca, for the Twinkle 'record-plugging'. You were going to pay us that as well, weren't you?' Edmund asked softly.

'How much do you want?' Delaney asked through his teeth.

'It's another fifty each, if you don't mind, Mr Delaney.' Paul looked like he was going to rip his head off.

'Brando would have been proud of him,' Edmund thought, 'And make it snappy friend.' Edmund shouted this time backing Paul up. The receptionist girl went white, still expecting trouble.

He was back in a flash. 'There you are gentlemen' Delaney gave them an insincere smile.

Paul grabbed the cash and swiftly counted it. 'Try that again and I'll....' Looking to get an Oscar.

'Let's go!' Edmund tugged Paul's sleeve and they both walked out. 'I guess we've just been sacked again matey.'

As they walked back to the bus station with the £250 each in their pockets, Edmund knew that this time they were to be going their separate ways. It was in fact the first time since they had left home together to go to France the year before.

'When would they meet up again? And in what circumstances would that be?' Edmund wondered.

Paul's London coach was already waiting in the bay and Edmund walked to it with him.

'Good luck in your new venture Paul.' Edmund patted him on his back.

'I'll miss you old matey, still, I'll see you in Hollywood eh!' Paul said as he jumped on the footplate and into the coach, just in time. The bus's engine soon fired up and with just one wave from the passenger window, he was gone!

Edmund knew that from then on, he was going to shape his own future without his best pal. The world was rapidly changing and he knew that any new opportunities were to be shaped by his own hands and no one else's.

12: <u>Excitement in Southbourne</u>

Indie & Freddie

'Vizards, can I help you?'

'Good morning, my name is Eloise Monks and I would like to speak to Mr Macduff, if that is at all possible'. Ellie rang as early as she could to catch him before the interminable meetings that most lawyers seem to be involved in.

'One moment, I will try to put you through.' The receptionist said.

'Mrs Monks?' The deep familiar Scottish tones of Alex Macduff came over reassuringly.

'Speaking' Ellie answered and tried to be as business-like as she could.

'How nice to hear from you, I must admit I didn't expect to hear from you so soon after your meeting with Clive Jameson. I trust your meeting was successful?' asked Macduff.

'Very successful and I have already visited the property and met the agent looking after it.' Ellie said.

'Well done my dear. Now what can I do for you?'

'I'm sure that you are not surprised that I have some important questions Mr Macduff, so I wonder if I could come up to your offices and meet you and hopefully get some answers. I would like it to be as soon as possible.' Ellie crossed her fingers in hope.

'I will look forward to that Mrs Monks. To save you holding on, may I call you back after I have spoken to my secretary. I realise this is very important to you, so I hope to make the dates as soon as possible.'

Ellie was opening her post as the phone rang. 'Mrs Monks?' Ellie confirmed. 'Do you have some paper and pen handy?' After a few seconds, she had retrieved a pen and a pad.

'Sorry Mr Macduff, but do you mind if I open this letter that arrived today, it's got your firm's name on it?' She asked.

'I'm pleased about that; please open it whilst I hang on.' He replied.

She ripped open the envelope and pulled out the letter with the phone receiver attached to her ear and shoulder. As she was reading it, something fell onto the carpet; it was a cheque that had landed face up. As she leaned over to pick it up, the telephone itself fell onto the floor and as she struggled to pick that up, the chair she was sitting on also toppled over!

'Are you alright Mrs Monks?' Macduff had heard the noise.

'Yes, sorry about all that. I was trying to pick the cheque up and, well everything fell over. I have now read the cheque, it says £110,550!' Then she started to giggle. Macduff started to laugh too and the whole conversation became hilarious.

'I don't receive letters like this very often Mr Macduff' Ellie tried to compose herself.

'The contents, Mrs Monks, are they to your satisfaction?'

'It's unbelievable, Mr Macduff.' Ellie spluttered.

'I take that as a yes, Mrs Monks. Now, where were we? Oh yes, I remember the dates for our meeting.' His secretary had moved some less important meetings around, resulting in two appointment spaces available for the following Monday and one for Tuesday.

'That is very kind of you Mr Macduff; I will tell you now, that the ten o'clock appointment on Tuesday suits me fine.' Ellie said, much relieved.

'Ten o'clock Tuesday it is then, I am very much looking forward to meeting you. Will you be bringing your husband to the meeting?' He asked.

'Sadly, no he is still in Belfast, so I will be coming up alone. Thank you again Mr Macduff, goodbye.'

'Goodbye, Mrs Monks, I'm so glad you are happy with my letter and I'll see you on Tuesday. If you have any problems before you arrive up here, you know where I am.' Macduff then closed the call.

She settled on the couch and re-read the letter, her eyes focused on the legal blurb.

'Enclosed is our certified cheque which represents the second part of the bequest of the deceased Eloise Mary McIntyre in full and final settlement after deduction of the firm's charges'.

She then looked again at the cheque. 'What do I do with this?' Unconsciously she was holding the stone in her hand at the same time and immediately she knew what to do.

The next morning as her bank opened, she was at the counter paying in her cheque. The bank clerk looked at her and asked if she wouldn't mind waiting to see her superior. Ellie just nodded and sat on one of the chairs opposite. A grey suited man opened the door at the end of the room and held it open for her to enter. She felt the stone warm again at the end of the chain.

She sat down in the dark panelled room, opposite the grey suited man, who smiled weakly at her. He could see that she wasn't in any mood to talk, so he tried the usual niceties.

'Mrs Monks, I notice that you have paid into your current account an unusually hefty sum.'

'The unusually hefty sum is my inheritance as you can see by looking at the payer and if you are asking, it is not the result of some drug dealing.' Ellie said sarcastically.

The grey suit again smiled thinly. 'I am not in any way thinking about the source of the income madam, I just wanted to take the opportunity to show you what the bank can offer you for investment.'

'Thank you, but some other time, as I am in a hurry. I have placed it in my current account on a temporary basis, for safety. I take it that it is safe with you is it not?'

Ellie did not smile as the man rose from his chair smiling again, which Ellie found a bit sickening and offered his hand, which she shook briefly and turned to leave. She turned the ignition in the Polo and headed for home and even from that moment, she knew what she was going to do next.

She rushed around the house, filling an overnight bag and then, finding an almost new Waitrose reusable shopping bag, took enough food out of the fridge and kitchen cupboard for breakfast. She headed out of Oxford, on the ring road and then the dual carriageway, south on the A34.

In an hour and a half, she was turning into the car park at Breakwaters. As she got out of the car it was raining and the wind was blowing in her face. Thankfully she was wearing her duffel coat so she was well protected. She struggled with the two bags in one hand as she juggled with the ring of three keys in the other.

The big brass Chubb key opened the heavy front door and she closed it behind her. The wild weather was suddenly shut out and silence reigned. She looked across the big hallway for the next door and opened the one marked 'West Wing Lift' and soon she was standing in the inside it. She looked at the smallest key and slotted it into the keyhole marked 'floor 3 private'. As she turned it the lift moved noiselessly and soon the door silently opened into the plush carpeted hallway.

She was mesmerised for a moment and then after nimbly walked out looking right and left, but of course there was no one there. The third key, of course, clicked open her own apartment door. She sank into the thick pile, put her two bags on the carpet and walked around the flat for a few moments.

She went from room to room, getting her bearings. She lightly felt the top of the soft leather couch, lazily opened the empty draws in the bedside cabinets in the bedrooms and at the kitchen equipment. She quickly came to her senses and switched on the Smeg fridge freezer and it immediately hummed into life.

After unpacking her clothes and putting the meagre food items away, she went towards the large glass patio doors that opened onto the veranda, but she stopped short from opening them.

The wind was lashing the rain onto them, but to Ellie's amazement the wild weather wasn't making a sound. She suddenly felt very hungry, as it was well past lunchtime and had nothing except breakfast things in the fridge, so she decided to make a cup of coffee and wait for the weather to change.

As she waited for the kettle to boil, she remembered that she had Internet connection on her mobile, so she set up an account with Waitrose home delivery, in readiness for next time that she stayed at her new apartment.

'And that won't be long either.' She said to herself.

As she drank her coffee on her new sofa, as if by magic the rain stopped lashing on the patio doors and looked like the wind was dying down too. Her hunger was not abating and had to be satisfied. She remembered the nearby café that she and Rowena had gone to, so she put her boots on and got into the old duffle coat again.

'It's time to eat and I'm starving!' She shouted.

The clouds were still heavy and were scudding across the sky, but at least it was dry. She looked at her watch, three thirty and hoped that they still had some food on the menu, but she needn't have worried. She was soon tucking into tomato and basil soup, then a generous steak of salmon on a bed of cheese and cream sauce with mange touts and new potatoes.

After the meal, she walked the short distance to the cliff top and leaned on the fence next to the Fisherman's Walk cliff lift and looked at the impressive sweep of the bay as it pointed toward Hengistbury Head. She smiled to herself, as from there, she could see the impressive block of luxury flats that she now owned. Her euphoria was marred by another heavy bank of cloud heading her way from the darkening horizon.

Back in the Breakwater's car park, it was like déjà vu with the wind blowing the hard rain at her, as she struggled to get to the front door. Heading towards the lift, there was someone just opening the lift door, so she ran to catch her.

As they entered the lift, Ellie smiled at an elderly woman, noticing that she was beautifully dressed as if she had just returned from the opera.

'Hello, my dear, are you a new resident?' The lady asked.

'Yes, sort of,' she looked down at her jeans and duffle coat, all wet with the rain. The woman pressed level two and looked at Ellie, who pulled out the 'Furse' key. She thought quite rightly, that the woman needed to get out at her floor, before she could operate the key mechanism for floor three.

'I see you're on the third floor, are you?' The old lady said, when lift door opened for her floor.

'Er, yes, my name is Ellie, pleased to meet you.' Ellie replied smiling.

She turned around for a moment to put her key in the keyhole when the lift quickly opened and the lady got out. She then turned around to continue with their conversation, but the door closed and the lift began to ascend again. Ellie felt a little uneasy that she hadn't had a chance to speak further, but that's what it's like in lifts, there just isn't the time.

She boiled the kettle for another drink, but she couldn't get the lady out of her mind. She glanced at her watch, four thirty and Brian the Estate agent would still be at his desk, hopefully.

'Ruddock and Partners, can I help?' Ellie recognised the cultured tones of Brian's voice.

'Brian, it's Eloise Monks here, I hope that you are well.'

'Mrs Monks, how nice it is to hear from you again.' He answered.

'Can I ask a favour, Brian?'

'Ask away'

'Could you please let all the residents know that I have taken over the property and will periodically be using the west wing third floor apartment?' Ellie asked.

'I typed out the letter, almost word for word yesterday when I got back to my desk. Not only that, my assistant posted it by hand to each apartment first thing this morning!'

'I'm very glad, because I met the lady on the second floor about an hour ago and we didn't get time to get acquainted in the lift, if you know what I mean.'

'Ah, that must be Mrs Cohen, lovely lady. Yes, she's in West 2, I'm sure that she is aware of the situation by now. Please don't be concerned, her son is very big on Wall Street in New York and he deals with all of her affairs.'

'Thank you, Brian, my mind is at rest. Bye for now.' Ellie was relieved.

'Don't hesitate to call if you need anything, Goodbye.' Once again Brian had proved his worth.

The wind had finally died down and the faint rays from the low sun were reflecting on the dark sea. As the light faded there were a few people taking their last walk on the beach before nightfall?

She leaned over the rail of the veranda to catch the final rays of light. A very tall man was walking past, quite slowly and she noticed a black and white dog's head bobbing in the surf. The man was throwing stones just ahead of the dog, so that it swam further out.

Occasionally the dog came out of the sea and shook its coat. She could then recognise the breed to be a border collie. She was surprised as she knew this breed didn't normally like the water that much, as they preferred the hills where the sheep were. As the tall figure passed he looked up at her and waved. She shouted 'Goodnight' and he waved again in reply.

Back in the flat, she took another tour of the rooms. There were three bedrooms all furnished, all slightly differently, but matching to a tasteful style. In the lounge that was quite large, the TV was an up to date model with digital reception. Considering that no one had ever lived there, someone had made sure that everything was up to date, Brian of course.

A quick run through the channels on the TV, came up with nothing to watch. Those days, most of the channels were commercial and if they screened anything remotely interesting, she had to endure prolonged periods of stupid commercials. On the wall to the left there was tasteful wall shelving with a mini sound unit. As she turned to the tuner, the Jupiter symphony by Mozart was playing on Radio 3, perfect.

Out on the balcony again, she looked west at the twinkling lights of the Bournemouth sea front. The moon was full and it was reflected onto the sea leaving a silvery beam as far as the beach. In a big curve, the lights of the promenade were stretching from Bournemouth, all the way eastwards to Hengistbury Head.

Further beyond Hengistbury Head, she could see the lighthouse which was flashing its blue light from the Needles, on the Isle of Wight. As she looked out to the black sea, there were a few lights on the horizon, ships anchored for the night. She imagined that the crew were probably watching the same rubbish TV programmes that she had seen a minute ago.

'Whoever designed this place knew what they were doing' she thought, as the lights from the promenade picked up the white of the surf crashing softly on the sand.

Her watch told her that it was nine thirty, beyond the time to ring Gary. 'Maybe he rang the home phone and thought I was out, I'd better give him a call.'

Gary's mobile rang a few times and she let it ring some more.

'Hello, who is this?' a female voice answered.

'Who are you?' Ellie answered indignantly.

'Ellie, is that you, Hello?' Gary quickly came to the phone.

She terminated the call. To say she was surprised would be an understatement, she was stunned. Her mobile rang and 'Gary' flashed up on the screen, so she diverted it to her voicemail and then switched it off.

'Why should a woman answer Gary's phone?' Her mind started to play tricks. 'What is he up to? How long has this been going on? Is this the reason he can't get back for the weekend?' She pulled out the stone and held it. She felt its power and the mental strength came back to her. She decided to listen to Gary's message.

'Ellie, darling, sorry about not answering, it was a little mix up. We are having a late dinner at the hotel, I put my phone down on the table and someone picked it up whilst I was talking. Sorry love, please call back.'

Ellie was still holding the stone as she rang him back. 'Hi Ellie, did you get my message?' She now felt calm and composed.

'I'm fine now Gary, just for a moment I thought you were with somewhere else.' Ellie tried to sound in control.

'Look Ellie, we're all having a meal and.....'

'Just put her on, the woman who answered.' Ellie heard muffled voices.

'Er, hello?' the voice sounded different this time.

'Are you the person who picked up Gary's mobile?' Ellie asked.

'Er, yes I was.'

'And why did you do that.' Ellie demanded.

'The phone was ringing and it was getting on my nerves, I just answered it to shut it up. Sorry, I'm sure.' The voice seemed partly sarcastic, partly condescending.

'Please put him back on, thank you.' Ellie was sharp with her.

'Hello Darling'

'I won't disturb you any further; you just go ahead and have an enjoyable time.' Ellie was holding back the tears.

'Look Ellie there's nothing going on here. As I said, we are just having dinner. Tell you what; I'll ring you when I get back to the room, OK?'

She suddenly felt cold, perhaps it was the call, but when she looked at the half open patio doors, she went outside again. Despite the cold, she took a deep breath of sea air which cleared her head and felt much better.

'Look Ellie I know what you must be thinking right now, but please believe me there is nothing going on. It's just work. I'd rather be with you.'

'OK Gary I guess I have over reacted. But answer me this, you were planning to take another weekend away, right?'

'Yes, I was.' Gary said.

'Are you really telling me that they all work seven days a week over there? I doubt that very much! Anyway, just to let you know, I won't be home this weekend. I'm going to Glasgow to see Macduff. He doesn't work weekends but I'm going there as a tourist and my appointment is on Tuesday morning, so if you're lucky I should be home next Wednesday, I say again, if you're lucky.' Ellie was in no mood to be submissive.

'I'll be home on Wednesday then and we can get this misunderstanding out of the way. I promise you that all I am doing here is work, nothing else. Are you flying to Glasgow?'

'Yes, I am, from Eastleigh airport. My flight arrives back at ten in the morning on the Wednesday.'

'How about that I meet you there and we can drive back home together?' Gary asked.

'I feel better now, now I've got things off my chest. Please don't worry, I can look after myself and I will see you then, Bye.' Ellie remained strong as she held on to her stone.

'I love you Ellie, talk soon eh?'

The bedroom was like a cocoon, silent warm and cosy. No wonder she had had a good sleep, there was nothing to disturb her. The following morning the sun was streaming through the open bedroom doorway. 'What a lovely way to start the day,' she said to herself.

She put on a thick dressing gown and slippers that she found in the wardrobe filled a bowl of muesli that she had brought from home poured over the cold milk and stood on the balcony, staring at the sea.

Someone was walking on the beach towards her. A figure was throwing a ball and two little white dots were chasing after it. They were barking with excitement. As they got nearer Ellie waved at them and the woman looked up and waved back.

Then she looked to the left towards Hengistbury and between the two man-made rock groynes she could just make out a solitary figure looking out to sea, not moving. She didn't have any binoculars but she stood still and stared.

'Is this the man who gave me the stone?' she asked herself.

The lady and her little dogs were heading that way, so she put down her unfinished breakfast, threw on her thick polo necked jumper, pulled her jeans and boots on and wrapped her duffel around her. In a few minutes, she was starting the car and driving east towards the Head.

About a quarter of a mile along the coastal road there was a signpost indicating a car park to the right. She bought a ticket for a couple of hours stay, locked up the Polo and ran to the cliff path. The wind was coming off the sea blowing the sand in her face. She ignored that and scanned the bay eastwards for the solitary figure, but to her dismay it was empty!

Ellie ran down the beach path to make sure, scanned to the east, but nothing there. To the west the figure with the two little dogs was getting quite closer and she could hear someone shouting. The little white balls of fluff were chasing towards her and the woman was obviously trying in vain to make them come back.

'I'm so sorry dear they are so excitable, but very friendly.' She looked friendly too. Ellie was very pleased that she had finally met someone who walked on the beach.

'Hi, I'm Ellie'

'Hello, my name is Ursula, pleased to meet you. I hope the boys are not too boisterous for you, they love people, but they get so excited!' She had a slight foreign accent.

'No problem Ursula, I love dogs, but I've never seen this breed before.'

'They are Bichon Frise, related to the poodle and they are related to each other too, having come from the same litter.' Ursula explained.

'How do you tell them apart?' Ellie asked smiling at them.

'Well, you see, this one has a red collar and is the naughtiest, he's called Freddie. This one with the blue collar is called Indie. I take them for a walk every day for my neighbours who are both out at work.' Ursula explained.

'It's a very good reason to be out in such a beautiful place. Are you from South Africa originally?' Ellie asked.

'No, I'm not, I'm Swiss, but you're not the first person to think that. Yes, I love this part of the beach, it is so unspoilt with no buildings and no ice cream vans either.' She looked at Ellie and smiled. 'I have a daughter about your age, but she lives in Turkey. Where do you live my dear?'

'Just there' Ellie pointed to the big building overlooking the cliff.

'Did I just wave to you? You were in white, I didn't recognise you dear.' Ursula laughed, looking at the boys, who were getting a bit restless.

Indie was sitting looking up at Ellie with his cute little button eyes and his head was leaned on one side. Freddie however was running after a little spaniel puppy that had arrived. She shouted at Freddie, who stopped for a second, looked back and then carried on running with the other dog.

'One word from me and he does what he likes. He is so naughty!' Ursula shook her head and smiled.

Ellie fell in love with them they were so cute. She could see that Ursula was ready to go back, so she tried a question.

'Ursula, can I ask you a question, please?'

'Yes of course my dear.' Ursula answered.

'Did you see a man earlier, standing over there?' She was pointing just past one of the groynes made from huge chunks of sandstone. 'He was staring into the sea not moving. Do you know him at all?'

Ursula looked a bit serious for a moment. 'Does he wear a long coat and a wide brimmed hat and does he have a silver blue Border collie called Zowie?'

'Well, you describe the man, but he didn't have his dog with him last time we met, but it was in the same place. He gave me something last time and I want to thank him. Do you know him?' Ellie bit her lip in anticipation.

'Well, all I know is that he is called Edmund and he is in his sixties and he lives in the New Forest, but that is all I know.'

'He never mentioned what town, did he?' Ellie asked.

'No, but there is someone who might know, John he walks with Mollie on this beach every day.'

'Is he very tall and the dog swims in the sea?' Ellie was crossing her fingers behind her back.

'Yes, my dear, Mollie loves the sea. John can't get her out sometimes.'

'Thank you, thank you very much Ursula!' Ellie shook her hand heartily.

She wanted to hug her, but thought better of it. Ursula said her goodbye and started back, shouting for the boys to follow. Freddie had had his fun with the puppy and then noticing that his brother was some distance off, ran very hard to catch them up.

About halfway between Ellie and Ursula, Freddie suddenly stopped in his tracks, turned around and ran back to Ellie. He then sat in front of her for a pat and a scratch under his ear, then jumped around and chased after his brother again. Ellie was in love!

She walked back to the car triumphantly. On her own she had found him, the secret donor of the stone and it felt great. On the way back to the apartment, which took only a few minutes, she had decided what to do. It was still only nine, so she decided it was time to go back to Oxford, as all her clothes and things were there.

She ran around her new apartment picking up the odds and ends that she had brought and before leaving, made sure that the big glass doors on the veranda were shut tight. The mobile rang as she was opening the entrance door and as it rang, she looked at the display, oh no! She remembered that she hadn't phoned work.

'Ellie, are you all right we are all worried about you here.'

'Simon, I am so sorry! There's been so much happening, you wouldn't believe it.'

She flopped back on the settee and gave him a shortened version of the recent events, missing out some of the more delicate points of course; however, he was still very impressed.

'Look Ellie you obviously need some more time to get this all sorted. Don't worry, we're all fine here; take the rest of next week off. You know that you are owed some holidays. If you need someone to talk to, ring me any time. I want to help, you know that.'

'You're a life saver Simon, thank you.' Ellie knew that Simon had strong feelings for her, although he was too much of a gentleman to admit it, but she knew all the same. After that call, she felt free to choose how to organise her forthcoming visit to Scotland. The stone felt warm in her hand again.

13: <u>Turn Shoes into Wine</u>

The shoe factory

On his return to Deal, Edmund was pleased that the shoe factory had kept his job open, even though he had given them no notice that he was going to be away on the Pirate Radio Station. Obviously, Winnie his landlady had pulled a few strings with her niece Sheila, who just happened to be the personnel manager there.

There was quite a ripple in the factory when Edmund walked in. A few smiling faces no less, most unusual for him. He passed the area where Paul used to work.

'On your own then, where's Paul, is he still on there?' One of the girls who worked with Paul asked.

'No, he's not still on Invicta, it looks like he's got a job as an actor in London.' Edmund answered.

One thing he did notice as he walked into the factory area, Radio Invicta was playing on the overhead radio. Dave Cash was introducing the Righteous Brothers' hit 'You've lost that loving feeling'. That gave him a bit of a buzz inside.

'We thought he might do something like that, he made us laugh with all his antics.' The girls all giggled. 'We liked his singing as well.'

Edmund walked on towards the offices smiling to himself, If Paul had been there, he would have milked that moment for all it was worth.

Pub life, for a while had also improved a bit. Some of the locals at the Brickmakers recognised him as the Invicta D.J. and he got a few drinks out of it. On Sundays, Spike the bull terrier in the Pelican had never heard of Invicta, but he liked Edmund just the same. In Divito's the same old crowd were at the same old tables. Pauline was as aloof as ever, so he spent much of the time walking alone along the shingle beach thinking of how things might have been.

He did however have some success at the factory. Six months had passed and the man in charge of him suddenly left, so Edmund was offered the job as production controller. That meant a bit more money and a lot more work. Ian Burrows, the chief accountant at the factory wasn't a qualified man, but he made up for that shortcoming with an excellent knowledge of the workings of the business.

Edmund in his new role, managed to get alongside Ian, when he had time from his own duties and looked at the company's accounts with him. Edmund asked Ian if he had made any suggestions to improve them, to which he replied that the boss wasn't really interested in anyone else's ideas.

This then became Edmund's first real challenge and he considered that there was 'Nothing to lose'. He knew that there was no benefit in direct contact with the boss, so he set about it another way. He put all the production records together and soon he could identify which shoe style made money and which ones made losses.

He wrote out a report and when completed, it didn't make very nice reading. There were many individual styles that made a loss and worryingly there were only a few profitable ones.

'It's a waste of time showing Whippsey this report, I've tried, but he just won't listen.' Ian said after reading Edmund's report.

Edmund thought he would try it anyway, so he put an unsigned copy of the report in an envelope, marked it 'Strictly private' and stuck it in the boss's post when the boss's secretary wasn't in her office. Nothing happened for a week, until Elaine popped her head around Edmund's door.

'Edmund, can you come into Mr Whippsey's office please?' The boss's secretary asked.

He felt the stone in his pocket and pulled it out for a moment, it felt warm in his hand. He kept it there as he walked into Mr. Whippsey's office realising that it was the first time he had ever been there. Sitting opposite was a little bald man, red faced wearing little round glasses perched on his nose. He reminded Edmund of the Dickens character Mr Bumble, but not looking as jolly.

On the desk in front of him was Edmund's report. In a flash, he noticed that it had previously been screwed up and then Mr Bumble must have had second thoughts and had tried to flatten it out again. He tried not to laugh as he gripped the stone stronger in his hand.

'You wanted to see me sir? Edmund asked.

'Does this belong to you?' Whippsey pointed to the crumpled sheet.

'As a matter of fact, it does, Mr Whippsey.' Edmund answered.

'What are you trying to do here, son?' Bumble pushed his glasses back. 'Why should I take any notice of this, Edmund?'

'Because I care about all the people you employ and if we go on at this rate, you won't have any business to employ them with, will you? Your Accountant has tried to tell you in the past, but it seems that you have given him the same response, am I right?'

Edmund gave him a defiant look and then turned on his heels and walked out of his office, not even waiting for a reply. The main outer office housed three girls and a young man. They were sitting at their desks staring at Edmund as he stormed past them.

'I'd better go and clear my desk for what it's worth,' he thought to himself.

'What the hell is going on Edmund?' Sheila caught hold of him as he was going in his office. He realised that he was still gripping the stone and put it back in his pocket.

'I made a mistake Sheila, sorry I lost my temper, I shouldn't have said those things to him. He's the boss and bosses demand respect.'

He started to clear his desk and smiled to himself, as he had noticed that there weren't enough of his own personal items in the office to fill a large envelope.

'Are you leaving right now, Edmund?' Sheila asked.

'I've made my mind up Sheila, it's not just the job, it's everything else, I can't explain, but I strongly feel that it's time to move on!'

'Look Edmund don't go before I've got your paperwork, you know what I mean, just sit at your desk. I'll be just a minute.' Sheila rushed out of his office.

As Edmund sat coolly at the desk awaiting her return, he suddenly felt much better inside and instinctively knew that the decision he had made was the right one.

'You'll never guess what has happened Edmund?' Ian rushed into his office with a big grin on his face, gripping a crumpled sheet of paper.

'What Ian? Old Mr Bumble had a heart attack?' Edmund asked, faking an expression of concern.

'No better than that, he has given me your report and told me to implement the changes you recommended. I don't believe it mate.' Ian's face then dropped as he looked at Edmund's cleared desk.

'No, you can't leave, not now, we've won!' The young accountant exclaimed.

Sheila arrived back with his cheque and employment card. She did give him a hug after all and tears were in her eyes.

'Give my love to Auntie Winnie please Edmund. God's speed, I hope you find happiness wherever you go.'

Edmund shook Ian's hand. 'Over to you mate, don't make a mess of it. If you make it work and he offers you a piece of the business, take it, with both hands.'

'Thanks for that advice Edmund, thanks a lot! I want to wish you well in whatever you do next. I'm sure that we will be hearing greater things about you in the future' Ian gave him a hug.

It was around lunchtime and Edmund was walking along the shingle for the last time. He'd said his goodbyes to Winnie, packed his small battered suitcase and now he was ready for his next adventure.

Edmund made a small detour before heading to the bus station, which brought him on the route past the Pelican Pub. Olive had just opened the bar for the morning business and was shaking the doormat against the outside wall.

'Coming in for a quick coffee, Edmund?' She asked.

Edmund nodded, stepped into the empty bar and settled on the nearest table to the door. Spike suddenly appeared and as usual leaned his huge head on Edmund's knee.

'He's not playing with you today Spike!' Olive shouted from behind the bar.

Edmund looked closely at the dog's mouth; there was no ball in it. He just sat on Edmund's foot and leaned heavily on his shin, Edmund patted his very smooth muscular back and Spike looked back at him with his little black eye and gave a little whine, as if he had realised there was something different happening that day for his friend. Alice brought the coffee and with a little wave indicated 'no charge' for it.

'You're leaving us, aren't you?' she asked perceptively.

Edmund nodded, 'I'll miss you Olive and you Spike.' He then drank his coffee, gave the bull terrier a final pat and he was gone.

He needed to pass Divito's, so he thought he would pop in for the last time. Old man Divito was wiping the tables and it looked like he was the only one there.

'Mr Divito, is Pauline about?' Edmund asked.

'In Canterbury, today' the owner replied.

'Will you give her a message from me?' Her father looked puzzled. 'Tell her from me, er that I... tell her from me goodbye. Will you tell her please?'

'I will tell her. Where are you going, young man?' Divito inquired, Edmund was already heading outside and the tears were streaming from his eyes so he couldn't look back.

'Goodbye Pauline. I did love you, but I'll just walk on by.' He said to himself.

He held the stone in his hand all the way to the bus station and at that moment he had decided to go west. He had still got the £250 from the Pirate station and with the additional cheque from Whippseys, he had enough cash to at least get a clean start somewhere else.

Deal station was very small, there was just room for one bus to turn around, with a small shelter for the waiting passengers. The shelter stood next to a small café and that was the total of Deal bus station.

There were no buses waiting to leave as he arrived and just a few passengers in the shelter. He went to the back of the queue not looking at anyone, but to his surprise a smiling face turned around to look at him.

'Edmund, you know me, don't you?'

'Rosalind, so sorry, I just wasn't looking.' She was shorter than Pauline, with blonde curly hair and the most beautiful blue eyes.

'Have you heard how Paul is doing Rosalind?' Edmund asked.

'It's good news, Eddie; he got that job with the touring company. They've been rehearsing till now. His first performance is somewhere in Wales, I think. He sends me a letter now and then. What are you doing here?'

'Fancy a coffee next door? It's a long story.' Edmund asked her.

As they walked into the café she put her arm in his, she could feel he was a bit down.

'I wish I'd met someone like Rosalind', he thought to himself, as he told her what had happened at the Factory.

'I'm sorry about Pauline; I know that you loved her. Paul told me in one of his letters, I hope that you don't mind.' She said.

Edmund stared into his cup and shook his head, he could feel the tears welling up. Rosalind put her hand on his for a moment, which only made it worse for him. Receiving any sort of compassion was difficult for him to comprehend.

He composed himself. 'I don't know where I'm going Rosalind, but I just want a clean start, do you understand?' They got up as a bus pulled in. 'I'm going west Rosalind, I don't know where, but far from here!' He looked up at the destination sign at the front of the bus indicating 'Folkestone'.

'This one will do for me.' He said.

Rosalind considered his eyes and wanted to say more, but she just hugged him tight. He paid the driver for his ticket, climbed on the upper deck and looked down at the blonde young woman and she waved furiously.

'Goodbye Rosalind and goodbye Deal forever.' he said to himself.

Edmund knew Folkestone from the time when he and Paul got off the ferry from their French adventure. He had no intention to stay long in that town, but decided that the best thing would be to stay overnight in a B&B, have a walk around and maybe get some ideas before moving on. He settled on a small hotel near the rail station, parked his bags and went to find the Acropolis café that he knew so well.

The Cypriot family were still running it and it felt good to be there. He even imagined that Paul was sitting at the table chatting up the girls a usual. The Jukebox had the usual pop records, but its choice was unique. It was the only one that he knew with Beethoven's 'Fur Elise' and Liszt's 'Leibestraum' on it. So, he played them again for old times' sake.

'One more song' he said to himself. He saw that Dionne Warwick's song 'Walk on by' was still on the selector, but his broken heart just couldn't take it.

He shook the hand of Spyros the owner of the Acropolis café as he left, not sure if he remembered him or not.

'I bet he would have remembered Paul.' He laughed to himself.

As he walked around the Folkestone town centre, he stopped to look inside a baker's shop window extolling all the delicious temptations they had on offer. The sign above the window said it all. 'Strickland's Family Bakers.' Edmund succumbed and went into the shop to purchase one of their jam doughnuts.

'We used to make these at the bakery last year.' Edmund remarked.

'I know you did' the older one of the two ladies turned and looked at him.

'How do you know?' He asked her.

'There was a man called Paul, he worked with my sister and she fancied him, but he got the sack. She told me it was for larking about and he was putting far too much filling in them.' She pointed at the doughnut in Edmund's hand. The two women giggled about that. 'Where is Paul, with you in town?'

Edmund shook his head. 'No, he's in London, acting in a play.'

'What happened to the Pirate job?' The other assistant asked. 'My cousin who lives in Deal told me; you went there over Christmas time didn't you?'

'We were sacked!' Edmund answered.

'Of course, we should have known.' They were still laughing as he left the shop.

He was eating the doughnut as he walked along the street and as usual some of the jam filling leaked out and fell on the floor. Edmund smiled to himself, picturing Paul with a broomstick in hand entertaining the girls in the confectionery section, singing 'A new kind of love' and imitating the one and only Frank Sinatra!

Most of the buildings around the station were of limestone and over the years had become blackened by smoke from the old steam trains and the wild weather that sometimes lashed the coast. The state of the surroundings of the town did nothing to endear Edmund to the area; in fact, he felt that moving as far away as he could, was his best option.

The entrance to the station displayed the usual timetables on the walls as well as some old but bright posters. One of the posters advertised the coastal line to Bournemouth, with a beautiful stylised picture of a sweeping sandy bay and a colourful pier. He remembered that Ben, who he had met in

France had said that his mother wanted to live there. He decided on the spot that that was where he was going. He smiled at the ticket clerk behind the office window.

'Yes sir, what are you wanting today?' The clerk asked him.

'I want to go to Bournemouth, is there a train tomorrow?' Edmund asked.

'There is a train that goes direct to Bournemouth, which leaves here every two hours, the timetable is over there.'

The clerk pointed over Edmund's shoulder, so he walked across the hall and looked at the departure times. It took in all the coastal towns including Brighton and Hastings. From Folkestone to Bournemouth took about five hours.

'I'll take a single to Bournemouth. I want to get the nine am train tomorrow, will it be full? Do I need to book a seat?' Edmund rattled off his questions to the clerk.

'That will be two pounds ten shillings sir and Tuesdays is not a busy day, you can just walk on the train without any booking, departing on platform two.' The clerk said.

The little B&B near the railway station didn't do evening meals, so he went in search of a fish and chip shop where he could sit inside and eat them. Spyros's baguette from the Acropolis café had soon worn off and he was quite hungry again.

The next morning was cold and wet, but that didn't matter at all to Edmund, as he was looking forward to the sunnier climes of his destination. The train was soon whizzing out of the station, no smoke or smell as the line was by then electrified.

The train eventually pulled into Bournemouth and the atmosphere was quite different to Folkestone. The sun was shining and the station was well turned out with flowers in hanging baskets and smiling faces of children anticipating their days on the beach.

He was soon on a local bus heading for the town centre and in a few short minutes he was mixing with the throngs of holidaymakers. A local news stand was selling the local 'Daily Echo' so he purchased a copy and then went to a very high-class café called Fortes, paid for a cup of tea and a thick slice of cake and sat down to look for somewhere to stay.

The top floor bedsit in a converted house in Crabton Close Road seemed to meet his needs, so he promptly paid the ten pounds deposit. It suited his meagre needs, one large room with cooking facilities, room to eat and room to sleep, very basic but clean. He shared bathroom facilities with the floor below, but he didn't mind that.

He was very lucky to get an interview the very next day for a job just down the road in Pokesdown. James & Co, a sizeable wine merchant that did its business delivering in Bournemouth and the New Forest. They offered him the job as manager of the whole operation. After he had started, he subsequently found out the reason why he had been hired so quickly. He was the latest of an extensive line of managers, most of them hadn't lasted more than a week.

A few days into the job, it was clear to him that there were many problems at the place. The biggest one by far was the pilferage by the staff. In fact, most of the staff in the yard was well out of it by lunchtime. He tried at first to get on with all sections of the staff, but they were very suspicious of him and kept themselves to themselves.

Tenaciously he realised that he had a job to do and was determined to make a success of it. He lay in his bed at the bedsit one evening after work and an idea came to him. He decided to do what he had done at the shoe factory. He was to present the owners a report that would solve the company's genuine problem of pilferage.

Without the knowledge of the staff, he kept a detailed dossier on each one of them. He had witnessed the yard staff helping themselves to bottles of beer, then having drunk them, secretly replaced them in a lower case in the stack. The drivers often took an extra case on the lorry and disposed of its contents during the delivery run.

On pretext of getting to know the workings of the delivery system, he worked on a van as a driver's assistant for the day, the route that day was the New Forest run.

It was common for the driver and his mate to pull in on a layby for a break, near Brockenhurst. The driver pulled out several bottles from underneath his seat and commenced drinking them. Recently Edmund had stopped drinking, as it played havoc with his skin, making it very blotchy and it was embarrassing.

The driver accepted this excuse for not joining him without suspicion and after a few bottles, relaxed for a while. He even showed Edmund the oak tree near to the lay by where they had hammered the bottle tops into the bark. Edmund estimated that there were hundreds of them stuck to the trunk and rusting. The driver called it the 'Worthy Green tree' after the maker's name of beer they had pilfered, 'Worthington Green Shield'.

He spent time with the cellar staff next and the area covered by the cellar was vast. It reached underneath several of the properties that were adjacent to the wine shop. Edmund wondered if the neighbours knew what was underneath them, ignorance was bliss, no doubt.

The drinking here was a more secretive affair. The cellar men used 'breakages' as an excuse and it was amazing how much Bristol Cream, Amontillado and other bottles of fine dry sherry was 'broken'. The foreman proudly showed Edmund the broken bottles as proof. It seemed strange though to Edmund that only the best sherry bottles had been 'accidentally' broken, especially as it was difficult to trace any pools of sherry anywhere!

As much as he tried to encourage them, none of the cellar staff could do their work efficiently after lunch, due to their obvious state of inebriation and it seemed to Edmund that the bosses were blissfully unaware of all the misdemeanours that were going on in their stores.

The morning after he had completed his fortnight of assessment; he went into Richard James's office to ask for a day off. When Richard asked why, he told him that he was putting a report together for him and his father.

Richard was just a couple of years older than Edmund and it was obvious that he had had a more comfortable upbringing and clearly had never wanted for anything. He had no resentment towards Richard, but he felt that his young boss had not accepted him; maybe he had considered that Edmund was too ambitious.

Richard accepted that he would wait until the trucks were loaded and on the road, before he called him into his office and agreed with Edmund that there was no need at that time to raise any suspicions with the yard staff.

The father and son partnership sat opposite Edmund in their office and initially it felt like he was in an inquisition. He had previously passed them each a copy of his findings and calculations at the start of that day. They had taken time to digest it and this meeting was called to discuss their reactions to Edmund's damning report. The partners both looked very serious and in some ways, that was just the response Edmund had expected, considering its gravity.

Mr James senior spoke first. 'Edmund, I would like to thank you for this report and may I say that I'm not surprised at it. Of course, it belies the lack of control that has gone on for too long, don't you agree, Richard?'

Richard was more aggressive to Edmund. 'Yes, this is all very well, but what are the conclusions and recommendations, reports like this are no good without them.'

 'Thank you, Richard, you are correct.' He handed them both another sheet of paper headed with the same word that Richard had wanted; 'Conclusions'. The partners sat and read the paper and this time Edmund didn't give Richard time to respond.

'It doesn't take an Einstein to see the value of what you are losing, but it's a bit harder to know what to do to make it stop.' Edmund smiled nervously.

'We can't offer those sorts of pay increases dad, it will bankrupt us.' Richard glared at Edmund, 'it's just not feasible. I vote no!'

'I can see what you are getting at Edmund and it is very bold, but I can see that there have to be difficult solutions for difficult problems Richard.' His shrewd father said calmly.

'Tell me then Edmund, how would you implement it?' Richard asked, a little more calmly.

'I would use the carrot and stick method, by getting the yard staff together in a formal meeting and hopefully one of you standing at my side showing support, I will offer the proposed pay rise to them, obviously this will appeal most to the men with families.

'That's obvious.' Richard rebuked.

'Yes, but here comes the stick. In return, I will expect each of them to do a weekly stock count of a designated area and this must be very accurate. The sheet will be pre-printed; one of the girls will type it out for me.' Edmund explained further to them.

'Yes, but Edmund....'

'Let me please finish Richard,' Edmund said, whilst his father gently restrained his son, by giving him a smile.

'I can see where this is going Richard. This will make them more responsible, as well as showing what the consumption levels are.' His father explained.

'Yes, yes dad, but how do we know if the count is accurate?' Richard remained sceptical.

'I've thought of that Richard. I will tell them that I'm doing constant stock checks and carry out my word. Any bad eggs that are revealed will soon break.' Edmund said confidently.

'How do you propose to stop this alcohol consumption?' Richard had calmed down somewhat.

'I intend to be firm as well as fair. I propose to you that we give the men a beer allowance, the same as the breweries do, then at the same time ban drinking on the premises. Obviously, the long-term heavy drinkers are going to need some help.

I'm very sorry about this, but firstly I will try to wean them off the drink for a period of three months. But if this does not work, unfortunately they will have to go, it is for their own health that I shall give as a reason. I need your backing on this one.' Edmund looked to the senior partner for support this time.

Old Mr James stood up. 'Well done, Edmund, you came through the fire and I personally was not disappointed with your response. Richard and I will discuss this further and get back to you very soon.'

Edmund was back at work without anyone noticing and it was still only 9 am. The trucks had been loaded for the afternoon run and all seemed normal. At lunchtime Edmund was just walking out of the yard gates to buy a sandwich, when he heard his name being called. Joyce, one of the office girls was waving.

'Perhaps it is the brewery on the phone; he thought.

As he walked into the office she said 'Mr James and Mr Richard want you to join them for lunch. They're in Mario's across the road, they're waiting for you.'

Edmund had never been in Mario's, but he knew that he liked Italian food. He opened the door of the small café and in the far corner, he made out two figures and one was waving at him. As soon as he had joined them at the table, he realised that he was starving hungry just with the thought of some pasta. The owners were drinking a bottle of Chianti and Richard was about to pour some in the glass for Edmund.

'No thanks Richard I don't drink, just water for me.' Edmund tried to smile at him.

'Edmund, my father seems to have great faith in you and you have certainly surprised me and that's no easy task as you well know. We have discussed all your proposals and we want you to go ahead with them all, so give it your best. That is all we can ask at this stage.'

'Thank you, Richard, you too Mr James for your confidence in me, I promise to do everything in my power to make this work. And before you ask, I expect you to see tangible results in less than a month, I really believe that.' Edmund answered confidently.

'Shall you arrange for the first meeting with the yard staff for next Monday after loading the Lorries?' Richard asked.

'Richard will join you at the first meeting, won't you son?' Mr James Senior smiled at Edmund.

'Yes, dad I will' and for the first time Edmund saw Richard confidently smile at him.

The meeting was over and then it was down to a huge plate of fresh spaghetti with the best homemade Bolognaise sauce that Edmund had ever tasted. During the meal Edmund entertained his hosts as he described the time on the pirate radio and his adventures in France.

A year had passed since Edmund had made his successful proposal to the partners. Initially there had been some difficulties to overcome, but as soon as he had witnessed the huge improvement in the staff's attitude, Richard was sold. Sadly, they had to lose two of the long-term staff; alcohol misuse over such a protracted period had taken its toll and try as he might to change them, it was just impossible and with a heavy heart Edmund had to let them go.

With Richard's approval, Edmund introduced an incentive scheme based on the business improvement and two of the drivers were happy to do some selling as well as delivering. The whole place was buzzing with the excitement of improved business.

At Christmas at the end of the second year, Edmund was invited to Richard's home in the New Forest. It wasn't the first time he had visited his home, but somehow, he felt that something had changed in Richard's tone, it was much friendlier.

Edmund had even been accepted as part of Richard's family by his wife and two girls. Old Mr James had taken a well-deserved back seat and because of the excellent trading enjoyed by the company, he had amassed a good retirement package and prepared for a well-earned rest. In that year Richard was branching out into property development, so he was rarely seen at the wine business.

He seemed very happy to leave the day-to-day running to Edmund; finally admitting the he could do it better anyway.

After a good Christmas lunch, Edmund was bursting with rich food. Richard had promised the girls a long walk in the forest with Bertie, their golden retriever, just as soon as he and Edmund had finished their meeting in his study. Together they sat down at the oak table; Richard's abrasive character was long gone, but Edmund held on to his secretive stone as Richard opened the conversation.

'Edmund, I have to admit to misjudging you, my father saw your qualities much sooner than I did. I know that we wouldn't be where we are today without your strong intervention. You did all the work and we, dad and I, have taken all the benefits. I'm going to change all that, I'll come straight to the point and I want you to become a full partner in the business. When can you give me your answer?'

'Richard, I am truly pleased that you've made me this offer, but I cannot bring any cash to buy into the partnership.'

Richard's face lit up. 'No Edmund, that's not what we want from you. We want your commitment and expertise, this time not as an employee, but as a full partner.'

'Then, before I give you my answer, I need to ask you two questions.' Edmund held on to his stone and it felt comfortingly warm in his hand.

'Ask away' Richard leaned back on his chair.

'The first one is for your father to tell me in person that he wants me to join the partnership. The second is that you allow me to qualify as an accountant. I'm already halfway there from a job in my past, so I guess it will possibly take two years.'

'To answer the first one, dad is already on his way here with mum. And the second; we will employ an assistant for you whilst you qualify.' Richard quickly responded.

'Before I finally accept your kind offer Richard, I hope you realise that taking me into the partnership, I shall automatically be entitled to a third of the business, sink or swim.'

'Edmund, it will be a half, as dad is stepping down, as you step up.' Richard's face was a picture of happiness.

Two years following that meeting, Edmund had qualified as an accountant in his company that had become very strong in the area. Most of the large hotels in Bournemouth had accounts with James & co. and at the same time, the people who worked for him were for once enjoying great rewards for their effort. All in all, so much had been achieved at the Wine Merchant's business.

Edmund had called Richard to a meeting at the usual little Italian restaurant. It was quite a painful time for both as dear Mr James Senior had passed away only a few months before. Obviously, Richard was hurting the most, but Edmund also had grown to love his father.

'Richard, I have something important to tell you' Edmund looked serious and Richard's face dropped, fearing the worst. 'I don't think that it's unwelcome news partner; we are being courted by Whitbread.'

'What does that actually mean Edmund?'

'Surely you know that we're causing them some pain in this area? That can only mean one thing Richard.' Edmund explained.

'Buy us! Surely not; we are too small for them, Edmund.'

'And they want to be bigger. You're in the property development business and you must have thought that this might happen one day.' Edmund responded.

'What sort of money are they offering?'

'I have sat back on this one Richard, but I have a suggestion. I think we should meet up with our lawyer and discuss it with him and then we ring Whitbread with our proposal. Do you want to think about it first Richard?'

'Meet me tonight at my home Edmund. I'll get Alex to join us there; please don't speak to anyone until then.'

'What do you take me for, partner?' Edmund replied.

Alex Macduff, the youngest full partner in a top legal firm called 'Vizards of London', was a tall Scot whom Edmund had got to know since becoming a partner in the business. He liked him very much; they were almost two of a kind, both enjoying success from their own efforts and Edmund knew that he could trust Alex with his life.'

'I know that your father started the business but you aren't particularly interested in it now, are you Richard?' Alex bluntly asked at the end of the meeting that evening.

'No, but I'm still hurting with dad passing on Alex, but you are right we must move on, do you think that you Alex, should make the first approach to Whitbread?'

'No, you two make the first approach, take the last year's accounts with you and my suggestion is that you meet on neutral ground, so they don't try to pull a fast one over you. They're not new to this game of takeovers, but you are.' Alex looked at Edmund this time.

'Alex, if it proceeds, I don't want to forget the staff in all this, will you remember that, when you draw up any agreements. Is that ok with you, Richard?' Edmund asked.

'Yes, Edmund that's fine with me.' Richard answered and put his arm over his business partner's shoulder.

They all laughed and promised to meet up again in Alex's office after the next stage. It was Alex who left Richard's house first, so Richard asked Edmund to hang on for a minute.

'You know, Edmund, I've got all this and you've got a little bungalow in Southbourne, yet it's you that thinks about the staff. My dad was right all along about you; you enriched both our lives and now, well....'

'Well partner, let's go and make some money, what do you think?' Edmund cleverly interrupted him.

'My dad would have been so proud of you Edmund.' Richard hugged him, with tears in his eyes.

Time moved on to 1975, four years since the takeover by the brewery. Edmund knew that he had achieved all he could have achieved there. The new owners had closed the operation in Pokesdown and incorporated the operation in their main southern distribution centre near Southampton.

Of course, all the staff that could not move to Southampton lost their jobs, but they were well compensated as per the takeover contract. Edmund, for his trouble was initially given a minor directorship with the holding company with a short contract, but that had soon come to an end and reliable Alex had secured a good exit deal for him too.

That marked the end of a successful period for Edmund, where not only did he achieve his dream to have some professional qualifications, but he was now able to look for the next phase in his life with at least some sort of security.

Still remembering that fateful meeting with the American on his yacht in the South of France he felt that he had made some steps at last to be on the road to success.

How much did he owe to that wonderful talisman? He pondered to himself.

14: <u>A Chance to help</u>

Keeping watch

Edmund had decided, after the events at James & co he would take a break and see if he could make the grade in a job in his own town in Derbyshire, now that his circumstances had changed. He had left his bungalow in Southbourne in the capable hands of his dear friend Brian Mulholland, a partner of the local Estate agents; Ruddocks.

He was quickly appointed as controller of a forty-strong team of ladies who ran the Credit Control and the huge Sales Ledger of a lingerie manufacturing group.

The woman supervisor had taken an instant dislike to Edmund, she was a bit of a battle-axe and most of the female staff hated her, but she wore the hate like a badge. He knew that the only way he could gain respect from her, was to do the job better than she could and so this was Edmund's first task.

She was dreadfully overweight and this had caused her to have health problems. At one point, she was sick and off work for several weeks and this gave Edmund the opportunity he was waiting for. He quickly computerised the Credit reporting information to the Finance Director. This gave his boss the opportunity to see what was happening to the £70 million ledger in an instant. He also took the opportunity to tell the Finance Director that it was the supervisor's idea, he had just written the program for her.

When the battle-axe finally returned, she was called into the bosses' office and was congratulated with a pay raise for her efforts. At the time, Edmund was working in the computer room looking all innocent, when she came in to apologise for her attitude to him and it was sweetness and light from then on.

Courtaulds was a big company. The division that he worked at employed six thousand people in eighteen factories all over the UK including Northern Ireland. Each month his other task was to print out the miles of paper that enabled the junior accountants to complete the monthly accounts.

This monthly task took the computer twenty-four hours to complete and Edmund had to work overnight to watch that the machines worked well. The Director was the only person who held the security key for the whole building, which had to be double locked at night and Edmund had to borrow that key from his secretary each month to perform that task.

At around nine in the evening, Edmund and his assistant would go down to the local pub for a pint and a game of pool to kill the monotony. This night, the director was 'working' late with his very attractive secretary and he'd forgotten that Edmund had the only key to the office complex. He wanted to leave, but it coincided with the time Edmund was at the pub and had of course double locked the doors.

Having not found the key the erstwhile director promptly tried to climb out of a ground floor window with her. Unfortunately for them, a police patrol had spotted him and put them both into custody, with no amount of explaining could help their embarrassment. The next morning all hell had broken loose, to all his staff Edmund was a hero, but not with the Director. Edmund knew the character of this man and he realised that his boss would use his power to 'return the favour'.

Just as Edmund had predicted, within a few weeks he was given the task to close a factory that the company owned in the Falls Road in Belfast. It was during the height of the troubles there; even the hotel in Belfast that he stayed at had been bombed thirty-nine times, called the Europa Hotel.

The unfortunate factory to close was 'Steegan' and the offices where Edmund worked were on the ninth floor of the block. During the first week, he was disturbed by a huge 'whooshing' noise that seemed to be getting louder and louder. As he looked out of the window, slowly rising from the lower floor was an Army helicopter. The two occupants looked inside the offices. One smiled and waved at Edmund before it sped away.

He calculated that the rotor blades were no more than ten yards away from the window and when Edmund looked around at the other occupants in the office; no one had even noticed or looked up from their work!

The second incident was even scarier. He worked at the Belfast factory for a full week at a time, leaving the East Midlands airport on a Monday and flying back from Aldergrove airport on the five o'clock flight on the Friday.

He always managed to get this flight, except for one Friday. The resident Director of the factory wanted to discuss some point or other with Edmund and he was told to wait in the boss's office at four.

Two things were making Edmund nervous. Firstly, there was no director in his office and secondly, he needed to get to Aldergrove in time for the five o'clock flight. It was gone five when the Director turned up and it was already getting dark.

After a short meeting Edmund arranged a lift to the airport and for once he was heading there at night. After driving out of Belfast, the road became narrow and devoid of street lights, the driver was apparently taking a short-cut. Edmund saw the lights on the horizon for the approaching airport, but the driver suddenly stopped to avoid an unmarked car in the middle of the road which was blocking their way.

The occupants of the car were UDF and after checking their papers, let them proceed. Edmund, however feared the worst and not for the first time thought that 'his number was up'.

Enough was enough! He decided on the spot to pack the job in, admitting that the scorned Finance Director at the head office had won.

Before he left, he decided to call on his old friend Paul's older brother Mark who still lived in the town. Edmund hoped that Paul had kept in contact with his brother, so that he could obtain his latest address and phone number.

In the whole time that he had spent at his hometown, he took all his holidays back in Southbourne, so that he could keep a check on his bungalow.

The journey back to Southbourne was arduous, but the closer he got the more comfortable he felt, until when arriving at the bungalow drive, he positively felt excited again.

Before he had set out from the north, he had had the forethought to ring Brian and let him know that he was returning permanently. Once he had unloaded his cases and put a few things away, he just drove along the cliff road to the café Riva at Fisherman's Walk and had a relaxing meal. Afterwards he walked the few steps to the cliff side and drank in the fresh air, something he had missed for three years.

'This is my fresh start,' he said to himself as he clutched the familiar stone. 'I'm ready now for the next stage in my life, bring it on.'

The local employment agency had placed him in a couple of temporary accounting assignments, but they were only short term. Edmund was not too concerned about that, knowing the most important thing was not to rush into any old job. He knew there was no pressure financially, so he decided to 'step back' from the rat race and give his old friend Paul a ring on the number his brother had given him.

'Well I'll go to Trent! How are you, old buddy?' Paul answered enthusiastically.

'What are you doing at the moment Paul, working?' Edmund asked.

'Well, Eddie, not just now, but I've just finished a TV ad for British Gas, not much in the way of real acting, but still it pays the rent.' Paul explained.

'I'm coming up to London at the weekend, do you fancy meeting up, my old pal?' Edmund asked him.

'Be great, have you got my address?' Paul asked and Edmund said he had. 'I'll see you on Saturday pal, we've certainly got some catching up to do after all these years, right?'

'I can't believe that it's been fourteen years mate, can you remember that day in Ashford when we disembarked from the pirate station and then went our separate ways? I'll tell you all about what has happened to me since then, when I see you.' Edmund chuckled.

'OK, see 'ya.' Paul's voice was still laughing as Edmund put the phone down.

Waterloo station concourse was full of travellers; some were looking at departure times, meeting friends and seeing people off or, just like Edmund, standing and just looking in awe.

He placed his weekend bag on the floor for a moment to look for the underground sign when suddenly a large man walked by him and tripped over Edmund's bag, fortunately he managed to stop himself from falling.

'Really sorry, buddy I guess I wasn't looking where I was going!'

'Hello Ben.' Edmund said calmly.

'Do I know you buddy? I can't quite place you, I.... Oh no, is it you? Yes, it's you ain't it? You're the guy we met in Cannes. You're Edmund, am I right? Vera, Vera!' Ben shouted across the concourse. 'Look who's here!

Coming through the melee and pulling her suitcase wheels over people's toes, she rushed over and gave Edmund a hug with tears in her eyes.

'Look you two, there's a coffee shop just there, fancy a quick cup before you go?' Edmund asked.

'Sure, we've got time Edmund; we're only catching the train to Bournemouth to see my mom.' Ben smiled.

'I live there too Ben, I'm just up here to see Paul, I haven't seen him for such a long time and he now lives in London.' Edmund said.

'I bet he's an actor, am I right?' Vera asked. Edmund smiled and nodded.

Ben placed his hand on Edmund's shoulder. 'I just can't believe it, meeting you here buddy. You know Edmund; since we met in '64 we have always wondered how you were doing'. That's right, ain't it honey?'

'Do you remember what you said Edmund, you were going to make a million, did you do it?' Vera asked inquisitively.

'Maybe not yet Vera, but I'm getting close. Things don't happen that quickly over here.' They all laughed together. 'Listen you guys, how long are you going to be over in Bournemouth?' Edmund asked them.

'We're flying back on Friday, why don't we meet up old buddy and we can catch up' Ben looked at Vera for approval.

'You bet.' she said.

'Have you got anything to write on, Vera?' Edmund asked her. She pulled out a couple of postcards that she had just bought. Edmund wrote down his address and phone number on one of the cards and Vera did the same and passed it to Edmund.

'We're staying at the Royal Bath hotel for the week Edmund, is that a good hotel?' Ben asked him.

'Sure, is Ben, it's the best one in Bournemouth. I'll be home tomorrow, I'll call you then' Edmund hugged them both and they soon disappeared again into the throng. 'Bye! See you very soon' as Ben looked back for a final wave, shouting over the noise.

After the surprising meeting with Ben and Vera, it was time to make his way to Paul's pad. He looked at the address, Kingsland Green, north of Dalston Junction tube station. He looked at a London Tube map and checked the route.

'Get on to the District line, go east and change at Whitechapel, then north to Dalston.' Edmund wrote on a piece of paper. It was a short walk, but he found it wasn't the most walker-friendly route. No one smiled at him and as he looked at the locals, he didn't really feel like asking anyone for directions either.

He finally approached the front door of a rundown Victorian three-story house. The door was unlocked and he knew that Paul was on the third floor. Lots of strange sounds and smells were coming from each door he passed on the way up there.

As he climbed up the final uncarpeted staircase, he couldn't miss the dingy green paint on the walls was flaking badly.

The sound of blues reached his ears as he approached the closed door and he recognised it as Van Morrison's 'Madam George' from the Astral Weeks album. There was only one person he knew that liked that sort of music.

He was about to knock, when it flew open. A beautiful yet unkempt blonde young girl with dreadlocks, wearing a multi coloured kaftan rushed by, leaving the door open.

'I didn't mean it love, honestly.' A voice said from inside the flat. Edmund could hear her banging down the stairs obviously very upset, so he quietly walked in.

'Oh yes you bloody well did.' Edmund jokingly shouted.

'Eddie old mate, come here!' Paul turned around and held his arms out and they hugged. 'How long has it been?' he asked.

'Fifteen years give or take a few.' Edmund sniffed the air; it was a mixture of acrid and sickly sweet. 'That's bloody pot. You're smoking pot!' He exclaimed.

'We're in a different time warp up here Eddie; we've thrown the rule book away here in Dalston.' Paul laughed.

'Is that the latest bird that flew out the door, none too pleased with you?' Edmund asked as he pointed towards the door.

'She prefers older men, if you know what I mean. She goes for the ones that appeal to her mind. The young guys are only after one thing.' Paul said sarcastically.

'I'll remember that one, next time I take up with a young filly like that, she can't be any more than eighteen.' Edmund said raising his eyebrows.

Most of the afternoon and evening was spent hearing all about Paul's work, his conquests, even about the jobs that he was in the running for, but never got. It was a trip into fantasyland for Edmund but he enjoyed every minute of it and hung on every word.

He gave Paul some money to get some fish and chips and a bottle of wine. Paul returned with a litre of Bulgarian red and Paul drank most of it by the time they had consumed their food.

'What's wrong mate, you used to drink me under the table at one time. Can you remember that competition we had on Invicta?' Paul asked.

'Do you mean, who could drink the most cans of Special Brew in one night?' Edmund laughed.

'Yes, matey and you were still going at eight.' Paul answered.

'There was nothing else to do on that rusty old tin can, was there?' Edmund remarked as he recalled the appalling conditions they worked in.

Edmund shacked up on the couch in the end; Paul staggered into his bedroom totally out of it with too much Bulgarian red. Maybe Edmund should have drunk some of it himself, as there was to be no sleep on the couch for him.

He looked at his watch, the room fronted onto the busy street and even at two thirty in the morning, no one seemed to sleep in that area, it was like a Caribbean carnival night.

Loud music, heavy drumbeat, shouting and screaming and car horns blasting under the window! There was no time for a shave or wash, he just wanted to leave that place, it was six am and he was ready to get back to some sanity.

During the previous night's talking, Paul had given Edmund a copy folder of his acting profile that he used in his job interviews and Edmund put that in his bag. He pulled out an envelope and checked inside, there were two hundred pounds in fivers, so he found a piece of paper on the floor tore off an unwritten part and found a pen in his bag and began to write on it.

'I'm not staying at this place any more, it's too expensive. Take care of yourself Paul,' and then signed it. He knew that Paul would see the funny side of that.

Edmund tiptoed into Paul's bedroom although there was no need to be quiet, as he was fast asleep. He placed the envelope on a wicker chair next to the bed and then quietly closed the door and went out of the flat.

'Bye old mate' he whispered.

He decided not to take the underground for the return journey. Instead he decided to catch a cab outside The Duke of Wellington pub on Balls Pond Road and thankfully it dropped him inside the concourse of Waterloo Station.

By seven thirty, he was on the train, looking out of the carriage window, watching those dreary grey flats of the

London suburbs roll by, quietly relieved that he was heading for home and the sea and sanity once more.

Edmund's mind was never at rest. Whilst sitting in the carriage, he was hatching a plan that would involve Ben and Vera and would benefit Paul, that is, if he had any sense to take the opportunity that would be offered.

'Hello?' A soft warm voice answered the phone and Edmund knew instantly who it was.

'Is that Mrs Cohen? This is Edmund; can I speak to your son Ben if he's there? I believe he's visiting you this week.'

'Are you ringing from New York, young man?' Ben's mother asked.

'No, I'm ringing from Bournemouth, Mrs Cohen.'

'Hi Edmund, glad you're home safe old buddy, what's up?' Ben's voice came on the line.

'I wonder if you might be free for a while tomorrow. I'd very much like to talk to you.' Edmund asked.

'Hi Edmund, Vera here, could you come to dinner tonight at our hotel, we'd love it if you'd come.' Edmund heard Ben's voice booming to tell him to come. 'Ben's mum will be here and I know she'll love to meet you.'

'I haven't got a dinner jacket Vera; I know you have to wear one in your hotel.' Edmund said apologetically.

'Well, come in your buckskins then, we don't care.' followed by loud laughter from Ben, who took the receiver again.

'Look buddy, you English are so self-conscious. Nothing to worry about, we are in the something suite, ah yes, the De Vere Suite and we have our own dining room with a waiter laid on, so come how you like buddy, we ain't dressing up neither.' Ben insisted.

Edmund had never been in the Royal Bath Hotel before, the hotel reception was awesome but he hid his embarrassment.

'Mr Cohen please, I am expected.' The doorman led him to the lift and pressed for the third floor and bowed to him.

The dinner was exquisite, the service was perfect and Ben was on top form, when he could get a word in between Edmund and his mother. When Edmund looked around at both of his hosts they were content to let Edmund make his mother laugh, it was a wonderful night. Near the end of the evening, Ben had finally got a word in.

'You said on the phone that you wanted to ask me something Edmund?'

'Well, Ben this isn't the time or place, but do you have any time tomorrow? I should like to invite you to my home, it's only a little bungalow, not far from here and I can ask you then.' Edmund said.

'Am I also invited Edmund?' Vera asked.

'Yes of course Vera. It's only a little bachelor pad though, nothing you're used to, you can certainly wear your buckskins there.' Edmund smiled at them.

'Will ten tomorrow be OK Edmund? Ma's having some beauty treatment tomorrow so we've got time to spare.' Ben looked at his mother.

Edmund leaned over to Mrs Cohen. I believe you're having some beauty treatment tomorrow Mrs Cohen?'

'Yes, my dear, my son is paying for it, aren't you dear?' Ben beamed at his mother.

'Well, Mrs Cohen, he's wasting his money.' The room went quiet. 'You can't improve on perfection.' Edmund smiled at her and Ben laughed so loud that the paintings on the wall nearly fell off!

'I told you Edmund, that one day I'd get you on the Ed Sullivan show. That was the best yet 'ol buddy!'

The next morning his taxi pulled up outside of his drive and Edmund had the door open ready for his American visitors.

'I like the views around here, Edmund.' Vera smiled at him.

He ushered them into the small living room; of course, Ben, being the giant that he was, had to duck his head to get under the archway.

'Duck or grouse Ben.' Edmund joked.

'Hell, I've just had my breakfast old buddy.' Ben looked confused.

Vera smiled, 'I know this one Ben and he means if you don't duck your head you will grouse with the pain. Am I right Edmund?'

Edmund nodded to her, but Ben was still puzzled. Just before they arrived, Edmund had made a strong cafetiere of coffee, thinking all Americans love their coffee.

'Edmund, do you have tea? I've discovered a new one at the hotel and it's called Earl something' Vera asked him.

'Earl Grey, I think I have some Vera.' Edmund answered.

'Well if you can find it, I'll make some for us, OK?' Vera shouted as Edmund went in search of the tea.

'Let's get down to business.' Edmund passed him Paul's folder.

'Do you know who this is, Ben?' Edmund asked as the American opened it.

'Sure, this is Paul, am I right? It's some sort of profile.' He leafed through the pages of mainly pictures of Paul posing in costume. 'I like this one, Shakespeare ain't it? What's he doin' now?' Ben asked in his usual drawl.

'No, he's not doing anything at the moment, I'm sure you know the situation about out of work actors Ben, that's the reason I want to talk to you. You have lots of influence with many people in the States I know that and with that in mind I need someone that I can trust, to do something for me.'

'No problem on that score.' Ben smiled at his friend.

'This is what I want to do for him. I've got some money put by, from a business deal and it sits in a bank account doing nothing. I want you to find someone, maybe someone in the entertainment business who owes you a favour, a big one, who would invite Paul over to the States to do some acting work over there. Are you with me so far Ben?' Edmund asked.

'I get your drift Edmund, please go on.'

If you can do this, I will fund the fare and his expenses up to $20,000. So, if you can find someone to help Paul, you then contact me and I will transfer the money to you. Do you see why I need a trusty friend now?' Edmund asked him.

At that point Vera came over to the table with the Earl Grey. 'That, Edmund is the most wonderful thing...Ben, if you don't do this for Edmund, I'm gonna ask my pop to do it and that's a promise!'

Ben looked seriously at Vera. 'Listen Vera if you think I'm gonna let your old man get the better of me. Honey I'm gonna make Paul bigger than Brando himself, you watch if I don't!'

'Just one more thing dear friend, if we succeed, I don't want anyone but us to know that I've been involved in this venture, I want him to think he has done it himself, do you understand Ben?' Edmund asked him.

'I sure do, ol' buddy, I'll drink my duke something tea on it.' Ben looked at Vera for help.

'Earl Grey Ben.' Vera answered her forgetful husband. 'I think that it's the most wonderful thing anyone can do for a friend. Especially that you don't want him to know about it. I promise that we will do our best for Paul.' Vera said, almost in tears.

'You two are my dearest friends, thank you very much. I'm confident that between us we can make him a star' Edmund hugged them both.

15: <u>The Great Challenge</u>

Share certificate

It was 1981 and Edmund had been offered a job in a small Pharmaceutical company in the New Forest. The first day that he started, he had discovered that the previous accountant had left in a hurry. He had forgotten initially to ask about why the vacancy was available because his interview had been conducted so quickly.

Within a day of his application, the agency called back saying the company had wanted him to start with immediate effect which still did not raise any suspicions.

He did however look at the previous accounts during his interview and it didn't make for enjoyable reading. It was certainly going to be a challenge, but not as big as when he got behind his desk.

Edmund had to pick up things very quickly; nothing had been done in the financial control area for over a month. His assistant, a young woman, had only been there herself for a few months and by the look of it, she was getting quite stressed herself.

The company had a proud history, founded by a scientist and a landowner; they trundled on serving the local veterinary needs and making a nice little profit each year. The landowner partner decided to sell the business to the current owners in 1979. Two large banks each had forty percent of the shareholding each and the two directors had ten percent each. He was soon to find out that they were 'lording it' over everyone else who worked there and that he was to be the next target.

There was one other director on the board, Tony was the remaining founding member of the company, who was tolerated by the new directors because of his knowledge. He was however, pushed out of any decision-making and kept in the background.

The other main player in the company was the sales manager Ivor. He was a firebrand and openly hated the two 'owners' and soon had disclosed to Edmund all the lurid facts about them. Some of the facts he felt were perhaps not true and could have been born of spite, yet he was soon to find out that Ivor was speaking the truth.

As is usual with small companies he worked for, Edmund often witnessed the pure selfishness of the bosses, wielding their power over their staff senselessly, never showing any respect and never rewarding their loyalty for the excellent work that they did for them.

The two owners, Kevin and Charles were completely different in character to each other. Kevin enjoyed the egoistic success of ownership although Edmund never saw him do anything in the company. He was always in meetings, or off out entertaining strangers that no one had seen before, certainly they were not customers according to Ivor the sales manager. Charles was more secretive and often shouted down anyone who dared interrupt him. He was apparently a qualified vet, but he had never practised as such.

After his first investigation into the company's affairs, it became very clear to him why the previous incumbent had left so suddenly. The rude owner Charles held a separate company chequebook, which he kept locked in his office. Edmund was expected to do the accounts ignoring the payments made from this book. He immediately saw that as a possible fraud.

'Even you Charles cannot stop me from seeing that cheque book.' he thought to himself.

The next day Edmund knocked on his door and waited, but there was no answer. He knew that he was in, so he went outside and looked through his office window; he was asleep. He couldn't believe it; Charles was lying on the desk asleep. He went back to the door and banged hard on it. A few seconds later, the gruff short man, his suit crumpled opened the door.

'What do you want?' Charles shouted.

'Can I come in? Edmund asked as polite as he could.

'No, what do you want?' Came the gruff reply.

'I want your company cheque book with all the stubs, I need to reconcile the bank and can I have it please?' Edmund asked.

'No! It's not here, it's at home and anyway you've no right to see it!' Charles retorted.

Edmund turned on his heels and went upstairs to his office, he was fuming.

'No one talks to me like that', he said out loud. He ran up the stairs and sat behind his desk thinking out a plan, the stone was gripped in his hand as he decided to take the challenge.

'That ignoramus must go and I'm going to make it happen!' Edmund said to himself.

Edmund was usually the first in the office, but not on this day. The Sales Manager, Ivor, was waiting for him.

'Got a minute Edmund?' Ivor asked.

Edmund followed him into his office over the other side of the site. 'So, you've had a run in with Charles, that didn't take long.' Ivor smiled at him.

Ivor had realised that Edmund's attitude to wasteful management coincided with his. When Edmund made any comments in this area, Ivor was always willing to listen, Edmund decided that this was the right time to make his play.

'I want to know Ivor, if push came to shove, whose side of the fence you would jump?' Edmund asked him quietly.

'Are you asking me if I would support them if I had to? Then I certainly would not. I've told what I think about them and it's no secret, no secret at all. Even the customers hate them.' Ivor was adamant.

'OK then, I have been in something like this before, probably not as bad, I'll grant you, but when I get the bit between my teeth I promise you I will get things moving. I can't give you details but I do have a plan. I'll ask you again, if I was to get....make things happen, can I count on you for support?' Edmund asked urgently.

'You got it, friend, sink or swim.' Ivor answered with a wide smile and shook Edmund's hand.

'I'm a better swimmer, a better swimmer than even you could imagine. By the way, would Tony come on board?' Edmund asked him.

'Leave him to me, old Tony needs a little shove but he'll be OK Edmund.' Ivor looked relieved.

They shook hands again on it and Edmund quickly left his office and went up the stairs to his own; fortunately, neither of the two owners had arrived at that point.

The annual accounts for some of the previous years were in the cabinet and he pulled them out. On the third page was the list of Directors for the previous year. Looking closely, he noticed that there was a fourth name at the bottom of the list that he didn't recognise.

Without delay he rushed down the stairs, greeted the girls who were just hanging their coats up and rushed back to Ivor's office. Thank goodness, he was still there, but one of his salesmen was in the office so he waited whilst the salesman was despatched to the factory to chase some product or other.

'Do you know who this is?' Edmund asked, pointing at the fourth man on the director's list.

'He's the man that the banks put in to spy on us.' Ivor answered bluntly.

'You mean the bank's representative on the board?' Edmund asked him.

'I think so; I'm not really party to that sort of information, all I get is hearsay.'

'Thanks Ivor thanks a lot.' and ran back to his office. 'A break through at last!' he said to himself.

The owner Charles who was so rude to him, passed him crossing the yard, but Edmund refused to acknowledge and rushed by. He knew already what he was going to do, but it would take time, he must keep his nose clean, do the accounts and don't cause any alarm to anyone.

Six months had passed and by then he had found his way around. He decided to start improving all the company reporting without raising any eyebrows, but at the same time he began to maintain a secret dossier on both directors.

His office was upstairs in the loft area of a converted bungalow; usually the only person to climb the stairs would be his assistant with queries. Considering the inflammatory nature of Ivor's conversation, Edmund would rather go to visit the Sales Manager in his own office across the yard. Occasionally Ivor would come over to the main building to see his support staff in their offices. Edmund always knew when Ivor was around, as he had the dirtiest laugh he had ever heard, but he was a likeable character nonetheless.

One day he heard someone climbing the stairs towards his office, very slowly and could also hear him groan as he struggled around the tight corner. As he appeared in the doorway and pulled himself in, Edmund could see that he was a good six foot six and twenty stone at least.

'Those stairs are too much for me young sir.' The man declared with a soft Scottish accent. Edmund helped him into the chair opposite his desk.

'Can I help you sir?' He thought it might have been one of the customers who had lost their way.

'Damned hot up here isn't it?' Edmunds office was in the roof space and even with the window open fully there was nowhere for the air to go especially in a sweltering day.

'Must be my pen causing all the friction heat, they keep telling me I work too hard.' Edmund joked.

'My name is Robin and I've come to see how you are coping with everything my boy.'

'You're the banks' representative on the board, am I right?' Edmund smiled at him with an inner relief.

'For my sins I'm the Chairman of the board, for what it's worth.' Robin answered.

'Then why haven't I seen you before? I've read up on you, you're on the board of many companies and you are a Chartered Accountant are you not, sir?' Edmund asked.

'Have you seen my fee, dear boy? It's only enough for one visit per year. Anyway, the banks seem happy enough.' He replied.

Before he said that, Edmund realised that there was very little Robin could do to help him in his quest in exposing the two directors' incompetence. It was nearly lunchtime and the great man invited him to lunch at the local pub, to which Edmund gladly accepted.

'Are you ready then, Robin?' Another voice that he'd never heard before shouted from the bottom of the stairs.

Edmund let Robin go down before him, as he didn't want the great man to fall on top of him whilst manoeuvring the steep stairs.

Waiting for them was Tim, the Investment Manager from Pegasus, the Lloyd's investment arm. Robin was showing him around some of the companies in the New Forest that they had invested in. It was Edmund's luck that they had reached his company at lunchtime.

Ivor was invited to join them but he had a customer, so he couldn't go. The two owner directors came along, but because Edmund and the two new guys were accountants, they fortunately sat at a separate table in the restaurant, which was a bit of a relief for Edmund.

In just five minutes Edmund knew that he would get on with Tim, as they seemed to talk the same language. Edmund talked about his friend Ben in New York and where he had met him. Tim was a keen sailor and of course talk of Wall Street sent him into raptures. After lunch, they all went into Kevin's very plush office that doubled as a boardroom.

Edmund suspected that Kevin and Charles had had too much to drink at the pub and he was so surprised that they had allowed him to stay for the Director's meeting.

Edmund didn't think he had ever met such a boring man as Kevin. He spoke for twenty minutes but he was sure that no one knew what he had said. Charles looked like he was asleep already. At the end of Kevin's 'sermon' they got up to leave, Robin was already getting in the car, but Tim held back for a minute.

'I'm not blind Edmund, so if you want to talk, here's my card. Best time to get me on the phone is Monday mornings, or come to see me in Bristol, I'm sure you can find an excuse.' Tim whispered.

'This is it!' thought Edmund. 'This is my chance and I'm going to take it. They won't know what hit them.'

Edmund rang Tim the following Monday morning and true to his word, he was available to speak. Tim realised that Edmund's call wasn't going to be a casual one, so he, with Edmund's permission, put the manager of the other investor, on a group call.

'I would like to set up a meeting in Bristol with you both as soon as possible. If you like, Robin could be there as well, but I don't think that will matter much, do you?' Edmund said boldly.

'You sound like you've got something important to tell us, right Edmund? By the way my name is David.'

'I think so and I don't want to wait too long, David.' Edmund said.

~ 241 ~

'We understand, Edmund.' Tim said this time. 'Believe it or not we have our misgivings as well. We've got a large amount of money tied up in the business, so we want to hear all that you have to say, lock stock and barrel.'

'Hear, hear! Can you make this week, Tim?' David said to him.

'How's Friday at two David?' Tim responded. 'What about you Edmund, can you make Friday at two?' Tim asked.

Well, I haven't had any holidays yet, I'll book a day off this Friday. Where shall we meet guys?' Edmund asked. They agreed to meet in Tim's office in the Bristol Lloyds head office.

'I'll reserve you a car park space underneath, just follow the sign 'private parking', OK Edmund?' Tim and David said their respective goodbyes and the stage was set.

Edmund had to pass the written request for the day off to 'old grump's' secretary, who came upstairs an hour later with his signature on it. Edmund smiled at her, but gave nothing away.

'If only you knew what this was for.' he said to himself as he absent minded looked at Charles's signature again.

It was a momentous meeting, not only did Edmund show them the awful facts, but he had spent the few days before the meeting with a proposal for the company's future once the incumbent directors had been despatched.

The two young investment bankers winced at some of the things Edmund had proposed, but broadly they accepted them and promised him their full support.

Charles was the first to go, just as Edmund had proposed. He was offered two choices, prosecution for fraud or sell his shares and get out, he took the latter and went the same day.

The day after he left, his secretary gave Edmund a letter, the envelope was in Charles's handwriting. He took it upstairs expecting the worst, but in fact it was a most glowing reference from Charles, thanking him for his 'Sterling Work'.

The factory was buzzing with rumours. 'The ogre had gone, who kicked him out?'

The atmosphere in the offices also lifted one hundred percent and for the first time Ivor came upstairs into his office. Edmund indicated to him to keep his voice down, as Kevin was still in his office downstairs.

'How did you do it Edmund? I know it was you, so tell me,' Ivor asked.

'One down, one to go Ivor, I'll tell you all when number two has gone.' Edmund whispered, pointing downstairs.

Ivor just couldn't suppress his huge laugh. Edmund was a bit scared that someone would add up 'two and two', but no one had made 'four', so he had got away with that one.

Three months later Kevin had also gone, he told everyone that he was starting up a new business, having sold his shares for a huge profit. So, Edmund wished him well and reminded him that the Inland Revenue would have to be informed of any profits made on sale of shares.

Edmund felt a bit sorry for Kevin, as he was so naive.

Firstly, he knew, through the bankers, that Kevin had only got face value for the shares he owned and that he had made no profit on them, but Kevin just couldn't get over the big ego that his position gave him. In the end, it was his ego that he had eventually tripped over.

The first stage was completed and now there were two offices to fill, so he went over to Tony and Ivor and asked them to join him in the boardroom. He laid out the new structure of the board, which was to be: Ivor as the Managing Director, Tony as the Technical Director and Edmund as the Finance Director. The banks would appoint a new representative who would visit every three months and Edmund would report to him.

The two men were delighted and Ivor congratulated Edmund on a job well done.

'Well Ivor, the job isn't done not by a long way. Firstly, before we get down to business, I expect you are wondering what has happened to the shares they owned. Well, I want to know if either of you are interested in buying any of them?' Edmund had convinced them that at a pound face value, the shares were going to be a bargain.

Tony who was nearing retirement and previously had had his salary held down low by the other two directors, as well as having been treated so badly by them, decided to decline the invitation. Therefore, thirty thousand shares were up for grabs, so Edmund and Ivor split them half each.

The new board of directors agreed to meet each week, to discuss what had happened in the previous week and as Edmund had requested, to discuss the plan going forward.

It was truly an exciting time for the three of them. Ivor proposed the promotion of his pet salesman Simon to be the Sales Manager, Edmund was initially a bit suspicious of him, but thankfully he was eventually proved wrong.

This was the time when the EU legislation was starting to bite in respect of Product Licences for the treatment of animals raised for consumption. The Company had some inherited licences and Edmund made the rest of the board aware that going forward, the only way for the company to survive, was to get more licences approved by the Ministry of Agriculture, Fisheries and Food.

Tony was charged to head up that part of the operation, but Ivor was the hardest challenge however. Edmund had to appeal to his greatest weakness, greed. There's nothing better than a hungry salesman and Ivor was always starving. He was utterly ruthless when it came to selling, that's why he was so good at it.

Edmund's aim therefore was to get him to sell profitable goods only. If he could prove to Ivor that selling quality over quantity would make him lots of money and at the same time it would change the whole concept of the way the company would be run, the whole company would be transformed.

Edmund could never win an argument with Ivor, but he knew someone who could, Ivor's protégé, the Sales Manager; Simon.

Simon was so ambitious he was like a Rottweiler. Say kill and he would kill! Edmund made a secret proposition to Simon; he outlined a new bonus scheme that would be based on profit, not sales. He illustrated how much he could earn by not selling some of the larger 25kg lines and concentrating on the 100g sachet lines. When it resulted in personal gain, then Simon was soon sold on the idea.

Edmund then asked the new Managing Director, for whom he had just bought a Renault 25 V6 Turbo, if he would listen to Simon's idea for a bonus scheme and that it would be self-financing.

Simon knew how to put it over to his boss and said to Edmund that Ivor would agree straight away and to Edmund's relief, he did. Immediately Ivor ordered Simon to arrange a sales meeting that week to spell the scheme out to the rest of the sales force.

That one act of profit before sales had transformed the company overnight. The previous year the turnover had been three million and the profit was fifty thousand. The following year the turnover was four million and the net profit was five hundred thousand, multiplied by ten times!

By the end of that year, Edmund had taught Ivor how to read the accounts, so by then, the whole of his thinking was focussed on three things, profit, profit, profit.

16: <u>No Comfort in Iberia</u>

Flamenco

Tony, who had agreed to expand the licences for the company, walked into Edmund's office one day with a very tall bearded man in his wake.

'Morning Edmund, this is Dr Wheeler.' The tall man leaned forward and shook his hand.

'Please call me Theo, happy to meet you.'

'Theo is going to help me get some new licences Edmund and I want you to approve his post as Technical Advisor. Theo, show Edmund your card.' Tony said confidently.

He passed his business card to Edmund and when he read it he was amazed. There were seven different sets of scientific qualifications on it.

'The Ministry think very highly of Theo, as you can well see, Edmund. He is I'm sure, the most highly qualified Vet on the planet.' Tony looked admiringly at him, though Theo looked a bit sheepish as he took back his card.

'Have you got any particular licences in mind for us Theo?' Edmund asked.

'Yes, I do Edmund; I have a Danish friend who runs a company in Barcelona. He has offered us a licence for a unique product for pigs which is my speciality, so we need to get over there to see how the land lies.' Theo answered.

'We, do you mean you and Tony?' Edmund asked him.

Tony looked up. 'No Edmund, he means you and him.'

'Look you two; I have no knowledge of Pharmaceuticals and even less in the licensing of them.' Edmund smiled at Theo and shook his head.

'Tony tells me that you know a lot about people, I don't. I need your support, every step of the way, Olaf is a nice guy, but I've never done business with him. You will ensure we get the best deal.' Theo explained.

'What does Ivor think about me going over there, Tony?' Edmund asked.

'He wants the best for the Company, so he wants you to go. It will take at least a couple of weeks though, that's what Theo says.' Tony answered and Theo's long black beard nodded in agreement.

'I suppose I don't have any choice, do I? When do you want to go Theo?' Edmund asked him.

'What about the day after tomorrow?' Theo asked.

'Are you serious? That's this Thursday.' Edmund gulped.

Tony put his hand on Edmund's shoulder. 'Where's your sense of adventure old son, you haven't got anyone at home to worry about you have you?' They all laughed together. 'You might find a nice senorita waiting there for you.'

'OK, Ok I'll get Suzy to organise the tickets and hotel, do you want to go up to Heathrow with me?' Edmund asked as he looked at the bearded Theo.

'No, I'll get up there under my own steam, as I live in the Cheddar Gorge and you're not on my way up there' Theo smiled as they left Edmund's office.

'What have I done?' Edmund thought, forebodingly.

As they walked through the airport arrival gates, they were an odd couple. One was an accountant who was dressed like one; the other looked like he had just been on the Silk Route to Kathmandu! However, Theo was fluent in Spanish, German and Portuguese and Edmund knew that attribute alone, was going to be a major help for him.

After checking in at the hotel, there was plenty of time to be tourists as Olaf was seeing them the next day, so they decided to look at Sagrada Familia the famous Gaudi unfinished cathedral in the city.

Gaudi had turned all the traditional rules of architecture on their heads, the spires are the most unusual in the world and Edmund was just awe struck.

The following day Olaf was waiting for them in his office, just off the Diagonal, the main thoroughfare that bisected the city. The first meeting wasn't a success, as Olaf was unsure what they really wanted from him, something lost in translation perhaps.

The following day was Saturday so Olaf took them to the outskirts of the city to view his manufacturing plant. Theo was a bit more interested in that than his colleague, he wanted to analyse the company accounts that Olaf left him to pore over.

That evening Olaf picked them up at their hotel early, to take them to his home for a meal. He lived in a small village high in the Pyrenees, about ten miles away, in the winter it was a ski resort.

The journey however, was a nightmare and a highly stressful one for Edmund. He was in the backseat of Olaf's Alpha Romeo 164 Lusso. Olaf was a very calm individual, but he drove like a maniac, especially on the narrow mountain roads. It seemed to Edmund that he was trying to prove something to them.

His house overlooked a spectacular green valley that stretched for miles, Maria his Spanish wife had obviously taken great pains to produce authentic paella, but the excess of garlic and the drowning of olive oil over everything was difficult for Edmund.

He certainly did his best, but it was hard to convince his hosts that he was new to that sort of food. It was obvious that she didn't understand and that made Edmund very sad considering all the effort she had made for them.

On the Sunday, Edmund was up early in the hotel and rang Theo's room, but there was no answer, so he trotted along and knocked on his door. A bleary-eyed Theo apologised as he wasn't feeling well and told Edmund to explore the city without him. Olaf had told Edmund about the Ramblas and not to miss it, so that was his target for the day.

'Walk down the Diagonal until you reach a large island, right opposite is the beginning of the Ramblas.' The Dane had told him.

Quite simply it was a dual carriageway with a difference. In the middle of the carriageway there was a very large tree-lined paved walkway where each Sunday many of the local people promenaded along its length all the way to the seashore. Along the whole of it, street vendors were selling such things as brightly coloured caged finches.

Music and entertainers abounded and everyone was dressed in their Sunday best. The sun was shining and even the most cynical visitor would have been forced into a smile.

Cafés, shops and bars were situated on both sides of each carriageway, tempting Edmund into them. About halfway down, he looked left and through a narrow lane off the carriageway he saw flashes of colour. He decided to investigate and crossed the carriageway, jumping out of the way of the usual suicidal drivers and then walked down the dark passageway heading for the light. It opened in a blaze of sunshine and Edmund had to adjust his eyes for a moment.

A Gothic church courtyard opened to him and sitting around all four walls, many painters were setting up their canvases and easels, chatting away to each other. Placed around each painter were collections of their finished work, all hoping for a sale. Some of their work was truly excellent, except of course for Edmund, the price.

Edmund noticed another alleyway in the far corner of the flagstone square, there was someone coming out of it, laden with something, so he decided to investigate. He quickly came upon another square, just as nice but this time the whole perimeter was festooned with trestle tables laden with all sorts of things for sale.

'A Barcelona Flea Market,' he said to himself.

Everyone was wandering around the centre, darting this way and that. It seemed to him that they were all local people. On the first table, there was a mountain of Roman coins all looking for a buyer.

The next table he went to was already attended by at least six other people, all talking loudly in Spanish. He gently prised his way between two of them, just to see what was so interesting to them. He was amazed to see thousands of little brightly coloured tubes in carefully documented rows. He plucked up the courage to ask the man the other side of the table what they were.

'Zigar? Comprendez?' The man tried to explain.

He was gesturing to Edmund that they were the little bands that once had wrapped around each cigar denoting the manufacturer. Apparently, there was a huge demand for them in Spain and America and collectors were always looking for the rare ones.

He was nearing the end of his walk around the tables and had arrived back to the place where he had begun. The final table was displaying paper money from all over the world. This of course interested Edmund and his eye was caught by an old Reichmark note dated 1923 denoting a value of fifty million marks, which he promptly bought for twenty-five pesetas. Edmund knew from history that the note was printed during Germany's period of hyperinflation and this huge value note would not have been enough to buy a loaf of bread at that time.

In the week following, the negotiations for the licensed product were making progress. The final agreement they had made was for the UK Company to sell the drug under their Spanish licence with a significant royalty to be paid to them for five years, with an option to buy out in three.

On Friday evening Edmund was preparing for dinner at the hotel when his phone rang.

'Olaf here Edmund, will you and Theo be my guests tonight at the local Flamenco bar? I'll pick you up at eleven.' He sounded excited.

'Did you say eleven?' Asked Edmund.

'Why yes Edmund, it does not open until then, is that OK?'

'Yes of course, see you then.' Edmund wasn't used to going out at eleven, but that apparently was the norm for Barcelona. They were waiting for Olaf outside their hotel, expecting the Alpha to draw up, but no, he arrived on foot.

'It's not far from here, so I thought that we would walk.' Olaf said.

They followed him around the back of the hotel, down a busy street, quickly turned left down another smaller street and then finally up a narrow alleyway where halfway down, Edmund saw a flickering orange sign. Then he realised that this was their goal. Edmund was a little apprehensive, but Theo looked quite relaxed, so he followed them gingerly into the place.

Opposite them was a sort of reception room, with a couple of children who were busy colouring a book on the floor. Beyond the desk Edmund could make out some tables, with a few people eating. A woman in a sombre black shapeless dress stood up out of her chair, smiled and indicated a door on the right of her. Olaf opened the door that revealed a set of steep steps with no carpet on them.

'Is this the bordello that people warned me about?' Edmund thought to himself, he was starting to get somewhat apprehensive about it all.

At the top of the narrow stairs, a very large man nodded at Olaf and let them walk past after he had opened another door. The place that they entered was very dark, but soon Edmund's eyes adjusted to it. He could make out a very large room with many tables, all occupied and each lit by just one feeble light from a candle. On the right-hand wall, there was a brightly lit wooden dance floor raised up like a dais. Suddenly they were being guided though all the candlelit tables on the way to their own. Their table turned out to be next to the dance floor, right on the corner of it.

Just as they sat down, the whole room exploded with cheering and shouting! Edmund looked behind him and threading through the tables were five dark figures heading for the light and Edmund's table, the visitors stepped onto the floor.

First there was a young man carrying a guitar, followed by an older woman and then three younger women. They were all dressed in the most striking clothes of the true Flamenco style of black and scarlet. The whole place was still applauding and shouting in Spanish.

Olaf leaned over to Edmund and shouted over the cacophony, 'you are in for the treat of your life!'

The troupe consisted of the brother, who positioned himself on a small stool in the far corner and standing alongside him, his mother. In the centre of the stage were the three sisters, tall, proud and statuesque, arms in the air and maracas inside their palms.

Suddenly the mother shouted, the guitar struck up and it began. The young women cracked their heels on the wooden floor and danced to the beat, ever faster and fierier. At the side of their table, against the wall a cameraman was training his huge video camera on the whole scene.

During the first dance the waiter brought them food and wine, but Edmund did not notice. He felt no hunger, no thirst; he just drank in the amazing sight unfolding in front of him. Theo and Olaf were chatting to each other, but Edmund's eyes could not be averted, he was totally hypnotised by it all.

After about an hour, the girls took a rest and it was time for mother and son to perform a gypsy song. They gave an eerie plaintive cry, which moved Edmund, although he couldn't help taking a glance at the three beautiful girls in the shadow at the back.

The raucous shouting from the audience behind them continued, then at the end of their songs, the mother and son returned to the corner and the sisters strutted forward again.

Theo leaned towards Edmund and said, 'it's your turn next.'

Edmund couldn't hear him over the noise of the crowd. One of the girls came over to his table; she leaned over to Edmund and put her hand out. Their table was immediately bathed in a spotlight, just as he was gazing into her dark eyes.

'She wants you to get up and dance with them.' Olaf shouted. 'You have to get up and dance, because if you don't, it will be a great insult to them.'

The audience at that point was utterly deafening as Edmund slowly and nervously got out of his chair all the time keeping hold of the beautiful slim perfumed hand.

Edmund's attempt at the Flamenco was utterly pathetic, but the three girls danced around him, taunting him. He tried to copy their movements, which must have looked hilarious. Their mother was singing very loudly and their brother was off his stool playing like a madman!

Then suddenly as quickly as it had begun, it was over. The three girls applauded him and in return he clapped them and their mother and her guitar-playing son. Then, with wobbly legs, he managed to get back into his seat.

'You were great Edmund, bravo! That's something for you to remember all your life, just look around you.' Theo shook his hand; his face was beaming in admiration for his friend.

Edmund sheepishly looked around; people were standing and applauding him as he looked back at the troupe. They were now ready to continue without him, so he sat down for the rest of the show. He also glanced up to the cameraman who had been filming them, who smiled and gave Edmund the thumbs up sign.

The whole evening was an enormous success for Edmund and as they made their way back to their hotel, Olaf gave Edmund a red rose accompanied with a calling card.

The card had a picture of castanets on one side and on the other was a hand-written message;

'Mas profundo amor de Juanita'

'Olaf, I can't thank you enough for such an amazing night.' Edmund looked again at the card and knew that he would never forget.

17: <u>A Dish of Sardines</u>

Traditional fishing

'I told you I was a millionaire, didn't I? What do you think of this?' Edmund showed Theo the Reichmark note he had bought at the flea market the previous day.

Theo gave the note a closer look. 'I've got a friend who will put this in a nice wooden frame for you, take it as my present for your fortieth.' Theo gave him a knowing smile. 'You know why they picked you out to dance with them last night don't you?'

'Yes, I expect it was all Olaf's idea, wasn't it?' Edmund asked.

'No, it was because you had your tongue hanging out the furthest, so they thought the only way for you to put it away, was to get you to dance with them.' Edmund looked surprised until Theo started laughing. 'I'm only joking, Edmund.'

'Seriously Edmund, our business has finished here in Barcelona and I think we've cut a really good deal with them. I have got a backup plan for just this situation, if you'll hear me out.' Theo said.

Theo explained that there was a manufacturing plant in Lisbon for sale, which made a drug called Chlortetracycline.

The company in the UK used substantial amounts of this drug in their compounds and if they had a manufacturing arm, they could steal a march on their competitors. Theo had a contact called Dominguez and had found out from him that the whole of the manufacturing plant was for sale for a very low figure. Edmund could see the benefits and told him to go ahead and book flights and five nights in a good hotel in Lisbon starting the next day.

Before Theo left to arrange things, Edmund left him with no doubt that this next part of the tour was for fact finding only and there would be no on the spot decisions made.

'Buying a licensed product and buying a company are like 'chalk and cheese' he said.

The flight early the next morning to Lisbon had to change at Madrid, but there was not enough time between the connection flights, to tour the city, so they stayed in the airport lounge and awaited their call.

Theo brought out of his bag a box of ivory black and white dominoes, with an old marker board and challenged Edmund to a game of 'fives and threes'.

It was a scientific mind versus an accounting mind. As soon as the dominoes rattled onto the table, all the other waiting passengers looked around at them. At least half a dozen brought their chairs over to witness the match of the day.

Edmund recalled his intensive training that he had had with his father in the local 'spit and sawdust' pubs in Derbyshire.

All the men used to play as if their lives depended on it and he knew from Theo's first 'drop' he was going to have to draw on all that skill.

By the time that the airport speaker called for the Lisbon flight they were about even, the crowd had swelled to about twenty and they cheered each time a game was won, by either of them. After Theo had claimed the match victory, he told Edmund that the Portuguese were mad on dominoes. As Edmund reached for his bag, one of the spectators warmly shook his hand.

'Maybe we will meet in Lisbon and I will challenge you for a game, OK?' The passenger said, so Edmund nodded and smiled back at him.

Theo had set up a meeting with the pharmaceutical manufacturing company whose offices were right in the centre of Lisbon. Dominguez greeted them at the reception desk. He was a very affable man, asking the questions about the personal lives of his guests and in return told them about his family and where they lived. He was the Sales Manager for the company and Edmund wasn't at all surprised at that sort of greeting.

They were taken into the Chairman's office eventually and what an effort it was. There were guards at the door and to Edmund it was like visiting the don of a mafia family.

Even Theo had to admit that the conversations that he had with any of the main people in the company weren't going well. Translations were the biggest handicap, but he did manage to get some accounts for Edmund to look at, even though they were several years old.

That night in the hotel, after dinner, Edmund invited Theo back to his room, he had spent all afternoon looking at the figures and he wanted to show him what he had found. The balance sheet showed a huge reserve for something and he told Theo to get details of it, as well as get some of the more recent financial information.

The next day Edmund was asked to speak to the company accountant with a translator. It transpired that the company had made many people redundant two years back, but to his amazement, all the workers had an agreement with the company that if they were made redundant, full wages would be paid until they retired. This meant that if the UK Company bought it, this agreement would stand. He explained this to Theo in the simplest of terms and they agreed to terminate negotiations straight away.

It was Edmund's fortieth birthday the following day, so Theo had made some interesting arrangements for them both.

The next morning, they were riding on an old metal-wheeled tram, very small but covered in old fading posters and beautifully coloured. The metal wheels clanged on the old bent tracks. The tram was so small that with only ten passengers, it would be quite full. They were careering around the main streets of Lisbon. One street was full of old shops, with many of them hanging out the traditional rows of dried fish. The tram of course stopped to pick up passengers outside one of the shops and the smell from the dried fish just about made Edmund sick.

'Where are we going?' Edmund asked.

'It's a surprise for your birthday.' Theo answered smiling.

They reached the main rail station and Theo spoke in Portuguese to the ticket clerk and came away with two tickets, not showing Edmund their destination.

The train was waiting in the station. It was going to Oporto.

'We're not going there before you ask Edmund.' Theo smiled at him knowingly.

The journey was a slow one and the train had stopped at every small station, but it was so relaxing. It was hot, so every window was open. Most of the passengers had fans; they were mostly asleep or dozing. The landscape that passed by was green, all the white walled houses were topped with bright red tiles and between each hamlet were rows and rows of short trees.

'What are those trees Theo?' Edmund pointed inquiringly.

'They're special oak trees, used for cork. The bark is very thick, it's taken off the tree and then it grows back again. Sadly, many of the plantations had been uprooted and replaced by eucalyptus as a cash crop.' Theo explained looking glum.

'Why is it so sad?' Edmund asked.

'Well, you see the vegetation around the oak trees? Animals can feed there, but with eucalyptus trees, all of the vegetation surrounding them is laid to waste and nothing can grow when they are there.' Theo said.

The train stopped at Coimbra and they got off and changed platforms to one marked Figuiera Da Foz. 'Ah that's where we're going, right?' Edmund laughed.

'Yes, I know that you are going to love this place. Whenever I'm in this country, I always come here and it's a magic place.' Theo explained.

The train travelled on a single track through paddy fields and red roofed houses, it was a most peaceful journey for them. The station that they arrived at however was quite large.

'This place is where many Spanish people come for their holidays, to avoid the drunken British holidaymakers.' Theo told him.

For Edmund, walking on the streets in the Old Portuguese fishing town was like stepping back in time. Of course, there were cars, but now and then the odd horse and trap would pass by with a couple sitting dressed in the usual black clothing, traditional for the area.

'Do you see that Edmund?' Theo pointed to a little shop where there was a carousel of postcards. 'I mean that card,' Theo said pointing at a postcard.

Edmund picked it out from the stand and it pictured two oxen pulling a large fishing boat out of the sea. The animals had huge great horns and were totally black.

'If we're lucky we might see them when we arrive at the Atlantic coast.' Theo smiled at his friend.

The beach in Figueira must have been the longest in Portugal, over three miles long and famous for surfers, as the waves come in uninterrupted, from right across the Atlantic. Also as Edmund realised, the distance from the sea wall to the water's edge was also a considerable distance and it all looked so unspoilt.

Theo pointed to some activity, some way off on the beach, so they hurried to see what it was. Sure enough, there they were, two huge oxen doing what the postcard was depicting, pulling a brightly painted fishing boat from the churning sea.

'It's a sardine catch; they are all sardine fishermen around here. They've been doing this since time immemorial.' Theo said catching his breath.

'Thank you for my present Theo, I couldn't have wished for a better one.' Edmund stared in awe at the timeless spectacle.

They decided to have their dinner in one of the seafront cafés and try some traditional food. Theo of course had sardines; Edmund chose a Portuguese lamb dish with plump rice, which for him was the best meal that he had had since leaving England.

They finally decided to make their way to their small hotel by way of the first street that they had encountered from the seafront. It was steep, narrow and flanked on both sides by old tall tenement houses. The street itself consisted of cobblestones and the pavement was made from flagstones, which were heavy and thick. Theo noticed a small black scrawny cat, which ran across their path then ran uphill, disappearing around the corner, he grabbed Edmund's arm for a moment.

'If I'm not mistaken, you will soon be seeing something that has not changed for over a thousand years.' Theo pointed upwards in the direction of the street corner.

As they turned the corner, on their side of the pavement sat an old woman sitting on her doorstep dressed completely in black, holding up an ancient set of scales. On one side of the scales there was a small tray with three large stones in it. On the other side of the scales was a shiny tray with a pile of what looked like shiny silver sardines.

Quite a few people were appearing from the adjoining houses, carrying empty wicker baskets and headed towards the old woman. As Edmund and Theo got a little closer they could see that the old woman was emptying her tray of fish into each waiting customer's basket. The purchaser then threw some coins into a rough tin tray where she sat.

The old woman nodded to the small child standing next to her and he plunged the empty tray into a barrel of fish and set it on the scales for her and so it went on until all the customers were served.

The two men stood and silently watched until all her customers had disappeared back into their houses. The final customer that was left on the old street was the solitary little black cat, so with the last fish in his mouth, he was finally rewarded for his patience. It was most comforting to watch something that had not changed for such a long time, in fact, why should it?

They checked into their hotel and decided to look for a traditional bar to round off the day. A few steps around the corner, there it was, lights ablaze, with a few tables and chairs on the pavement. Theo laid out the dominoes and marker board as he'd done at the Madrid airport and Edmund went inside to buy the drinks. Inside the bar was very noisy with a group of locals playing darts, not dissimilar to any British local pub.

As soon as they realised that Edmund was English, he was invited to join in with the darts game, but he indicated that he was playing dominoes outside and once again they immediately had a large audience around them.

Theo insisted on a new game, this time called 'Maltese Cross', thinking that Edmund didn't know this one. But he was to be disappointed, as Edmund wiped the floor with him. It was a pleasant end to a wonderful fortieth birthday for Edmund and he was pleased to have shared it with Theo.

The next morning was the beginning of the long journey home, but it would be a long time until Edmund would have such a wonderful time again.

On the plane from Lisbon, Edmund pulled out the small card with the picture of maracas on it, turned it over and read the scrawled message again;

'Mas profundo amor de Juanita'

Previously Theo had translated it for him as 'fondest love Juanita' and Edmund dreamed about the dark Spanish beauties he had once danced the Flamenco with in Barcelona and sighed deeply.

18: <u>Alex's Story</u>

Time to listen

Back at home, Ellie knew that she had to decide about the coming weekend. The last conversation she had had with Gary had not been the nicest one. The fact that a woman had answered his mobile when she rang still hurt quite a lot. It was all down to trust however she knew that, but the big question of the day was; had his excuses been good enough to calm all her fears?

She turned on the computer and looked at the possibility of flying to Belfast on Saturday, staying at the Europa hotel on Saturday night, flying out to Glasgow on the Sunday and then flying back home on the following Wednesday. The benefit of going over to Belfast would be the opportunity to see if Gary was hiding anything from her.

That at first seemed like an excellent idea, but what would she say to Gary if he was to discover her ploy, it could destroy their relationship forever. She also considered that the whole trip could prove rather stressful, not to mention expensive. She even considered hiring a private detective, at least there would be no recognition problems, but she rejected that idea as being a bit 'low life'.

Ellie sat on her sofa and was deep in thought. She held her stone in her hand and suddenly her mind became clear again. I am not the jealous type, no I'm definitely not! I will and I must trust him. She walked towards the full-length mirror. You're worth more than that Ellie. Make all those stupid jealous tendencies disappear and forget all that forever!

'Vizards, can I help you?'

'I do hope so, my name is Eloise Monks and would you please pass a message on to Mr Macduff.' It was the day before her appointment and she was in the Glasgow Airport lounge. 'Certainly madam, as soon as he gets out of his meeting, what should I tell him for you?' The receptionist asked.

'Just tell him that I have arrived at the airport and I am making my way to the Ramada hotel and I look forward to meeting him tomorrow at ten.' Ellie explained.

The taxi dropped her outside the hotel and the moment she started up the steps, the tall concierge picked up her bag and carried it to the reception. She had booked a suite at the hotel and she wasn't disappointed. The concierge led her to her room, opened her door and it made her feel so comfortable. When she closed the door, she looked around at the panelled bedroom and the furniture was exquisite.

Adjoining the bedroom was the sitting room with a leather suite and a mahogany table. She approached the table, which had a bottle of Lansing Black Label in a cooler with two glasses and at the side was a simple calling card. It had Vizards on one side and a little hand-written note on the other.

'Welcome to Glasgow, see you tomorrow, Alex.'

'Please call me Ellie, I would really like that.' She said as she walked into Alex MacDuff's impressive office.

'Thank you, Ellie, from now on please call me Alex. I really think that we are going to get on well, I have cleared my morning for you and I hope you will join me for lunch. Do you have a favourite meal Ellie?'

'I like Italian best of all.' She said.

'Good' he said and picked up the internal phone next to him. 'Maggie, can you book a table for two at Fellini's at twelve thirty. Ring me back if there is a problem, otherwise we don't wish to be disturbed.' He instructed his secretary.

'Firstly Ellie, I must ask if you have any preconceptions of what you might expect to hear from me tomorrow?' Alex asked her.

'Yes of course I do, but I would rather get on with the meeting. I promise you that I won't get upset with anything I might hear.' She felt calm and in control, the stone was working once again for her.

Alex invited Ellie into his Glasgow offices, amazed to see how composed she looked, so he started with a question.

'You were probably wondering why someone with the same name as your own would leave you with such an inheritance and yet you don't even know of her, am I guessing correctly Eloise?' The lawyer asked.

'Yes, Alex, it has certainly given me some sleepless nights since I had that meeting with your Mr Jamieson in Salisbury.

'Well Ellie, I can now reveal to you that the deceased Miss Eloise Mary McIntyre, was your natural mother and before I tell you why, I want to know what your feelings about that are.' Alex looked somewhat serious.

'Ellie looked quite coolly at Alex. 'I suppose you're going to say that my dad then, is not my natural dad, at all, is he?'

'We're racing ahead Ellie but you are right. The person you have always regarded as your father is in fact your foster father and your mother your foster mother.' Alex tried to raise a smile.

'Right, then so who is my father?' Ellie asked.

'Ellie, I really don't mean to prolong your agony more than I need to, but would you please grant me this wish and let me take this step by step for you. I realise this is very hard for you, but I have secretly known you since you were born!'

'You're my father, Alex, are you?' Ellie looked at Alex searchingly.

'No, it's not me Ellie, I promise you. A man far better than me has that privilege.' Alex said.

This calmed her down a little. 'I need a drink.' Ellie suddenly said. Alex looked surprised at that comment from her. 'I mean I need a cup of tea.' They both laughed and Alex rang Maggie for some tea.

'Your mother, let's get back to her, shall we?' Alex asked.

'Your mother was one of the really lucky people. She was beautiful, she was a gifted veterinary surgeon, she was well travelled; spoke several languages and most of all she cared, caring was her life force. There were two things that changed your mother's life and they happened close together.

The first was when she met your father in New York and the second, not much later, was when she went to Tanzania. Your mother and father met through a mutual friend, a rich stockbroker on Wall Street called Ben Cohen. Your mother had set up a charity in Tanzania and Ben was able to get together some rich people and like-minded influential people, to make the charity a strong one.'

'What sort of charity was it?' Ellie asked.

'Your mother found some people who were concerned about the care for working animals, like donkeys and goats that were badly neglected and dying needlessly in Tanzania and she wanted to help them.

Your father was involved with a Veterinary Pharmaceuticals company in the New Forest, so not only were they interested in the same thing, but also, they fell in love the moment they first met.

'I sense that something bad must have happened Alex, what was it?' She looked at Alex puzzled.

'They were only together for a few months, when she got the call to go to Tanzania, where they urgently needed her help. There was no way that your father could stop your mother going there, it would have been a waste of effort for him. However, what she didn't know was that as she was flying out to Dar as Salaam, she had been caught pregnant with you.

She had booked a flight out a week later and as she had sorted the problem out early, so this gave her some time to go on safari in a local game reserve. They were camping near a lake and she was bitten on her neck by some sort of tropical fly. Within a few hours she was showing signs of an acute reaction, which was getting worse by the hour.'

'She was rushed by helicopter to the airport and then flown to London on the first available plane. She was taken to the department of tropical diseases at the St Pancras Hospital. They quickly found the cause of the problem and were able to stabilise her body, including her foetus, I mean you.'

'But what happened then?' Ellie looked enthralled with the story.

He looked gravely at Ellie and said, 'that wonderful brain, that lively character, that needle-sharp memory, all gone!'

Ellie looked at Alex and she was desperate to know, 'What happened?'

'That part of her couldn't be saved. It had taken her too long to get to the hospital and her brain had been attacked by the virus and had done irreparable damage. She was kept in some sort of suspended animation, whilst you were growing inside her. It was a desperate time for your dad; he was totally powerless to help.'

'When you finally came into the world your father was at the birth and I know he held you, but your mother had no idea what was happening. After that, your mother went downhill for a while, needing round the clock care.

Your father had to decide, one that had to be the best for you both. Your mother had a brother who had a lovely wife and no children. They wanted to take care of you and he made the decision to let you go there. Do you think he was wrong to do that Ellie?' Alex asked.

That was a tricky question for Ellie. How could she know? What would it have been like being brought up in a one-parent family? Her adopted parents were wonderful to her; she was given everything she needed. Eventually after a long pause she answered.

'I think dad was probably right, but I really don't know Alex.'

'Shall we break for some more tea?' He asked. She nodded and he rang Maggie. After about fifteen minutes he saw that she was refreshed and that she was ready to carry on.

'I'm sure that you must have noticed that your adopted father was not a strong man physically and in his later years could only work part time as a carpenter.'

'Yes, I had thought about that, just recently. I wondered how come we lived in such a nice house in Bradford on Avon and that I was able to go to Herriot Watt with such support, in fact we as a family never struggled with anything, come to think of it!' She looked at Alex and he smiled, knowingly, back at her.

'It was my real dad wasn't it, Alex. My real dad was looking after me in the background. Am I right Alex?' Ellie pleaded with him.

'Well, yes you are right Ellie, like I said to you earlier; your dad is a very special person. He always considered others and wanted the best for them, especially you of course.' Alex explained.

Ellie thought about what Alex had said. Initially, she felt proud of her dad, but then frustrated because she had missed so many years of knowing him.

Alex looked at Ellie, struggling to comprehend all these things that the lawyer had revealed that she hadn't known about. There was one more thing that Alex was wrestling with. He was going to tell her but then thought better of it, at least for the time being.

He was going to tell her that in all the years of care that her mother had received, towards the later stages of her life she had enjoyed a few little flickers of memory recall. Good enough at times to be able to leave the nursing home in Edinburgh.

During these brief spells, Edmund took her for a walk around the park next to Herriot Watt University. She liked to sit on the bench on her own and look at the ducks. Edmund kept a wary eye on her from the next bench when sometimes a young blonde student would come over and sit with her and they would chat for a while.

Edmund would sit on his bench and watch his own daughter and her mother chatting happily, neither knowing who the other was; he was utterly heartbroken about it. As he watched them, he dreamed what it would have been like if that untimely insect bite, so many years ago hadn't ruined their entire world.

'Have you got anything else to tell me about my mother Alex, I have so little of her?' She asked.

Alex was almost in tears himself. He wanted so to tell her that she had met her mother several times, but if he did, it would break her heart too. Instead he gave her some photos of her mother before her illness.

There were some of the last fundraising party in Manhattan, some old family portraits and finally a graduation photo from Bristol University. Remarkably like the one Ellie had had taken at Herriot Watt.

'Just one other thing Ellie, your inheritance is rather large in value terms and your dad even thought about that for you. He took out a policy to cover the tax you would have to pay. For most people, they would have to sell the property to pay it, but I have sorted the policy out and the insurers have settled the whole amount for you.'

'He thought of everything didn't he?' Ellie was close to tears.

'Yes, Ellie, he thought of everything but himself.' Ellie got out of her chair, she was sobbing and she hugged Alex as hard as she could.

'Glad no one can see this,' he thought. 'A lawyer and a client hugging and sobbing at the same time it would blow their mind.'

19: A Reward for Effort

NYC

A year had passed since his visit to Spain and Portugal and the company had just celebrated its first-year end with the new directors in charge. Edmund had arranged a sizable bonus for the new Managing Director, who was as happy as 'a cat with two tails'. As the company had done so well, he had also asked Ivor to agree a company profit based bonus for all the staff, to which he readily agreed.

That remained Edmund's quest, to always get the rank and file staff rewarded for their loyalty. Also during that year, with Tony's help, the company reached the highest level of quality production that the old Technical Director had seen in the whole time that the company had been in existence.

Things were going swimmingly even the banks were happy. He could have guessed that, as there had never since been any interference from them. At last it was time to take his foot off the pedal a bit.

Edmund was in Charles's old office and once or twice he took a call from Ben in New York, telling Edmund his latest news and how Vera was getting on with her latest exhibitions. He had also updated Edmund on Paul's progress in L A. his 'lucky break' had been converted into a successful career.

'Hey, buddy, I want to offer you my personal invitation to a party I'm throwing in Manhattan and I really want you to be there. C'mon buddy, you keep saying yes but you never do make it. Are you short a' money or somethin?' Ben joked.

'When is it?' Edmund asked.

'Next month, on the fourth of July, it's a holiday over here. You gotta be here for this one, whaddya' say ol 'buddy.' Ben pleaded.

'I'll only come if you get someone to meet me at JFK Airport.'

'I'll tell ol' Vera, she'll be tickled pink! Send me your flight details and leave the rest to me, Yippee!'

'Bye Ben.' Edmund sat and smiled to himself. He had finally bought a dinner jacket and this was his first opportunity to wear it. Buckskins were out this time!

As he passed through customs at JFK, he walked into the airport's huge concourse into a large wall of people all waving banners and cards with names on them. There was no mistaking who was waiting for him though!

A huge black man in a black suit with black sunglasses stood right at the front with Edmund's name on a huge card. The other folks were screaming and shouting at the sight of their loved ones arriving, but not him, he stood slightly apart, towering over all the others and looking straight at Edmund. He didn't speak, just pointed to the bag collection point.

Edmund thought it better not to say anything either and just followed him out of the airport to the waiting car.

A stretched limo, with four doors each side, awaited them. Another huge man got out of the driving seat and opened the door for him. No one spoke throughout the whole journey. They were soon heading into the New York business district and pulled up outside the Waldorf Astoria on Park Avenue.

His door opened, his suitcase was being carried to the reception and so he just followed. He got out his wallet to pay the man, but thought better of it. The man just nodded his very large head and walked away.

He introduced himself to the concierge and the man looked at him and smiled and then gave him his key. He waved to the bellhop who picked up his case and entered the elevator. He pressed the twenty sixth floor button which made Edmund gulp with surprise. He was on floor twenty-six, wow! The door said on it 'Presidential Suite'.

'What a man that Ben is!' Already the white phone at the side of the bed was warbling.

'Is that George?

'It's Mr Vice-President to you, Mr Cohen.' Edmund laughed.

'How did you arrange this, it's unbelievable? How did you manage to swing this one old buddy?'

'I guess you know it's a holiday tomorrow being Independence Day, so Vera and me, we'll pick you up at ten and show you the sights, Mr Vice President.' Ben was so pleased with himself.

'Everything was like a carousel for Edmund. They drove around the whole of Manhattan in their limo and Vera was pointing out the sights of 42nd Street, Fifth Avenue, Greenwich Village, Chinatown, Broadway, over the Brooklyn Bridge and back again and finally a short walk in Central Park eating a hot dog as they relaxed for a brief time.

The driver of the limo was waiting at the other end of the walkway and Edmund could hardly get his breath before it was time to get back to the Waldorf. That was where Ben was throwing the party he had been invited to.

'I guess you know that anyone who's anyone in this town, has stayed at the Waldorf, Edmund. And only the best of the best has stayed in your suite' Ben said.

'And you are one of the best to us.' Vera gave him a hug.

The party was in aid of an animal charity in Tanzania. Did Ben have some friends? They came from all over the States to help him with the fundraising. Edmund was talking to one of Ben's guests when he felt a tap on his shoulder. He turned around to see a beautiful blonde woman in her late twenties smiling at him.

'Hello Edmund, Ben tells me that you have come over from England to support my charity. I just want to thank you.'

'That's a pleasure Miss...? Edmund asked her.

'Oh, sorry, I'm Ellie McIntyre.' She smiled sweetly at him.

'You're not American are you, where are you from Ellie?'

'Well originally, I'm from Edinburgh, but when I qualified in Bristol I got a place near there, a small town called Bradford on Avon,' she explained.

'What are you qualified as?' Edmund asked.

'I'm a vet.' She answered modestly.

'Well it's a small world; I'm involved with a Veterinary Pharmaceutical company in the New Forest!' Edmund smiled.

'Yes, I know,' she said, looking over at Ben, who smiled and waved trying to look innocent.

Edmund looked at Ellie, 'beauty, brains and caring as well. Tell me, what is the charity all about?'

The whole evening went by in a flash. They talked about everything and anything and after a while it got a bit noisy for Edmund, so much so, that he had to shout over the noise.

'Are you staying at the Waldorf?' Edmund asked her and she said that she was. He invited her to his room; unbelievably he was met with no opposition.

'What, this is your suite Edmund?' She was looking at the notice on the door.

As he opened the door, she walked in without hesitation. 'How did you manage to get this room?'

He explained about Ben and their friendship and how they had met in the sixties in Cannes, he felt so comfortable with her. Why did she keep smiling at him? He just couldn't get it into his head. How he wanted to kiss her, but hadn't got the nerve. He remembered the mess with Pauline all those years ago in Deal and couldn't stand another rebuff, so he held back.

Ellie stayed the night with Edmund and several more nights. Ben was going to call him up the day after the fundraising party, but Vera tactfully stopped him.

'Look here Ben, you darn well set this up didn't you and so we'll leave them to it hun and let's see what happens, OK?' Ben smiled and nodded.

They were inseparable in New York; she didn't mind that there was fifteen years between them. The third morning as they lay in bed together, he asked her why she had chosen him.

'You look so vulnerable to me Edmund, it's as if you've got some big hurt inside you and I want to get rid of it with all of me.' She smiled and cuddled up to him. 'No rush to get out of bed yet is there?'

20: <u>The Big Question</u>

Edmund was sitting in the comfy leather chair in his cottage in the forest, his face reflecting the glow from the log fire. Zowie was sitting at his side and he was stroking her head unconsciously whilst reading a letter from Alex. In the letter, he described how Ellie had received all her inheritance with good grace, as well as detailing the discussions they had at his office on that Tuesday.

He wrote that he had told her that she was adopted and who her real mother was. She had taken the whole thing very well, even to the point of understanding the difficult decision that Edmund had had to make when she was born.

Alex also made him aware that her step parents had moved to South Africa soon after Ellie had graduated, so as far as Alex was concerned he saw no impediment to Edmund now contacting his daughter.

'Don't you think it's time to change and make both of your lives a little better?' Edmund read that passage several times.

Edmund had spent so much time alone. He had had no visits and visited no one apart from the trips to Edinburgh to see his beloved Eloise. Now that that part of his life had ended, there were times of melancholy and so much of his time was spent dwelling on the past. After re-reading the letter, he decided to walk towards his little secret pond through the thick copse of trees and took the letter with him. The little bench was there and the atmosphere was perfect. Man and dog seemed to melt into the surroundings as the quiet surroundings enveloped them.

It wasn't the same on his return though! Zowie was nervous, she had her tail between her legs and her ears were flat to her head. She looked around her front and back. Edmund followed her gaze but could see nothing. There were the usual shadows and dark areas, but that was normal.

'What is it, girl?' She looked up at him, almost pleading, Edmund knew that she was feeling something, that humans cannot feel or even see, but to her it was not anything she liked at all! He instinctively felt in his pocket for the stone, his long-term friend, but it wasn't there. No comfort, just emptiness inside his stomach.

He put Alex's letter down to think about what to do. Alex had a point. The way was clear and maybe Ellie did want to see him, but he still felt that she wouldn't forgive him for his enforced absence from her life.

Edmund thought back to the times when life had been so good, that wonderful night at the Waldorf, coming back from the States, those wonderful months coming home from the office to Eloise, who was by then working from the bungalow in Southbourne. Then of course, not long after, their world had been shattered by her illness. The birth of Ellie had been so traumatic. Then, he recalled the subject of his daughter's adoption that he had always struggled with.

Dark thoughts spun around in his head and so he sank back into the chair, so tired, so very tired! His strength was sapped entirely. He lapsed into unconsciousness trying to call out her name, as if she was in the room with him.

  'Ellie, please forgive me I did it all for you, my darling daughter.' Then it all went dark, so dark.

21: <u>The Payoff</u>

The winner

At the Pharma Company in the New Forest, Ivor was great through it all. He even got support from the investment banker Tim for the day to day finance questions. Despite Edmund's protracted absences, the company still went from strength to strength.

Edmund was very grateful to Tim for holding back on the sale of the company for the time being as usually banks sell their investment in less than five years, but Edmund promised a significant improvement in a few more years and that Tim would get a better return if he held on.

A year had passed since the birth of Ellie; Edmund had done his best to get some normality back in his life. He had received several caring calls from Vera in New York but thankfully she never pressed hard on his grief.

For once, Paul had actually written! He had just finished a supporting role in a film and said that he was taking American Nationality courses and most surprising of all he was getting married. Elvira was apparently an heiress of a wealthy industrialist. He had certainly 'fallen on his feet' this was great news for Edmund, Paul had now made it in his own right!

'Can you come over to L A for the wedding? I want you as my best man old matey!' Paul wrote.

Edmund wrote back immediately explaining why he couldn't go and suggesting that Brando double for him. He also sent a telegram of congratulations to Paul and Elvira on their nuptials, but never got a reply from either, but that was Paul. Edmund didn't really expect one anyway.

The eventual sale of the company went through in 1991 and by then Tony had retired, but then suddenly died of a massive stroke shortly afterwards. Ivor was very shocked and it brought the thought of his own mortality that much closer.

Ivor and Edmund were on the train to London and Edmund was outlining the deal that they were offered. Their shares were valued at seven times their face value, but he explained that there was an additional deal offered to them. The deal was to be, that they agree to stay in the business for a further year and enable the new company to get their strategy right for it, any shares they didn't sell on the first deal, the value of them would be calculated on the profit made in that year.

Alex had given Edmund the benefit of his advice on the takeover, after an invite to stay with him for a short holiday in Southbourne. So, when Edmund explained the deal in layman's terms to Ivor, he hit the roof, having quickly recognised the possibility of great gains!

The potential was enormous. All Ivor had to do was ramp up the sales and they would 'rake it in'. He rubbed his hands so much they nearly caught fire. They sold half their shareholding that day at seven times and the poor owners had to pay twenty times the face value, on the anniversary.

Along with a nice pension pot and a golden handshake to boot, Ivor could now retire a rich man, something he thought could never happen before he met Edmund.

Of course, Edmund had received a similar sort of payoff, but that sort of money had to work very hard, it couldn't be used in the same way as Ivor's. Before he left the company, he was called to Bury St Edmunds for a briefing with the Managing Director of the new owner of the business.

Jack Defors had a very strong persona and had a hard reputation for getting what he wanted. Many people avoided contact with him due to his abrasive nature.

Edmund was pleased to have been warned about him by Ivor, before going to Bury. He needn't have worried. Although Jack had Edmund's file on his desk, Edmund had the stone in his hand as he went in.

'That was a job well done Edmund.' Jack looked up from the file. 'You and Ivor really took us to the cleaners, didn't you?'

'It's like this Jack, you set the ducks up and we shot them down.' Edmund replied confidently.

'I've got a friend in New York who's a lot like you, he's not as quiet, but he knows what he's doing.' Jack closed Edmund's dossier. 'You're the kind of person I need in this organisation. I want to make you an offer. Will you give it some consideration, or am I wasting my time Edmund?'

'In short, I have two offers for you to consider. The first is to head up our Petfoods UK Co. in Leeds. The second is to do what we did to you and help us to take over other companies, ones that you can identify as good for our Group. We're looking for a big expansion in two countries, Spain and Portugal and we want to buy ourselves in there.' Jack explained.

'It's great to be considered for these.' Edmund looked straight at him.

'What's the 'but', Edmund?'

'But, I have some difficult personal problems that are going to take up too much time to allow me to do any of these fantastic offers you've got on the table for me. Please understand Jack, that under any other circumstances I would jump at the chance and you know that I would do them well, but I have to say thanks but no thanks.'

'I believe you know a guy called Ben Cohen, is that right?' Jack asked smiling.

'Yes, we go back some way.' Edmund answered.

'Well so do I, in fact I was at the Waldorf at the same time as you, at that fund-raising bash. I never met you of course, but Ben thinks so highly of you. It's an honour to meet you

Edmund and I wish you well in your new life.' Jack walked around the table and shook Edmund's hand warmly.

'God's speed, Edmund, all your friends are rooting for you.'

Edmund didn't know what to say, he was so shocked, so he just smiled at Jack and walked out of the office, then drove all the way back to Southbourne and home.

In the quiet of the journey he pondered how the people that had been involved with him in the past, like Ben for instance. These people seemed to pop up in the most unexpected places. To think that Jack could have been standing next to himself and Ellie on that day in New York.

'That', he thought to himself, 'was an amazing coincidence. Or was it?' Once again that stone talisman glowed in his palm.

22: <u>The Betrayal</u>

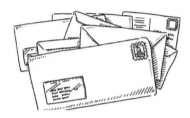

Three days mail

Back in her hotel suite in Glasgow, Ellie was exhausted. The meeting with Alex had gone on longer than she had expected, but he was determined to explain every little thing that Ellie needed, this was his top priority. She was so glad that he didn't keep referring to the time, so everything went smoothly.

She felt so safe with him and could understand why her dad had kept him as his advocate for so many years. At the end of the meeting Ellie did not press Alex for the identity of her father, because of the promise Alex had made to him. However, lying on the mahogany four-poster bed, she knew that she would make every effort to find her dad, with whatever means she had.

Gary would be working right then, so she left it until around seven before she called him on her mobile. It was all clear in her head, she was to tell him that all the details were now sown up and they could get on with their lives once again. She held on to her stone whilst her mobile rang his number, the phone continued to ring this time, with no answer.

She waited for the voicemail message, but it cut off before anything occurred. She thought perhaps the network had accidently put her through to the wrong number, so she tried again, but the same thing happened, no answer and no voicemail. 'No worries', she thought, 'I'll wait until after dinner and try then'.

As she walked back to her suite after dinner, she felt sure that all would be well with her call to Gary that time, but it wasn't. She still however refused to feel any suspicion, it must be the network. She then remembered that they hadn't spoken since Sunday and that conversation was just to confirm that he would meet her at Eastleigh Airport around ten on Wednesday morning.

'So, what am I worried about?' she said and sent him a quick text, 'Gary please call as I can't get through to you.'

She slept fitfully and was awake at six, dressed and packed and down at the reception at seven. She left her case and briefcase with reception whilst walking in for breakfast, she kept her mobile with her, but there were no messages or calls, nothing!

As she looked out of the window of the small jet the patchwork fields flashed by. Sometimes she could see a motorway, sometimes a little piece of woodland, although sadly forests in England were few and far between those days.

With no large suitcase to pick up, she was soon heading for the exit to the car park at Eastleigh airport. She stood near the automatic doors, but there was no one waiting for her, no one to hold her. Suddenly she felt cold, unwanted and a bit desperate.

The little Polo was in the far section of the car park and she continued to look around, expecting to see him running towards her, perhaps he'd got held up with traffic?

He'd have called, wouldn't he? She dropped the bags in the little boot and before she got into the car she opened her mobile, still no message. She finally took one last look around the car park, but there was nothing and her heart sank.

She drove home to Oxford; confused, dismayed and now hurt. Why is this happening? As she approached the house, there was no car in their drive and the house seemed dead. As she opened the front door, she could feel the cold inside. Nobody had been in the house since she left for Glasgow on the Monday.

There were three days of post on the hallway carpet and she looked for a handwritten letter. There was only a pile of typewritten letters, so she dropped them on the kitchen table to look at later. After she had restarted the hot water and heating, she checked the home phone for any messages. There were two messages, one from Simon from work, just checking that she was OK and saying if she needed to talk to him to give him a call. The other one was from Rowena.

'Hi Ellie, I wonder how you are, hope you got back safely, please call me when you can, I've got something to tell you. Can I come over to see you? Love you, Bye.'

Ellie had things on her mind, as she sat on the sofa, the house was now getting warmer and she was taking a sip of coffee that she had just made. Feeling more herself again, she thought she would look at the mail on the kitchen table.

Bills, circulars, a couple of charity requests and this white one, on high quality paper. It was addressed to her and when she looked at the top of the envelope, the franking was from Gary's company and the date was Monday, according to the Belfast sorting Office.

She opened it and it was typewritten like the envelope.

'Dear Ellie, sorry to break the news to you like this, but I shall not be coming home. You have probably guessed by now that I have found someone else and we have both decided to make the break from our respective lives and partners and to set up home together. At first, I really didn't think that this relationship would come to this, but it has. I wanted to end all the lying I have done to you and to bring everything into the open. I'm really sorry Ellie, I really am. I will write to you with the address of my lawyers next week and I think it would be better if we didn't contact each other except through them, I think that's the way it is done.'

Ellie was stunned and couldn't take it in, so she read it again. Mixed emotions ran through her head like an express train. Anger, helplessness, frustration, sadness and then back to anger again!

'How long has it been going on? Was it before he went to Belfast? How long has he been lying to me?'

It was time to answer Rowena's message. 'Hi Ro what's up darling?' She looked at her watch; it was two o'clock in the afternoon 'aren't you in the shop?'

'Well no I'm not, it's a long story Ellie and could I come to see you please?' It sounded urgent and Ellie did need someone to talk to, so she agreed.

'I'll be with you in an hour'. And then Rowena rang off.

Ellie hoped it wasn't unwelcome news; she had enough to handle already. As she waited for her friend to arrive, she thought again about Gary's letter. Why did he type it, perhaps someone else typed it for him, perhaps that woman who answered his phone that time typed it?

The whole thing seemed to have a ring of inevitability. He hadn't called her; he wouldn't answer his phone, even deleting his voicemail. The whole thing was planned from the start. She pulled the stone out from her top. She would show Rowena the letter, but as time passed, her mind became clearer and she already knew what she was going to do. Ellie was opening her front door just before three.

'You've done well Ro, great to see you' Ellie said and hugged her best friend tightly.

Rowena looked at Ellie's eyes, the green wasn't so sparkling and there was more than a touch of red around them. She followed Ellie into her living room. Ellie had made a fresh pot of coffee and that would have to do now; she didn't feel like offering anything else to her.

'Now, why aren't you at the shop, I thought that you were doing so well?' Ellie asked, desperately trying not to mention her own problem.

'I've shut the shop, I'm selling up and I'm moving to Bath.'

'Zach?' Ellie guessed.

'Ellie I'm truly in love, so much so that it feels like the first time in my life! He has asked me to move in to his home; by the way it looks just like a castle.' Rowena giggled.

'How did you two meet?' Ellie asked.

'It was about six months ago at a seminar in Bath. A friend introduced me to him. He had not long lost his wife and wasn't up for talking but I just couldn't help it Ellie, I just fell for him like a schoolgirl. I know that there is a big age difference, but I just don't care! He has asked me to marry him and I said yes. We already have a date in September in Bath Abbey; will you be my maid of honour?' Rowena was breathless as she explained everything.

'It's like a fairy tale Ro, but don't tell him to kiss my hand again, you know what happened last time in that car park.' They giggled together and hugged again.

'You've got some news too Ellie, haven't you and it's not good is it, love?' Rowena reached for her friend's hand.

Ellie looked at Rowena's sparkling brown eyes, what a lucky man Zach was, she was probably the most staggeringly beautiful woman she had ever seen, tall, dark and mysterious. She picked up the letter and handed it to her. Rowena began to read and suddenly the warm atmosphere changed, her brow furrowed and she took her time before handing it back.

Rowena just looked at Ellie, who was again holding her stone hanging from that exquisite chain. How she wanted to tell her what the old woman had said about it that day, but she was afraid to speak. An oath is an oath and not to be broken.

Ellie told Rowena of the events leading up to the letter, from the time that the woman picked his phone up, to the subsequent unanswered calls she had made in Scotland.

'Why don't you ring Alex in Glasgow, Ellie? Ask him to represent you, it's only just after four, his office will still be open.' Rowena urged her friend.

She rang Maggie, his secretary, but of course, he was in a meeting. She did promise to make him call back the moment he was out.

'I'm staying here with you tonight, if that's alright?' Rowena could see the obvious strain that this terrible situation was having on Ellie.

'I do need your support right now Ro, it certainly would help me a great deal.' Ellie answered gratefully.

'Tell you what, while you wait for your call, I'll go into the kitchen and make us up a meal with whatever you've got.' Rowena squeezed Ellie's hand tightly and disappeared. Surprisingly, it was only a few minutes before Ellie's phone was warbling.

'Glad to hear you've got home safe Ellie, what can I do for you?' Alex asked.

'This is very awkward Alex. I have had a letter from Gary, my husband and out of the blue, he wants me to divorce him. Could I email you a copy and if you would agree, would you represent me? Of course, I want you to represent my interests in everything, just as you represented my father.' Ellie asked and crossed her fingers.

'Of course, I would, Ellie that is if I were somewhat younger. But to be frank with you, after I had fulfilled my obligations to you with your inheritance, I had made a promise to my long-suffering wife that I would finally put the old warhorse out to pasture. You know I'm the same age as your dad and he retired from the cut and thrust quite a few years ago. However, I can be replaced you know.' Alex explained as courteously as he could.

'But who is good enough to replace you Alex? I need someone who is good and I can trust.' Ellie pleaded.

'I have a very good replacement in mind, young as well.

'Do you mean Clive?' She asked.

'Yes, I do, he's a good all-rounder and much closer to you than I am. Would you like me to ring him?' He asked her.

'Yes, please Alex and by the way, thank you again for all your excellent work, not just for me but for all the years with my dad.'

'I'll ring him now Ellie, I'm sure that he'll contact you just as soon as he can. Bye for now!'

23: <u>A New Address</u>

A different view

It was 1996 and as he looked back on his working life, Edmund had been both lucky and unlucky. The lucky times were of course, when he had been given the opportunity to improve the businesses wherever he worked. On the occasions when he had benefitted financially, he was very careful not to unduly risk any of the capital sums, considering the responsibilities thrust on him by Eloise's illness. His only luxury at that time was the purchase outright of the little bungalow In Southbourne.

Five years after the sale of the Pharma Company, his opportunities became somewhat non-existent; he put it down to age. Understandably the employers of the day were ignoring experience and focussing on younger go-aheads. When one is past fifty it is time to lower one's sights a little.

Ben had been over to the UK a couple of times, to visit his mother, whom he had moved to a little flat in the centre of Bournemouth, near her old pen-pal. He wanted to get his mother into something better, so Edmund offered to look out for him.

During the summer months, Edmund preferred not to seek work, but enjoy the more relaxed environment in the local area. One Saturday morning he was strolling along the high street when a banging on a coffee shop window broke his chain of thought. As he looked, he saw Brian beckoning him inside.

'Just the man!' he said. 'I've got something really interesting to show you Edmund, not far from your house and it's got the right potential.' Brian often had coffee with Edmund, so he knew basically what he was looking for.

'Tell you what Brian, I'm going back home just now, but come and pick me up at the bungalow at one this afternoon and show me what you've got.' He gripped the stone and smiled to himself.

As usual, Brian was prompt, especially when there was money to be made. They drove into the Overcliff Drive and then eastwards towards Hengistbury. Brian stopped the car next to a rough piece of grassland on the cliff top.

'Where's the property?' Edmund asked him.

'No property, just this piece of land for sale.' Brian smiled at Edmund.

'Don't see any for sale signs, Brian.' Edmund joked.

'The seller doesn't want to attract any attention Edmund. This piece of land is about half an acre, from the roadside to the cliff edge.' Brian said.

They got out of the car and walked towards the cliff edge over the rough coarse grass and as they reached the edge, Edmund drew in breath.

'Spectacular views Brian, they are beautiful.' Edmund said and Brian smiled knowingly.

'The owner of the land has been trying to get planning permission for an apartment block and has run out of money and now he wants to sell it to cover his losses.' Brian explained. Edmund once again thrust his hand into his trouser pocket and squeezed the stone in his hand for a moment as his mind flashed into action.

'OK Brian, let's get back to the bungalow and see what we can do.' Edmund had already formulated a plan in his head and Brian would have a very big part of it. 'But is he up to it?' He asked himself.

'Without planning permission, the land is only worth about fifty thousand.' Brian stated knowingly.

'OK then, what would it cost to get planning permission for the site old buddy?' Edmund asked.

'With fees from a good architect, permission could run up to twenty thousand.' Brian told him.

'Right then, here's the deal Brian.' Edmund's eyes lit up and Brian's eyebrows lifted in anticipation. 'Tell your client that you've found a buyer, by all means. Tell him that I will fund the full planning permission for him. I will, today, make a binding offer for the land, for a hundred and ten thousand, less the planning costs that I will have paid on his behalf.'

'If he agrees, I will get Alex to draw up a legal agreement to that effect that we both sign at the onset. Now then,

Brian, what would your fee for this project be?' Edmund was on fire again.

'I would do it for a grand.' Brian hesitated.

'How about this then Brian, complete everything by the end of 1998 and I'll make the fee two grand!' Edmund smiled at his friend.

Brian completed the sale of the land by the end of 1997, a year ahead!

Edmund then retained the architect for the next stage. He wanted him to design and build the highest quality apartment block ever seen in the area with no expense to be spared inside or out. Brian also agreed to project manage this also. They agreed a fee with another bonus to be paid on the successful completion by the summer of 1998.

Brian had checked his database for all the surrounding houses and blocks of flats in Southbourne and came up with a few suggestions for the name of the new building. 'Breakwaters' seemed the right choice. At that point Edmund invited Ben over from New York to be the first person to see the completed block. He was so delighted with it that he put his mother in straight away!

'The Breakwaters' was completed and Brian had soon filled it with tenants. He had been very careful to vet all of them and in the process many prospective applicants were rejected due to Brian's high criteria. Edmund did not interfere with the selection process as he wished to avoid a rift between owner and agent. He knew that Brian was the best in his field and wanted to retain him at all costs.

The following year heralded the turn of the Millennium. It was Brian who noticed that Edmund had become more introspective and he saw less and less of him on the High Street in Southbourne and rarely got a reply from Edmund's home telephone.

One autumn Sunday, he made a detour from his usual walk, passing Edmund's bungalow. It was a sunny day, so with no reply from the front doorbell, he went around the back and checked in the garden.

Lying asleep on an old deck chair, Edmund was stretched out with an open book on his lap and the sound of the gate latch woke him from his slumber.

'Not been back long, Brian' Edmund blurted out, trying to explain his situation.

''Back from where?' Brian asked.

'Edinburgh; the journey takes it out on the old bones these days. What I could do with is somewhere in the Forest, a little cottage would do.' Edmund looked to the sky wistfully.

'I've got just the place, needs some work though. No mains services and probably in the most isolated position you could imagine.' Brian somehow knew that this statement would spark something in Edmund's imagination.

'How did it come on the market?' Edmund asked.

'Through probate, I don't think it's been lived in for decades. The owner passed away last year in a nursing home not far from here.' Brian explained.

It was easy for Brian to sell Edmund's bungalow, as that sort of property was scarce and many newly retired couples were always on the lookout for one.

On the other hand, Edmund had found his Xanadu. The little thatched cottage was exactly as he had imagined. Virtually nothing had been done to it for a century and by the look of the position, deep in the woods, his dream of real isolation would be complete.

'Have you ever been to the show in the New Forest?' Brian asked.

'When is it on?' Edmund asked.

'Well, it's on until the weekend and as it happens I've been given two tickets for tomorrow if you would like to go as my guest. It really is a great show, not just horse-jumping and farm animals either.' Brian said.

'Sounds like an excellent idea, why don't we make a day of it?' Edmund seemed to be back to his old self again. 'Let's find a nice pub for lunch and then spend the afternoon there? I'll pick you up in the Morgan, we can put the soft top down and the weather forecast looks like we will be able to do just that.' Edmund said enthusiastically.

They found a thatched pub just south of Lyndhurst that served great food and at about two they were parked in the car park near Brockenhurst. The sun was glinting through the trees, lighting their way towards the entrance to the showground.

'Hey, did you hear that?' Brian suddenly stopped in his tracks. 'I'm sure...' He was interrupted by the repeated message over the tannoy system.

'It can't be for me, must be for someone of the same name, how could anyone know that I'm here of all places? It's just impossible!' Edmund shook his head and continued into the grounds.

'Look over there, let's just go over to that caravan marked 'Ringwood Public Address', we'll soon find out if it's you they want.' Brian insisted.

Edmund shrugged his shoulders and followed Brian over to the little van, which sported two huge loudspeakers on its roof. Brian interrupted the occupant just before he was going to read out the message again. He persuaded him to pass over the handwritten message and handed it to Edmund.

As Edmund read the note, Brian asked the man in the van, 'who is the person who wants to see him?'

'It's some foreigner over there.' The man answered, pointing across the clearing.

Edmund looked a little agitated when he gave the note back to Brian.

'When we reach the stall, we'll just look at the goods on sale, but don't say anything. I'll decide what to do when we see the lie of the land.' Edmund murmured to Brian.

As they approached the stall they could see that it was brightly decorated and the items on it were delicate carved boxes of all shapes and sizes.

Brian picked up a hexagonal box and inspected it closely. The woodwork was intricately carved and as he took off the lid, the workmanship made it fit perfectly. The design was indicative of Arabic styles like latticework.

Edmund watched the owner of the stall as he watched Brian holding the box. He was short in stature, olive skinned with slightly slanted eyes but not Oriental. He was wearing a long coat that was brightly coloured, underneath was a white shirt with a high gold embroidered collar, which carried on down the centre of the garment. Overall, he looked most impressively dressed.

In the shadows, he noticed a small dark figure dressed in black sitting in a corner. It seemed that this person was doing some sort of crocheting, but as she looked up at him, Edmund recoiled in shock. Her dark face was covered in lines indicating great age and she reminded him of the old woman that he had met many years ago in Deal.

'Let's go, now!' he shouted to Brian and turned to leave. The man stood in Edmund's way however, smiling at him.

'Sir, please do not leave, my mother wishes to speak with you. Allow me to introduce myself. We are Uzbeks, the boxes that your friend is inspecting come from my country Uzbekistan. Have you heard of my country, sir?' The man held his head to one side as he looked at Edmund who shook his head and tried to look away.

'My name is Yusuf and my mother over there is called Nila. We have come all the way from Samarkand to speak with the man who owns the Great Protector. Nila has a message for him from the Spiritual Guide.' Yusuf looked appealingly at Edmund.

'What's all this rubbish?' Brian asked the Uzbek.

'Will you tell me, what is the name of this Spiritual Guide?' Edmund asked challengingly.

Yusuf's mother stood up from the stool and quietly stood next to her son. She looked at Edmund with dark eyes and then spoke to Yusuf, who then interpreted it to Edmund.

'His name is Abdul. Nila knows that it is you she has to give the message to and asks for you to show her the Protector.'

'Is this what you mean?' Edmund pulled out the stone from his trouser pocket and held it out to her in the palm of his hand.

Brian leaned over to take a closer look at the small glowing object. The old woman looked closely at the stone and nodded at her son.

'I've had this, Brian, for many years; it was given to me when I lived in Kent by an old woman not dissimilar to this old lady here. In all those years, I have never shown it to anyone until now.'

Edmund looked at Brian's face, it had gone quite white and he looked troubled about what he had heard. 'Don't be concerned Brian, everything is OK; I'm just going to speak to these people for a few minutes. Go and find us a cup of tea and I'll catch up with you.' Edmund said so as not to frighten him. Brian quickly walked into the showground and didn't look back.

As Edmund, turned to speak to the two Uzbeks, the old woman passed a small piece of paper to her son, who then handed it to Edmund. It was a little crumpled, so Edmund carefully unfolded it to read what was written on it. The message was beautifully written in thick black ink but he had no idea what it said.

'My mother wrote this down exactly as she was told, in a dream that she had last night. I am sorry, but I cannot understand the language sir, so I don't know what it says for you. It is in the mother tongue of Russia and I was never taught it.' Yusef looked despairingly at Edmund.

'How does she know then, that it is a message for me?' Edmund asked.

'In her dream, a voice told her only who it was from and who it was for – you, dear sir.'

Edmund stared again at the note, how could he not believe them, it was too fantastic a story not to be true!

'Yusuf, please ask your mother this question for me.' He nodded and bowed. Pointing to the stone he asked Yusef, 'Ask her if she knows anything about this.' He held out his hand again, the stone was still glowing softly.

Yusuf asked the question to his mother, who gestured to Edmund to hand over the stone to her and he didn't hesitate. She looked at the stone and then quickly spoke for quite a while to her son, which he then sombrely translated to Edmund.

'Nila says there is a legend in our country, which has been handed down from a great many generations ago. The story begins with the Great Temujun, Lord of all the Mongol tribes.'

'Once he was in the mountains of Kashmir and he came across a great serpent. This serpent had been killing many of the Kashmiri people. Temujun discovered the monster in his lair, asleep. Quickly, he killed the beast with his sword. He wanted to bring its head back down the valley, but it was too heavy for Temujun to carry, so he took out the Serpent's eyes to show them'.

'Is she saying that the stone was a serpent's eye?' Edmund turned to ask Yusuf, but he was already serving a customer at his stall.

Nila looked at Edmund and for the first time, she smiled at him and said:

'Tanishganimdan hursandman – hayir!' Then she returned the stone to Edmund and walked away from him.

Even without understanding what Nila had said to him, he knew that the conversation was over between them. Edmund folded the piece of paper into his coat pocket and went in search of Brian.

He hadn't been that long, as he saw that his friend was still in the queue to be served at the tea bar. Edmund found a free table and was relieved to see that Brian had regained his colour.

'What happened? Brian asked, as he poured the tea.

'Not much, except the old woman gave me this.' Edmund passed the small piece of paper to his friend and Brian squinted at the small print on the paper.

'It looks like it's in Russian.'

'Good guess, that's exactly what it is, but unfortunately there was no translation from either of them. It looks like another mystery that I've got to solve.'

'Well, I know someone who can translate Cyrillic for you.'

Edmund laughed heartily. 'I thought you might old friend, I just thought you might.' They sat and finished their tea and planned where to go next on their day out together.

24: Coming Together

Just in time

Ellie was amazed to hear the phone ringing, only ten minutes after speaking to Alex.

'Is that Mrs Monks I'm speaking to?'

'Please call me Ellie, can I call you Clive?'

'That would be a pleasure Ellie. Alex mentioned you have got a problem that you want to see me about.'

'Yes, I do Clive and as soon as possible please and whilst we are speaking, Alex recommended that you take over all my needs Clive, legally I mean. She heard him clear his throat and she smiled to herself, knowing that her last statement could have a double meaning. 'So, Clive, that's two questions, do you have an answer or do you need to get back to me.'

'Er the answer Mrs...sorry Ellie is yes to both questions, with immense pleasure.' He said. She could feel the warmth in the young lawyer's voice and she liked it.

'I'm very pleased Clive, I suppose tomorrow is out of the question, is it?' Ellie asked.

'Where would you like to meet?' Clive asked her without hesitation.

'Do you know Breakwaters, the Apartment block I inherited?'

'Yes, I think I could find it, what time tomorrow?' He asked.

'Could you make twelve?' Ellie's fingers were crossed.

'Yes, I could.'

'If you could ring the intercom W3, I'll come straight down and let you in. Thank you for making yourself available at such short notice.' She uncrossed her fingers in relief.

'See you tomorrow Mrs.... I'm really sorry, I keep forgetting.' She distinctly heard him giggling. 'I mean Ellie, till then.'

Ellie was going to shop for the house in Oxford, but now it was time to make the first order on the Internet for delivery to the Breakwaters with the Waitrose account and got confirmation for her delivery at ten in the morning.

Over a lovely Spanish omelette that Rowena had quietly made for them Ellie finally relaxed somewhat. Once again, the level-headed Rowena had taught her how to cope with such a critical situation. Gary had been a louse, but she realised that lashing out wasn't the way and would in the end achieve nothing. Her stone was securely clasped in her hand and she could feel its glow through her fingers.

After the meal, they cleared the dishes and began washing them and Ellie was smiling again, as she was having a real girly chat with her best pal. Rowena made some suggestions on how to look after Clive the next day as she had overheard the phone call with her new lawyer.

It was hilarious and they were crying with laughter, but in the end, she knew that he was a true professional and based on their last meeting in Salisbury, he probably would be immune to all her charms.

The rest of the evening was spent with the two women discussing Rowena's plans for her wedding with Zach. All this was a useful distraction for Ellie, thankful of not having to face the evening alone.

The next day after a quick breakfast, Ellie and Rowena left Oxford together, Rowena to Salisbury and Ellie drove on to Southbourne. As usual Clive had arrived at Breakwaters fully prepared, knowing that they were to be discussing the divorce procedure.

Clive pointed out that the letter from Gary would prove decisive in his negotiations with his lawyer. His opinion was that Gary already knew that and he expected a speedy resolution. Ellie agreed to email him with the name and address of his lawyer as soon as she got it.

'I would cook you a meal, but I suppose you've got to get back.' Ellie asked.

'Actually, yes, I do, but not to London, my mother lives in Dorchester and I will be staying there tonight.'

She looked at him, in his well-cut suit, nice and tall and he smelt nice. 'What was that perfume? Perhaps his girlfriend had bought it for him for Christmas'. Clive noticed that she was looking at him, sort of sizing him up. It made him feel a bit self-conscious, as with all the pressure at the office he had little time to get any meaningful relationships with women.

'Ellie,' he thought. 'She's too good for me, too classy and too rich and yet she is smiling at me! What does it mean?' Clive broke the silence.

'We seem to have got that pretty well tied up Ellie, would there be anything else while I'm here?' He asked. Ellie sighed deeply and loud and Clive was desperate to hold her, 'but she's a client and I mustn't give in to my feelings.' He said to himself.

'Yes, there is something else but this is very difficult for me.' Ellie gazed into his eyes as she stood up close.

'Ellie, I think I know what you are going to ask me, it's about your dad isn't it?' Ellie's eyes were filling up and Clive desperately wanted to dive to those dark pools of emerald.

She looked up at him and at the same time pulled out her stone on the necklace. He was mesmerised and could not resist reaching out to her. A second later she was in his arms and he felt her shaking against his chest. He placed his lips on her hair and for that moment he couldn't breathe.

'My God what's happening to me?' She was still shaking and he couldn't move, as she had her arms firmly gripped around him. Slowly he managed to release her grip and held her at arm's length. It was a sacred moment for him as she looked up at him like a lost child.

'My father, Clive, I can't explain it, but something is telling me that he needs me right now. He's in some sort of trouble, but I don't know where he is. Help me, please, if you can.' Tears swelled up in those big green eyes again.

'How would I feel if it was happening to me?' He thought. 'Look Ellie, I know you want me to find your dad for you, but you also know that if I do this, I could lose my job.'

'S... sorry Clive, I know I shouldn't do this, but I feel my dad needs me. Don't ask me how, but I just know.' At that moment in her vulnerability he realised that he loved her. His heart was full of love for her and damn the consequences!

'Do you want to go and see him right now, Ellie?' Clive asked.

She ran to him, flung her arms around him, he responded and kissed her deeply, he just couldn't stop himself any longer. He felt the whole of her body pushing against his. Yet he had to stop, right now! She wrenched herself free and collected their coats.

'Let's go.' Ellie said excitedly.

In two minutes, they were standing in the car park. He pointed to the car he came in, a Jaguar XF.

'I don't think that it will take us where you dad is Ellie.'

Then they were looking at Ellie's little Polo, suddenly a huge Range Rover pulled into the car park and stopped alongside them.

'Are you OK pal? You look like you've lost summn.'

'Are you residents here?' Ellie asked with a smile.

'Well, not exactly, we're here visiting my Mom in W2.'

'You mean Mrs Cohen? You must be her son, she mentioned you when I spoke to her recently. My name is Ellie Monks.'

'I'm Mrs Monks' lawyer and the reason we look a bit odd Mr Cohen, is that we have to get deep into the New Forest and neither of our cars can take that sort of terrain.' Clive pointed to the Jag.

Ben spoke to his passenger Vera for a few seconds. 'Look buddy, we've only been to do a little shopping for mom, my wife here will take them up for her.' Vera smiled and waved as she disappeared into the building. 'Looks like you're in a hurry so do you wanna drive son?'

'I'm Clive.' He said, shaking Ben's hand.

'I'm Ben, all the way from New York.'

'Thank you, Ben, this really means a lot.' Ben slid across to the passenger seat; let Clive in the driver's seat and Ellie happily sat on the spacious leather seats in the back.

As they were driving through Christchurch and Clive was getting used to the controls, Ben turned around to look at Ellie.

'Forgive me ma'am, you look kinda familiar to me. You look like someone I once knew.'

'You mean my mother, Ben. I have a photo of you and your wife at a party with my mother!'

Ben turned around fully to Ellie. 'You'd better believe this honey, Vera and me; we loved your mom and your dad too. But somehow, we just lost contact with your dad. I guess that's just life. Do you know where he is?' Ben asked.

'We're on our way to see him now Ben.' Ellie softly touched his arm.

'Jiminy Cricket! You mean we're going to see him right now? Hey Clive, is it alright to make a call?' Clive nodded, concentrating on the road. 'Honey you ain't gonna believe this, were on our way to see Edmund, can you believe it? Me neither, talk to you soon. Yeah, I will try. OK bye.'

'Look Ben this will be the first time I'll see my dad, my very first time! And I don't know what to expect!' Tears were running down her face.

Clive looked through the rear-view mirror at her. 'We're both here for you Ellie. Don't worry, everything will be OK.'

'You betcha' Clive, I'm with you all the way buddy!'

Clive drove slowly through the last village, then slowed right down as he approached a dangerous bend. He stopped to check oncoming traffic and then turned sharp right into a narrow track. The overhanging branches were scratching both sides of the new car noisily, as they drove down the lane, it was so narrow. Clive looked furtively at Ben.

'It's only a car buddy. Let's not worry about that, these cars are built for such things ain't they?' Ben chortled.

Through the twists and turns of the lane they went and it finally opened into a clearing, revealing a small brick built cottage. Clive's heart sank as he noticed that there was no smoke coming from the chimney. That increased his concern somewhat, but he didn't want to alarm the others.

As they rounded the back of the cottage he stopped the big car and they all got out. Ellie could hear the bark of a dog, not a vicious bark, more of a yap.

Clive looked through the kitchen window. 'I can see him; he seems slumped in an easy chair.' He banged on the window. The dog barked but there was no movement coming from Edmund.

'We will have to break in!' he shouted.

'Please God, that we're not too late' Ellie said.

One shoulder charge from Ben burst the door open! Clive rushed inside first and sat alongside the seated man. He felt for a pulse on his neck, it was faint but still there.

'He's unconscious, but he's still with us. It looks like he's been there for quite some time. Ben, we've got to get him to hospital and the only A & E is in Bournemouth.'

The two men gently eased him out of the leather chair and carried him towards the car. Ellie ran outside and opened the car door for them. She then rushed inside again and up the tiny stairs, found a heavy blanket and gave it to Clive.

With it being such a large vehicle, she could slide in on the other side of the car and cradle her dad's head on her lap.

'Don't die, daddy, please don't die, I love you!' She remembered the dog, where was it? 'Clive, where's Zowie?' Ellie remembered that Ursula had told her the dog's name when they met on the beach.

Ben had seen the silver collie dive into the undergrowth a few minutes ago whilst they were carrying him into the car. He shouted her name with his booming voice, whilst opening the tailgate.

In a flash, she was in and looked over the back seat at her prostrate master and then lay on the floor quietly. 'Call of nature, I guess.' Ben smiled to himself. He looked for Clive and watched as the young lawyer tried to pull the back door of the cottage, but it was somewhat bent by the heavy persuasion from Ben.

The three of them sat together in the A & E waiting room for about two hours. Ben got up to stretch his legs. 'I guess I'd better check on the dog, Ellie.'

She didn't look up, too scared to. As he looked at her, she had one arm around Clive and the other holding a thin chain of some kind. The doors slid open, but he didn't go through them, as a nurse came into the waiting room with a clipboard in her hand.

Clive and Ellie jumped up together, as she was standing over them.

'He's out of danger. We've managed to stabilise him and he's sleeping right now. We need to do some more tests on him, so we'll keep him overnight. When he comes out, will he have somewhere warm to stay and someone to look after him?' The nurse asked.

'YES!' The three of them shouted in unison. Ellie gave her a contact number and she took the number of the hospital, in case she wanted to contact them.

On the way back to Ellie's home, Zowie jumped into the back seat with Ellie, who hugged her and told her all about her master in hospital and said that she was going to see her master the next day, no matter what.

'That was a job well done, son.' Ben smiled at Clive.

'I couldn't have done anything without your help Ben, thank you very much.'

Ben had called to let Vera know that they were on their way and as they arrived, she was waiting in the car park for them. Ellie ran straight to Vera's arms the moment she got out of the car.

'I know how you feel hun.' Vera said in a calming voice, let it all out, you've had one heck of a lot to put up with, haven't you?' Ellie nodded, still buried in Vera's arms and then she held her hand as they walked back to the doorway.

Clive looked at Ben as this was happening, but Ben was looking away. Zowie was following the two women close behind.

'Sorry about the mess on the car Ben, are you alright?'

'Sure, I'm OK, I don't often see Vera like that, if you know what I mean. Anyway, shucks if I'm bothered about some damn hire car, eh?' They both laughed.

As they were entering the lift, Clive called to Ellie to stop. 'I don't think that Zowie would take kindly to going in the lift.

I'll take her up the back stairs and you open the door when you're up there, OK?' She smiled while he gave her a little peck on the cheek.

Before Vera and Ben got out of the lift, Ellie just held on to Vera's arm. 'Vera, if dad's still in hospital tomorrow, will you come with me and Zowie to visit him?'

She gave Ellie her phone number, 'Gimmie a call when you know and wild horses won't stop me.'

Ellie rushed to the service door and let them in. Clive took Zowie on the veranda and he could tell that she could smell the sea and the crashing of the waves calmed her down, as if it had evoked some sort of memory in her. Clive told her to stay and she lay down looking at him with those silvery eyes.

He looked in the fridge, found a tin of chicken and chopped it up for her. She wolfed that down whilst he found some strong cord, waited for her to finish the food, then tied the cord through her collar. With plenty of slack he tied it to the upright on the corner of the veranda. Before she settled down, he washed her feet, as she had been in the woods earlier.

'It's to protect the carpet, Ellie.' He said.

Ellie was watching him do all that. 'Not bad for a city boy.' She teased.

'Well, my mums got a dog, so I instinctively know what to do.' His face dropped. 'Oh no, I've forgot to tell mum what time I was arriving at her house, she'll be frantic.' He dialled his mobile 'Hi mum it's me sorry about not ringing you'.

At the same time, Ellie had gently come up very close to his chest, sliding her arms around his waist and was looking up at him with her dark green eyes. She was pulling at his shirt button with her teeth now. He started to get hot and red around his neck!

'S... Sorry mum something has come up, I ring you tomorrow, bye.'

He peeled her from him and reached for his coat.

'Where are you going?' She frowned, but then followed him to the veranda where Zowie was sitting up straight and wagging her tail at him.

'I think we need a little walk girl, to cool down a little, if you know what I mean. Lend me your keys, Ellie, so I can get back in will you.' Clive looked at her sheepishly.

The next morning, having had the best night for a long while, with not too much sleep however, she turned over to find the duvet thrown back. She walked into the living room and looked at the veranda. There he was, bent over, tying Zowie to the pillar. She could hear him talking to her. He turned around to see her completely naked, without any inhibitions walking towards him.

'Have I died and gone to heaven?' he thought to himself.

As she wrapped herself around him, he struggled to tell her what he had been doing whilst she slept.

'I've rung the hospital, Ellie.' She was stripping his clothes off now. 'He's improved and he's asking for Zowie. So, I told the nurse that Zowie was a dog and could she come to visit today. She agreed for a brief time and about two would be best for them. Phew!'

'So, we've got some time until then have we?' Ellie smiled mischievously.

'Er, yes darling'. He followed her into the bedroom and closed the door.

She woke up and the bed was a mess. She walked into the living room and noticed that he had left a note for her to find on the coffee table.

'Sorry darling, I do have to get back to London. I'll be back tonight, that is if you want me to. I'll call you before I start back. Love to your dad. Keep safe. Love Clive X'

By two o'clock, Vera, Ellie and Zowie were getting out of the Polo and making their way to the ward that her dad was in. No one had said anything about Zowie being with them and if they had, Ellie was going to say she was a petting dog for the ill people.

They approached his bedside. Although he did still look very weak, they could see his face light up as they came near. Zowie sat at the side of the bed tail wagging furiously. Edmund let his hand out of the bed. She licked it and then let him rest his hand on her head.

It was Vera's turn next. She just leaned over to him and kissed him gently then whispered something in his ear. He smiled and she stepped back. He raised his head.

'My darling daughter, my darling daughter, there you are!' Edmund summoned up the strength.

Ellie leaned over gently. 'Daddy, I thought I'd lost you, your stone told me you were in trouble.'

The nurse appeared at the other side of the bed. 'We mustn't upset him too much, he's still very weak.'

'Will you come to see me tomorrow Ellie?' Edmund whispered. She nodded but couldn't speak. He looked at Vera, 'and bring that cowboy with you next time.' He looked tired and his head dropped onto the pillow his eyes closing. Zowie lifted her paw and put it into his hand. He moved his fingers a little and she knew!

On the third day of Edmund's hospital stay, it was Ben's turn to take Ellie and Zowie to see him. As they were walking towards his ward, Ellie could sense there was something different ahead. She gripped Ben's thick forearm in fear and Ben looked down at her reassuringly. As they approached the ward door she distinctly heard the loud laughing of women's voices.

'Sounds like a party going on, hun', Ben said to her.

They walked into the ward and looked in the direction of Edmund's bed; the whole area was festooned in flowers. At least three nurses were surrounding her dad's bedside. Everyone laughed again at a joke from a man, who was leaning over her dad. Ellie looked at Ben, who also started to laugh. Only Ellie and Zowie couldn't get the joke! Zowie gave a sharp bark and the man stood upright and turned to look at the visitors.

As he turned to face them, she noticed he had a six-foot, athletic frame with a deep tanned face and a salt and pepper goatee beard. His light blue mohair suit fitted him well and he smiled broadly at Ellie.

She looked past the stranger at her dad. Tears were running down his face with laughter.

'This is someone I really want you to meet, Ellie. This is Paul Arlington!'

'Not the American actor, the one in.......?' Ellie blushed deeply. 'But dad, tell me why has he come to visit you?'

'I guess that's my fault Ellie' Ben put his big arm around her shoulders. 'I rang him in New York the same day we found your dad and he caught the next plane.'

'But dad, why should he do that? I don't understand.'

Before anyone could say anymore, three more nurses appeared, autograph books in hand, they were giggling at each other as he signed each one. They quickly ran out of the ward again, mission accomplished!

'Look, Paul old mate, why don't you go for a coffee in the hospital restaurant, let me see my visitors and then they'll catch up with you in about half an hour.' Edmund said, waving him away. 'I'm really sorry about this Ellie, but Paul and I go back a hundred years, well nearly anyway.'

Paul kissed Ellie on the cheek, gave Ben a hug, patted Zowie and headed to the ward exit, closely followed by two more giggling nurses.

Ben shook Edmund's hand warmly, passed on his mother's best wishes and then stood back a little to let Ellie give her dad a hug. Zowie lifted both paws onto the bed, letting Edmund give her a hug too.

Ben looked at Ellie and laughed. 'Don't worry about the dog's feet on the bed Edmund, all the nurses are in the restaurant with Paul.' They all laughed at Ben's remark.

After their visit, they finally got Paul to themselves. Apparently, he had also secured the prestigious De Vere suite in the Royal Bath hotel in Bournemouth. The hotel had moved some important Arabs out at short notice, to accommodate him. He invited everyone to his suite for dinner that night.

Ellie asked if Clive and his mother could join them, to which Paul responded with, 'the more the merrier!'

Ellie had a plan; she wanted to take that opportunity to get together with so many people who had known her dad over the years, all of them that she had missed. It was of course an enormous success and the huge gaps in time were well filled by all the tales, especially from Paul.

Edmund needed a week to recover in hospital, but they had built him up sufficiently, to walk with the aid of a stick. He agreed to give up the cottage with little resistance. He realised that TLC was the order of the day and let Ellie take care of him.

Ben and Vera stayed long enough to see Edmund settled in W3 before going back home. Mrs Cohen well advanced in years, was getting very frail, so they went home to consider their options. Vera was even talking about living in the UK, but that was one thing they had to discuss at home.

Brian, the agent for the property, was the first outsider to visit Edmund at Breakwaters. He told him that he had found someone interested in the cottage and would like to negotiate with him personally. He asked Edmund what he thought of that idea.

'What's his name Brian?'

'Ian Burrows', Brian answered.

'Ian Burrows, where does he come from?'

'I think its somewhere in Kent; Deal, I think.' Brian answered.

'I definitely want to see him, when can it be arranged Brian?'

'Well, I think he is renting a bedsit in Boscombe. He works for the power company but I don't know what he does.'

'Get hold of him Brian and tell him to come to see me tonight at seven. Also tell him we are expecting him for dinner. Is that OK, Ellie?' Her dad asked her.

'Why are you inviting someone you've never met to dinner, dad?'

'You'll see, Ellie, you'll see.' Edmund wistfully smiled.

Ellie asked Brian if anything could be done to the lift operation. 'Is there a fault on it?' he asked her.

'Not exactly, but you know where you turn the key to get to the third floor, I want that to be normal access now.' Ellie explained.

'If you'll follow me, I'll show you what to do.' She pressed the button to get down to the ground floor. Brian asked her for the key, put it in the slot and turned it ante clockwise one whole turn. 'There you are Ellie, simple as that!'

'You're the best there is Brian' and gave him a peck on his cheek. Brian looked at her with mock surprise and laughed.

Seven o'clock soon came and Edmund didn't know who was the more nervous: Ellie, fussing in the kitchen, or the young man coming for the dinner. Clive was also invited and he was currently lying on the couch, with Zowie lying on top of him. The bell buzzed and Ellie pressed the intercom.

'Is that Ian?' He confirmed and she automatically opened the main door for him. 'The lift door is opposite you and just press three and you'll find us from there.'

Ian gulped for a minute. 'What a place, it's a palace, what sort of people live here,' he thought to himself.

Edmund came to the door and let him in. Zowie jumped off Clive and ran to Ian. He got down on his haunches and she licked his face.

'I noticed that there was only one door on this floor, is this the only apartment? I hope you don't mind me asking.' Ian asked meekly.

Clive came over and shook the young man's hand. Ian was about twenty with a stubble beard, not used to wearing a tie. He had blonde hair that looked like it could need a combing and he had an engaging smile.

'Let me introduce you to Ellie, she's your cook for the night. She not only owns the flat, but the whole building as well!' Clive proudly stated. Ian's mouth was open as he shook her hand perhaps a little too hard. 'And this is the man you have come to see.' Clive stood back smiling.

Edmund stepped forward and shook Ian's hand. Ian noticed that the older man's face was brown with outdoor weathering, but he looked like he had not been outside for a while.

'Pleased to meet you sir, Brian has told me a little about you, but may I ask you a question?' Edmund nodded. 'I don't understand why I'm invited to dinner when you have never met me before.'

Edmund waved for him to sit at one of the easy chairs, he was surprised that Zowie had stayed with Ian instead of anyone else and she sat so close to him as if she already knew him, it was amazing.

'Well now Ian, I invited you because of your name and where you come from.'

'But I'm certain that I've never met you sir, I would have known that, this is definitely the first time!' Ian looked at Edmund totally puzzled.

'Let me put you, Clive and Ellie out of your misery. It was your father that I knew; I worked with him in Deal, at the shoe factory.'

'Whippseys! Yes, now I know who you are. My dad still talks of you all the time. He told me that you gave him his break in life. It's an honour to meet you sir, I can't wait until I talk to my dad about this. He'll be over the moon!'

'Ian, I have had a signal from my daughter that dinner is ready so shall we go into the dining room? We'll talk business after, OK?'

Ian talked at length about his job during dinner. He worked for a power company, spending much of his time checking out new ecological sources of energy. He talked a lot about the misuse of fossil fuels. Edmund was most interested in that area himself, having spent such a time at the cottage without basic utilities.

'Ian, you are aware that there is no mains connection, no water no gas and no electricity at the cottage, aren't you?' Edmund asked.

'Yes sir, I am aware of that. As it happens it fits my needs perfectly for my job. I will be able to showcase my green ideas as well.' Ian explained.

After dinner, Clive and Ellie decided to take Zowie for a walk, so that her dad and Ian could talk business. Zowie didn't want to leave Ian at first, she wanted to stay with him and it was most surprising that he had hit it off with the collie so quickly. They had only begun their walk on the cliff top when Ian was walking out of the main doors smiling.

'You haven't closed the deal already have you?' Clive stopped him for a minute. Ian nodded and started to walk home after a quick pat of Zowie's head. 'Do you want a lift home Ian?' Clive shouted after him.

'No thanks Clive, by the way, your dad is a great man Ellie and thanks for dinner. Tell him I'll see Brian tomorrow.' He started to run home and jumped in the air. Ellie chuckled at Clive to see such happiness.

Around a year had passed since the meeting with Ian at the Breakwaters. Ian had bought the cottage and asked Edmund if Zowie could come with him. He wouldn't think of it at first, but Ian worked on him and he finally relented.

Edmund really missed her, but he knew that the apartment wasn't the right place for a collie, so he relented, only on the condition that Ian brought her down to the beach now and then. Edmund had also given Ian the pickup truck for free and had just held on to the little Morgan.

Clive had given up his job at Vizards in London and Brian had helped him sell his little maisonette in Hammersmith and then found him some large premises in Southbourne. It used to be a dental practice and on the first floor, there was a huge self-contained flat.

This was to be his new lawyers practice and once he got settled, Brian promised him that he would find plenty of work for him in the area.

Clive had done sterling work representing Ellie in her divorce. He had sensed correctly that Gary did not want to prolong proceedings, so with Ellie's agreement, he offered a cash settlement of twenty-five thousand pounds to Gary's brief that related to half of the equity value of their house in Oxford.

Her divorce was finalised in three months and as soon as Gary had signed over the deeds for their house to her, she paid off the mortgage and handed it over to Brian to sell it. As usual, with some incentive, on advice from her dad, Brian had sold it for the asking price and Ellie used the funds to help with Clive's business premises.

Clive was living at his mother's whilst the move was being completed. He thought that it was right to let Ellie spend as much time as she wanted with her dad.

One morning in the Breakwaters, Ellie was cooking a special breakfast for her dad, when he called her from the lounge.

'Ellie, I've just remembered that I have got something here to show you. I found it in the top pocket of this old sports jacket. Some people from Samarkand in Uzbekistan gave it to me, over ten years ago.' Her father said and he passed her a small piece of folded paper, written on both sides.

'I've seen this language somewhere before. When I was in Bath with Rowena, we went into a shop which had a sign above it in this Cyrillic script.' She then turned the paper over, 'is this the translation?' She asked, Edmund nodded and smiled at her and asked her to read it out loud.

'Abdul says that one day someone that you love, will save your life.' She read.

'And that's just what you did!' Edmund smiled at her with tears in his eyes.

In a brief time, they had made a beautiful home above the office on the High Street in Southbourne and Ellie had been given the best gift of all from Clive, a beautiful son! They called him Edwin, after his great grandfather.

There were times of course, when Ellie spent time with her father, talking over his past. Inevitably the subject of the stone came up.

'How did you know when to pass the stone on to me dad?' Ellie asked, as she pulled it out to show him.

'After your mother had died, I knew then that it was time to pass it on and now I realise it was the perfect time for all of us.' Edmund explained and smiled warmly to her.

'But dad, what about Edwin, when will I know if it's the right time for him?' Ellie asked her father.

Edmund smiled at Ellie. 'You'll know when the time comes my darling, you'll just know."

Sometime later, Ellie had a call from her dad. He wanted her and Edwin to call at the apartment as he'd got something to show them. As she walked with the buggy, she wondered what surprise he'd got in store this time.

They had reached the Breakwaters and Ellie rang the bell. She waited and rang again. 'Hello?' a woman's voice answered.

The voice played tricks with her mind. The door unlocked and she pushed the buggy into the lift and in a moment, was standing at the door, just about to knock, when it flew open.

'Mum, what are you doing here?'

'And who is this little chap?' Her stepmother asked, as they walked into the lounge with Edmund standing and smiling behind her.

'Your stepdad has passed away Ellie and I was all alone in Johannesburg and your dad invited me here. I'd got no one, Ellie!' She stepped backwards and held Edmund's hand. They looked at each other eye to eye, then back to Ellie.

She ran to hug them both, so full of joyous emotion.

The End for now...

(To be continued)

Printed in Great Britain
by Amazon

23455007R00189